RINGER

RINGER

BRIAN M. WIPRUD

MINOTAUR BOOKS ✖ NEW YORK

RINGER. Copyright © 2011 by Brian M. Wiprud. All rights reserved. Printed in the United States of America. For information, address St. Martin's Press, 175 Fifth Avenue, New York, N.Y. 10010.

www.minotaurbooks.com

Library of Congress Cataloging-in-Publication Data

Wiprud, Brian M.
    Ringer : a crime novel / Brian M. Wiprud. — 1st ed.
        p. cm.
    ISBN 978-0-312-60189-8
    1. Mexican Americans—New York (N.Y.)—Fiction.   2. Relics—
Mexico—Fiction.   3. Billionaires—New York (N.Y.)—Fiction.
4. Conspiracies—Fiction.   5. Mistaken identity—Fiction.   6. Trials
(Murder)—Mexico—Fiction.   I. Title.
    PS3623.I73R56 2011
    813'.6—dc22

                                                    2011008724

First Edition: July 2011

10   9   8   7   6   5   4   3   2   1

For Joanne

ACKNOWLEDGMENTS

Special thanks to:

Mike Miller: A friend and fine attorney, Mike gave me a tour of One Centre Street in Manhattan that was very cool, and it helped me immensely with the courtroom scenes. He continues to be my go-to guy for legal matters, but by way of indemnification, any inaccuracies are purely mine. Thanks, Mike!

Newcombe Baker III: A friend and graphic artist of the first order, he created the awesome graphics for this book, and I can't thank him enough. Thanks, Skip!

The Gauntleteers: I more or less had the choice of writing this book or something else. It was only with the help of these friends that I was able to decide to write about Morty one more time, which I hope the readers agree was definitely the correct decision. It was also in their company that I was able to visit and research La Paz, Mexico, where parts of this novel occur. Thanks, Ken, Chuck, and Jeff. See you in Baja 2011!

Jon and Ruth Jordan: Few have done more to help keep Garth, Morty, and Tommy alive. You guys are the best.

 **Sema4** Development Group

Todd Branch, Executive Producer
Sema4 Entertainment
20101 West Jefferson Blvd.
Culver City, CA 90232 3195

Hi, Todd:

See attached — the Martinez property we discussed. We feel the Purity Grant buzz could

make this stick if we throw it against the wall. Is Antonio Banderas still doing voice-overs for

the Nasonex bee commercials? He'd be cheaper than Benjamin Bratt. We'll need all the

residuals we can get for the screen candy. Locations are cake.

See you at the Globes.

Jennifer Stevens
Associate Producer, Acquisitions
Sema4 Development Group
1660 Broadway
New York, NY 10019

Jennifer Stevens
Associate Producer, Acquisitions
Sema Four Development Group
1660 Broadway
New York, New York 10019

Dear Jennifer:

I am grateful that you took an interest in my story and for
the good fortune you tuned into *Entertainment Now's* feature on my
predicament. That was months ago, so sincere apologies for the
lateness of this package to you. A few pages were all I intended
to write and I raced to revise it in the last weeks as more
information became available. There were so many details. And
without the details I look like an idiot, and nobody wants to see a
movie about a fool. Unless it is a comedy, I suppose, but when you
see that my very life dangles in the balance, there is nothing
funny in my story. Here in Mexico they have no sense of humor when
it comes to murderers of the famous and rich.

A book on screen writing assisted me in my task to shape the
actual facts into an epic film treatment. Even if my strange-but-
true tale never graces the silver screen, writing this has given me
hope that some small part of me might survive tomorrow's execution.
Do you think Antonio Banderas is too old to play me in the movie?
Benjamin Bratt would be an excellent choice as well.

As they say here in Mexico, *adios*.

M. Martinez
Centro de Detención Naval
La Paz, BAJA CALIFORNIA SUR 23000
MEXICO

PS: I have put it in my will that any monies from the movie that I
would have gotten were I not being shot tomorrow should go to The
Orphanage at Nuestra Señora de Cortez, La Paz, BAJA CALIFORNIA SUR
23000 MEXICO

FATHER GOMEZ ENTROPICA WAS AN aging brown fireplug topped by a bush of white hair. Judging from his rough visage, fate might have made him into a deadly gangster had God not made him a priest. He stood behind a desk that was as large and rough-hewn as an overturned native fishing boat. Save for a crucifix on the wall behind him, the stained plaster walls were bare. A tropical breeze scented the room with bougainvillea.

I had been summoned by Father Gomez to Nuestra Señora de Cortez, a castle-like church in downtown La Paz. This town is located in the Baja peninsula, a commanding finger of Mexico below California that points into the blue Pacific. La Paz is the ancient seaside village where I live. Or lived, so it would seem.

Why had I been summoned? I had every reason to believe that Father Gomez wanted to thank me. After all, I had given his orphanage a hundred thousand, cash. That is a lot of scratch, let me tell you. It had been at least six months since I had given it to Father Gomez, and to be brutally honest, it had started to bug me that I had not even received a thank-you note. Back in Brooklyn, people used to send such things even after a small bowling party or tar beach cookout. So it seemed to me that the priest could have at least sent an e-card or dropped by my hacienda to shake my hand.

I wore my white suit and Panama hat for the occasion. There's no sense being rich and living in a sea-view villa if you do not have at least one white suit, and I think a fancy walking stick is also a nice touch. I was, after all, no longer a house cleaner. With a few million in the bank, I no longer cleaned houses. I was La Paz gentry.

I sat across from the priest in a heavy wooden chair that was cold as stone, my legs crossed, hat and walking stick in my lap, a jaunty beneficent smile on my tanned face. Part of me hoped the priest did not weep with gratitude and kiss my hand. Another part wished he would. Show me a man who does not like gratitude and I will show you a woman who does not like a compliment.

Instead of blubbering, the squinty brown fireplug in the cassock and collar slid what looked like a small gilded humidor across the desk.

"Open it," he growled in Spanish.

This I had not expected. A gift! I thought to myself this was better than a weeping, grateful priest. I could put this humidor on my mantel and savor cigars of the holy gratitude I had earned.

"There is no need, Father. It is enough that I have helped those less fortunate." I was speaking Spanish, too. In Brooklyn, I spoke very little, but in my new homeland, I had picked it up out of necessity. "My father was an orphan here, so I feel in some small way beholden to this beneficent institution."

His pinched face became more pinched, and he growled once more, "Open it. It is very old."

"If you insist, but this is too much."

I lifted the lid of the box, and there was only one cigar. It did not look like a very good cigar, either. Still, as gentry, it is my obligation to always be gracious, so I forced a smile and said, "They do not make quality cigars like they used to, do they, Father?"

One of his tiny blue eyes popped out of his wrinkles like a bird on a cuckoo clock.

"It is a severed finger, señor. Not a cigar."

It didn't look like a very good finger, either, but on closer inspection I could see a fingernail at the tip and smell the faint musk of decay.

"Oo, very nice, Father." I opened my eyes very wide to keep from looking like I might decorate his desk with vomit. "I do not have a finger. Except on my hand, of course. A finger in a box, it makes for an excellent conversation piece, does it not?"

Father Gomez covered his face with his hands. "This is not a gift, señor. This is a holy relic that has been desecrated."

"It does look dried up, I agree."

Father Gomez sank into his chair and took a deep breath. Then he took his hands away from his face. "The finger in the box is that of Hernando Martinez de Salvaterra."

"The conquistador?" I sat forward. "I am descended from him. I think."

"Hernando Martinez de Salvaterra wore a gold ring bearing the cross of Caravaca. It is a double-crossbarred crucifix. It was cast from a golden Hapsburg medallion that encased a part of the true cross. Hernando Martinez de Salvaterra wore this ring, and he believed himself invincible as long as he wore it. That is, until the finger was cut from his hand while in battle defending a monastery in Peru. Only the finger was recovered and returned to his family in La Paz, and the brave conquistador's fortune helped establish this orphanage. Hernando Martinez de Salvaterra was himself an orphan raised by the church. The finger was enshrined in the altar."

"Where is my ancestor's ring now? It is not on the finger."

Father Gomez put his hands together as if in prayer. "Fifty-five years ago one of the boys entered the sanctuary at night and pulled the ring from Hernando Martinez de Salvaterra's finger."

"I hope you gave the boy a stern talking-to."

Father Gomez's lip twitched, and somewhere down the street a dog yelped. "Had I discovered who had perpetrated this abomination, I would have done more than talk, Señor Martinez."

"So you never discovered who stole my ancestor's ring?"

"We did not know. The ring was lost. Forever. Until this."

Father Gomez reached into his cassock and slid a picture across the desk. It was part of an article from *Forbes* magazine about someone named Robert Tyson Grant, apparently the founder of a successful discount chain called Grab-A-Lot. His teeth were very white and his hair very silver, the black eyes sparkling with the guilty glee of the super-rich. Dressed in yachting togs, he was posed aboard a large catamaran. His right hand grasped part of the rigging close to the camera. On that hand was a buttery gold ring.

The ring bore the double cross of Caravaca.

I stood, my face warm.

"So this scoundrel has the sacred ring of my ancestor?"

Father Gomez looked down at the desk. "I regret I did not properly thank you for your kind donation to our charity, Señor Martinez. Under the circumstances from which it came, I thought it perhaps better that we did not meet. As you know, Mexico has many unsavory people. It is not unusual for the drug cartels to donate cash to churches to try to buy off their guilt. Our lawyers advise us against making any acknowledgment that we receive these gifts, and yet the money does go to a good cause, to God's work, and so we accept it. In your case, well . . ."

"I understand, Father. Say no more. I gave the money out of respect for my father's memory. And for a good cause, not for the gratitude of the church."

"After your generosity, it makes it all the more difficult to ask a favor of you. I would like to ask you to go to Robert Tyson Grant in New York and ask him to return the ring."

Yes, I had been a humble Brooklyn house cleaner, and then I had a windfall and retired to La Paz, my father's ancestral home, to fulfill my destiny and birthright. All the same, since getting myself set up in my villa, and becoming white-suited gentry, I had felt like something was missing. I had begun reading to see what some of the world's great thinkers like Abraham Lincoln had to say about what makes life complete. Well, a good woman, of course. I had started sorting out the local females, but it was hard to find one that was at once chaste and would also put out. This is a problem all men have, and in Mexico I had found the girls tend to be all one or the other. It may sound like what was missing was that I was not getting laid, which was factually correct. Yet there was a hollow feeling beyond my loins. What was missing from me was the Holy Spirit, a purpose as God's minion. It would be as the instrument of God that I might earn contentment, and at the same time earn a gorgeous woman I could call my own.

My epiphany was such that I could hardly breathe. I croaked, "Why do you honor me with this task?"

"You are a wealthy American. He is a wealthy American. I do not speak English well enough. Also, your 'letter' to me"—yes, the white-haired brown fireplug actually made air quotes with his fingers before continuing—"about that money you generously donated to the orphanage gave me the impression that you are blessed with resourceful ways."

"I should have Robert Tyson Grant arrested for the theft is what I should do."

Father Gomez waved his hands in the air. "No, Señor. If you appeal to Robert Tyson Grant's conscience and tell him the story of the ring, God will touch his heart and he will do the right thing. Have faith in God to guide him. We have no idea how Robert Tyson Grant came upon this ring. He likely bought it, or it was given to him, legitimately."

"I see." My chest swelled. "I am to be the instrument of God, the hand of the Holy See. I am to brandish the sword of the Almighty to return this holy relic to La Paz and restore the honor of my birthright."

"Eh, something like that. Señor Martinez, I just ask that you go to Robert Tyson Grant and ask for the ring. As a favor to the orphanage, and as a favor to Nuestra Señora de Cortez."

I cinched my Panama on my head and pointed my walking stick at the priest. "Father Gomez, I am all over this, like butter on a bagel."

"Take the finger with you." His palm held the gold humidor. "It will help authenticate your story."

I exited through the vaulted chapel of Nuestra Señora de Cortez, the finger of Hernando Martinez de Salvaterra under my arm, into a blue June day. My boots clacked across the sunlit cobbled plaza, my heart full of purpose and without doubt of my success in recovering the Caravaca-Martinez ring.

God was on my side.

Unfortunately, Satan himself was on the other.

T W O

YES, SATAN. PERHAPS YOU THINK I am exaggerating? That I am engaged in hyperbole? I am a deeply spiritual person, let me tell you. I embraced a religious quest for the ring, and I do not talk about God or any of His angels, in heaven or in hell, as though they do not exist, as though they aren't right here with us. Because even if they do not exist for you, they do for me. As they did for Hermes Pacifico Diego Ramirez. His mother called him Paco. His friends called him El Cabezador. The Headhunter.

Now, to discuss Paco, I must help you direct your film. You have to turn away from me and Father Gomez in La Paz and point the camera lens at the Mexican town of Juárez. Perhaps you have heard of it? It is across the border from El Paso, Texas, and it was a very dangerous place. Drug cartels had wars there, and then the Federales—that's the Mexican army—had to sweep in to calm everybody down. When the Federales departed, the wars started again, and there was much killing as the two leading drug gangs fought for supremacy over the flow of money and drugs across the border. Killing and killers were like hot dogs at a baseball game, everywhere you looked. In fact, the gangs stocked up so heavily on killers that there sometimes wasn't enough killing to go around. Having more killers than they needed, they began to export them also, along with the drugs, to the United States. They even advertised in newspapers and online so Americans could shop for them.

We have all read about how Americans try to find someone local to kill their wife or girlfriend or husband, and each time we read about it, the newspapers tell us the same story. The murderous spouse contacts cheap hoods looking for a reference for a hit man. These local crooks inform the police about the murderous spouse in return for favorable treatment the next time they are pinched. The cops then pose as hit men, meet the spouse, and record the clumsy conspirator's proposition. In court, this recording makes the prosecutor's job easy. Really a very sad thing, when you think about it, for all concerned.

So here we are in Juarez, a sweltering, dusty, fading tourist town that had become too dangerous for the gringos. Restaurants once bustling with tortilla-munching Americans soaked in margaritas: shuttered. Pharmacies that once sold sex pills and tranquilizers by the sack: *cerrado*. The trinket markets jammed with piñatas, statuary, sombreros, and switchblades: *nada*. Things like food markets and auto repair shops were still open, but the streets teemed with groups of dark men of dark purpose going this way and that, eyes darting. Nobody but these types went out after dark unless they had a death wish.

Here our camera turns on Paco. He was a small man with a big head, a thin mustache, and green eyes, almost yellow, like a cat's. His black hair was crinkled and carefully plastered to his head, a part in the middle. He wore only black.

Our camera finds him kneeling in his small, sparse room, where he has finished his preparations to carry out an assignment across the border. He was to be ferried by the drug gang across the border at night and be driven to Houston, where he would take a bus to New York City. His duffel bag was packed with clothing and a number of aging pistols, ammunition, and his trusty axe, all of which was easy to carry on a bus but only an idiot would carry into an airport.

The hot desert wind blew the curtains into the room. Between the two windows was a foot-high statue surrounded by flickering gold candles. Paco was kneeling in front of the statue. You would maybe imagine that this was a statue of Mary? Our Mother of Guadalupe? You would be wrong. He was praying to Santa Muerte.

Saint of Death.

You may think I am joking when I tell you this, but the drug gangs had their own religion, and they prayed to this shrouded skull monster, a grim reaper, that was at once Death and Satan. I suppose they figured that they needed a protecting saint to be involved in such a dangerous line of work as killing and drug smuggling. One could hardly imagine God helping them with such activities, much less that they could have had the balls to seek His protection. These murderous scoundrels had no hope of ever going to heaven. The way they had it figured, it was Satan in the form of Death who would come for you in the end, so why not pray to the cloven-hooved reaper himself and ask him to cut you a break?

So Paco had his yellow catlike eyes on the evil skull head of the satanic Santa Muerte. A miniature scythe was in the statue's right hand, a tiny globe in the left. Paco's palms were pressed tightly together in reverence, and the lips under the thin mustache uttered a prayer:

"Oh, Santa Muerte, I call upon you so that through your image, you may free me from failure in my mission. Do not abandon me from your protection, and I ask your blessing upon your devotee Paco, and that I am blessed with wealth for accomplishing what has been denied me. I go without fear, but if they direct that I should die and you do not protect me from failure, come and take me. So be it."

Paco lifted a chain around his neck and kissed a gold amulet of Santa Muerte three times before dropping it back down his black shirt.

Paco was a killer who had not yet killed. His history was humble, the son of a Honduran pineapple farmer who joined the army. Lured by the promise of wealth, he, like many Honduran soldiers, deserted his post and went to Mexico to become a contract killer for the wealthy cartels. Like most sparkling opportunities that twinkle on the horizon, the rewards were elusive, and the Mexicans considered Hondurans cannon fodder in the cartel wars. Most of his friends had gone home or been killed. Even so, Paco persisted in the face of bad odds, and was given chances to improve his station. Unfortunately, something always went wrong. One time he was late for a gun battle and everybody was dead when he got there. Another time his partner killed the target while Paco was in the bathroom. Another time he was sent to kill someone who had died. Not killed, just died from a bad heart. His troop of killers had begun to joke. This was why he was relegated to reaping necessary trophies.

You see, when there is so much killing, it is necessary to take credit for your kills so that your kills are not confused with someone else's, or that someone else does not take credit for your kill. After all, killing in this way was intended to intimidate the opposition.

Paco's gang cut off the heads of their victims. Not all, just the most notable ones. Cell phone photos of the heads or the heads themselves were then delivered to the opposition.

I do not pretend to be some kind of expert in beheading, but I once read a book about some New York gangs on the West Side of Manhattan, and they gave details. I could go find that book and supply details, but I won't because I do not think a film audience would sit through this part of our movie without throwing up their cheese nachos, popcorn, and Mr. Pibb on the person seated in front of them, and then the poor ushers would have to clean up a tremendous mess. As a wise man once said—perhaps it was Abraham Lincoln—some things are best left to the imagination. I do not think anybody, much less old Abe, would imagine that cutting off someone's head is a pleasant undertaking. Which is why this task was left to Paco, the one who hadn't killed, the one they jokingly called the Headhunter. El Cabezador. His experience with harvesting pineapples was not lost on this new skill. His tool for both was the same: a rustic hatchet. The blade was curved in from use, the gnarled handle worn smooth from work, dark with sweat.

Paco's lowly station was not his making. He practiced, and was a good shot with the guns. He had good eyesight and good hearing and was smart enough, certainly as smart as many of those around him. He prayed and made offerings to Santa Muerte constantly. In his black clothes and with his yellow cat eyes, he looked dangerous.

Like an unloving parent, Fate had not rewarded his talent.

So it had come to pass that one of the American jobs had been assigned to him, one that had come in through the classifieds, a job reserved for beginners and those the gang wished to weed out. The gang got money up front, and then more money when the job was successful. If a new killer failed, no loss, the gang at least got something. If the killer actually succeeded, all the better. The cartels sent some killers to practice on Americans before graduating them to full soldier status. Or to weed out the losers.

El Cabezador knew this was his last chance.

He stood. Grim and determined, he wiped a tear from his eye and slung the duffel bag over his shoulder. The zipper on the cheap bag split, and the contents tumbled out onto the floor behind him.

Paco's sad eyes looked at his broken bag, at his scattered black clothes and guns, and then fixed on Santa Muerte.

"Por qué, Madre?"

THREE

THE FILM AUDIENCE MUST WAIT to know how Satan fits into my story, because I think it best to turn the cameras on a girl in a bikini. Why? Because every movie needs the promise of sex, and you do not want to keep the audience waiting too long or they will text their friends to pass the time until things get more interesting.

While the Baja peninsula is a commanding finger pointing into the Pacific, Long Island is a hand waving vaguely at Europe. Long Island is the eastern part of the same land mass as Brooklyn, where I used to live, which is sort of the ball of the thumb of the hand that waves at Europe. Yet as close as East Hampton was to Coney Island, it might as well have been on the moon. They do not eat hot dogs and french fries there, or drink canned beer. They do not live in apartments and ride the subway.

East Hampton is where the smart set owned big houses on the beach, with cars in the driveways that cost what many condos do on Mermaid Avenue. On Friday evenings in the summer, the tycoons, rock stars, and celebs fly out of Manhattan over the evening traffic jams in their helicopters or seaplanes. You get the picture. Hollywood on the Atlantic.

If you think about it, rich people are not often ugly. So it was with Purity Grant. She was draped on a lounger by a pool in East Hampton, June's ocean waves crashing just beyond the dune. Behind her were a pool house and cabanas, and behind that a large gray mansion.

Purity's hair, as seen in the tabloids, was always worn with long pigtails. On this day it was in a ponytail to stay out of the way of the sun's rays. Her five-hundred-dollar thong bikini was not wasted on this body. There are many such women strewn about poolsides next to mansions, yes? My answer is no. The eyes were limpid pools of aquamarine, blue yet green at the same time, like the Sea of Cortez, and when these eyes beheld you, it was as if they were asking a question, searching. These eyes wanted to see *more*. Yet the sea green eyes seemed to quickly settle for less, turning mischievous, looking for fun. Just the same, the eyes had a dark flicker, and it was the icy flame of revenge.

Of course, what is fun to some is trouble to others. (That sounds like something Lincoln might have said, too.) This was why a helicopter swooped low over the beach, twirled, and settled onto the helipad next to the tennis courts in a storm of sand.

Purity took a deep breath and wished she had not left her cigarettes in the Bentley GT, which was not in the driveway but with the police. In Westhampton, it wasn't like there was a deli on the corner where she could buy some more smokes. She wondered if she could borrow the helicopter to go get more cigarettes.

Footsteps clomped across the patio. Purity knew those angry footsteps anywhere. She could almost hear the steam whistling out of Bobbie's brain.

A folded newspaper landed on her navel, and the tycoon Robert Tyson Grant loomed over her. "Did you see the papers, you little cunt?"

"How do you know it's little?"

"Did you see the papers?"

She pushed the newspaper off her stomach. "I read *Easy Rider*."

"Well, the rest of the planet read about your escapade last night. It is going to cost a fortune to keep you out of prison, if we can even keep you out of prison."

The headline on the newspaper next to the lounger read: PURR-SUIT. Below that was a flash picture of mischief-eyed Purity flanked by police, captioned: CATTY HEIRESS LEADS HI-SPEED CHASE.

"So what is this nonsense, Purity?"

Grant's dark silhouette shimmered at the edges, his steely hair glinting.

"Hi, Bobbie. You're blocking my sun."

"I thought we had a deal."

"You mean about the . . ."

"Yes, about staying out of the papers, about staying out of jail, about staying out of lawsuits. I thought it was a pretty fair deal. You get an allowance and I get peace. You get to buy almost any-thing and do nothing. That sounds pretty fair to me. Did that not sound fair to you? It must have, because you agreed to it."

"That *allowance* comes from my mother's estate, not yours. This whole house was my mother's. So I'm really not sure what you should have to say about it."

"This house is now mine, and that *allowance* you throw away comes from a trust fund. I'm the executor. You may not like it here with your very own seaside mansion and open bar tab at El Rolo, but if you want out, I have the keys, and I'm not letting you out until you put these outrages behind you. There's still that Central Park matter to clear up."

"You know, I think in that sick, twisted soul of yours you get your jollies keeping me locked up here. It must have something to do with guilt over my mother's death somehow, I don't quite get it. Maybe you fantasize that I'm your sex slave."

Grant flashed crimson. "Making me this angry is the wrong thing to do. I have a heart attack and that won't help you—not a bit of it. I die and you don't get one red cent."

"Bobbie, can I borrow the Bell 430? I'm out of Dunhills."

Ah, you think perhaps Purity was joking about the Bell 430, a helicopter? She was not.

I have found that while we typically like to see people as this way or that way, they are more often both ways.

True, Purity was a layabout and a rich brat. She never finished all the schools she went to, even though she got all A's while she was there. She never had a career—other than as a tabloid queen. She went through cars almost as fast as she went through men.

Who would think that such a person would have a passion for helicopters?

Perhaps this is where we go into a flashback, the lens becomes fuzzy . . . I will leave that up to you.

Her mother married Robert Tyson Grant when Purity was sixteen, and it follows an almost inevitable course that she was not a fan of her stepfather then or since. Soon after her parents' union, her mother became fatally ill. Purity had been kicked out of another prep school about the same time, and so was grounded indefinitely at the East Hampton mansion. Her mother's illness made a change in Purity. It made her both sad and angry. The anger was the result of being left alone with "Bobbie" and without the love of her mother. That sounds crazy, I know, but it is a fact that we can be angry at the ones we love for dying. There is resentment, they tell me.

Already expelled from school and a castaway on the sandy shores at the East Hampton mansion without a car to destroy, she acted out in the only way she knew how. She bought something expensive.

Why a helicopter? Perhaps the size of the purchase matched the size of her emotional isolation and resentment. In any case, Purity knew that buying a helicopter would enrage Bobbie, which was becoming her life's work.

When the tractor-trailer delivered the helicopter to East Hampton, Purity soon realized that she'd ordered a helicopter kit as opposed to an assembled helicopter. The house staff rang her stepfather to tell him of the latest outrage, and he arrived by his own helicopter and confronted Purity in almost the same way he had eight years later about leading the cops on a wild chase.

She got the reaction she was looking for, of course. It was the first time her stepfather told her what he really thought of her. His tirade was brutally unflattering, to include but not limited to the irony of her first name. After he flew back to Manhattan, to his Grab-A-Lot empire and his dying wife at the clinic, Purity realized that the helicopter would be a hard fiasco to beat. Especially because Bobbie also blocked all lines of credit available to her.

A fiasco hard to beat unless, of course, she actually *built* the helicopter. Then learned how to fly it. At least that might provide an escape pod from East Hampton.

She had to enlist the help of a number of aviators from the local airport, but I think it is best once again to leave it up to the imagination of the theater audience as to how that was accomplished. She was, after all, only seventeen. Yet her charms were undeniable.

Purity outdid herself. That sweltering summer, she successfully charmed the right people to help her assemble and learn to fly the helicopter, though she did not manage to obtain a license to fly solo. She also successfully reenraged her stepfather. The only thing parents hate more than an unruly child is one that proves them wrong. She proved to him that she could apply herself, if only to spite him.

Purity came to think of it as her Golden Summer.

Bobbie's counteroffensive to the helicopter was to deny Purity the chance to say good-bye to her mother that September.

Robert and Purity Grant had been at war for eight years.

OK, time to get back to the girl in the bikini, and see if she takes it off.

"So, like, Bobbie, what do you want me to say? That I'll suddenly become a different person? That I'll go to work for your ho Dixie who runs the Grant Foundation, rubbing the crotch of fat old dudes at receptions so they'll sign fat checks to cure cancer? You know this is not going to happen, OK?"

"While I might wish that you would find something useful to do, I have never asked that of you, have I? I just do not see why you insist on making a spectacle of yourself. Though I suspect it's entirely to torment me, and that the twisted soul here is yours. Which is a shame because your mother was a fine woman."

To parry Grant's thrust, all Purity had to do was smile. She knew it was a smile that reminded him of her mother, his gorgeous loving wife, before the cancer, back when she was young and healthy like Purity. She had taken a beautiful vestige of her mother's and turned it into something malicious. It was the smile of spite.

Crimson again, Grant wondered once more what he had done to deserve this legacy. Dixie was right, there was only one way out of this hell.

"Bobbie, not everything is about you." Of course, for Purity, everything was about him. Something was different, though; she could feel that she was truly getting to him in a way she never had before. There was something about the way that vein stood out on his forehead, and the dull look that entered his eyes. She was getting deeper, killing a part of his soul the way he had hers. "If you want to fuck me and pretend it's my mother, just say so."

Grant went from crimson to ashen gray: He could take no more.

"The lawyers will be here this afternoon, with a limo."

"Spiffy."

"Be dressed and sober, for God's sake. You have a court hearing in town tomorrow morning, so will be staying overnight in Manhattan, at the Mandarin, and no, you don't have a tab at the bar." Grant stalked back toward the tennis courts, toward his helicopter.

Purity sat up and removed her bikini top, exposing healthy young breasts that were like God's own fruit. "Bub-bye, Bobbie!"

He shot a glance back at her and marched away even faster.

I'm actually winning, Purity thought. Yet what was the endgame? How did the war end? How would she finally break him and have him gone? Suicide? No matter that when he was gone, she would have no money at all and no place to live. Up until then, money in the form of her allowance had only been a weapon against her stepfather. If he were gone, she would have no need of that allowance. Fascinating, I think. Nobody would have guessed that she didn't care about her father's money or her trust fund. In fact, she hated that money as much as she did him.

Purity removed her bikini bottom.

Take a look at the "little cunt," Bobbie.

She lay back out on the lounger and waited for the helicopter to fly over her back to New York.

Bobbie will never kill himself no matter what I do, and waiting for a fatal heart attack is taking forever. He has to go.

But how?

See, she did take the bikini off, though perhaps the removal of the bottom may have to be done tastefully and without too much detail. We have to do what we can to ensure our R rating.

FOUR

THAT NIGHT, EVEN AS I was packing to come to New York, Robert Tyson Grant was in a swarm of penguins in a ballroom at the Grand Hyatt. He was attending a gala cocktail reception for a charity of some kind; he had forgotten which, and probably most of those in attendance would not accurately recall the next day. The checks were already written, so there was no need to remember. Men wore tuxedos, women gowns.

Yes, I say penguins because the men wore tuxedos, but also because they were huddled close together murmuring to each other the way penguins do on the documentaries. It was as if they enjoyed the collective, self-reassuring sound they made as much as what they might have been saying of import to each other.

I'm being figurative about these penguins, of course, but in the movie, perhaps we could cut in shots of penguins? I think an audience would understand.

These charity events are not what many would imagine, because most people are not rich and do not understand high finance or write off large sums of money to charities. While there are of course worthwhile charities, many that the rich put their money in are as much a tax dodge and financial scheme as anything else. Have you ever wondered how the rich always seem to have their own foundations? It is because they all give to each other's pet foundations, tax free, and then only five percent of the charities' money actually goes to help the victims of some horrible mishap or unfortunate circumstance. Yes, but where does the rest go? Well, as it so happens, the foundation is administered by the extended family or friends of the beneficent sponsor rich guy, and then money is siphoned off for administrative operations and gala events. So while they are making donations they are all really paying the others to employ their family, friends, and mistresses, tax free, and to drink and dine tax free at such events.

You have to envy the rich for their unrelenting craftiness if not for their lack of scruples.

Anyway, Robert Tyson Grant was a popular penguin at this gathering. He finally managed to peel away from a particularly loud group of squawkers and take the arm of a beautiful woman who looked perfectly and deliciously naked in a black halter sheath gown with red sparkles. The way the rich scoop up the most delectable women is sometimes as infuriating as it is predictable. As you would expect, this one was younger than Grant, pushing forty, though she would probably have pegged her age at a little closer to thirty. To her credit, she had the body of a much younger woman, and her age only showed on her face.

Who was this lovely, raven-haired creature? An actress? A model? Dixie Faltreau had once been a beauty queen in Georgia, and so went into media. That means TV. She had been an anchor in Atlanta but had realized the benefit of working for rich people's foundations, of working her way up. While she did actually administer charities shrewdly, she coveted the fat salaries and glamorous life. Of course, for the older patrons she would be the southern belle arm candy, but sometimes she was more. Such as with Robert. She was the director of his foundation, the Grant Charitable Trust.

You see? These charities are a delightful way for the rich to spend their money. Even the sex is sometimes tax free. It works both ways, too. You will notice that many older rich women have their nonprofits run by younger men with fine physiques.

Dixie and Robert peeled away from the crowd for a private conversation by a curtained pillar.

"So I flew out to East Hampton and the little tramp had no contrition, none. She flashed her pussy at me as we flew back overhead to New York. I can't understand what's taking our Mexican so long to arrive. Sooner he takes care of Purity the better."

"When was he to contact you, sugar?" She found her lip gloss tucked into her cleavage.

"Yesterday."

"You expect a Mexican to be punctual?"

"Yes. I expect anybody I hire to—"

"This isn't just anybody you hired." Dixie rolled her lips to even the gloss and gently tucked the lip gloss back in her bosom. Grant took the opportunity to stare at her tits a moment before scanning the crowd nearby for eavesdroppers.

"Robbie, stop looking so guilty." She pouted her lips and adjusted his tie. "Just think about how hard we're going to fuck later."

He had a real vixen on his hands, didn't he? Some men have all the luck, and usually all the money, too.

Robert shifted uncomfortably. He loved it when she talked dirty in public, but it meant he had to make sure his manhood wasn't on display. Their eyes met, and she gave his cheek a stroke.

"Relax, the Mexican will get here and we'll get it all taken care of."

"We? You mean *me*."

"I'm here for you, darling. In fact, I've been thinking, perhaps you should let me handle this. Best you not be seen with the Mexican. More discreet if I handle him, since the money is coming from the foundation anyway."

Grant winced. "I hate this."

Dixie put a hand on his chest. "Honey lamb, you're pooped. You've been trying for eight years. Enough is enough. Who would blame you? For all the cruisers they've wrecked chasing her around and all the grief, the Suffolk County police would probably be happy to take care of it for you for the right donation to their Toys for Tots campaign."

"Well, how long do I wait for him to show up, Dix? We made a ten grand down payment."

"Give it another week. If he doesn't show, we'll worry about it then."

"So I have to go to the coffee shop every day for lunch to see if he shows up?"

"*Aw.*" She drifted closer and gave a stroke to the front of his pants. "Only one more week of coffee shop, and I promise to be very bad. Remember the belt?"

Grant felt a sudden loss of blood pressure and couldn't be sure he wouldn't lose his balance. "OK, one more week of coffee shop. Can we leave?"

Dixie licked her lips, slowly. "Darling, they haven't done the refugee presentation yet. Have a . . . *cock*tail."

She turned and moved back toward the other guests.

Robert followed with short careful steps.

I think we need somebody very sexy for this role of Dixie. No Oscar winners.

FIVE

THE SCREEN IS FILLED WITH the picture of my jet landing at JFK, a puff of smoke from the wheels of the plane as they touch the ground.

After my meeting with Father Gomez, it was a small matter to find Robert Tyson Grant. The Web has many exposés about the sixty-five-year-old billionaire that detail his accomplishments, charitable works, and lifestyle.

Such tycoon exposés are much the same. They start by trying to impress you with a man's wealth. Grant was worth a lot, billions. They list all the companies the tycoon owns—in this case only one, Grab-A-Lot. Then they play back some history, about the humble beginnings or the inherited fortune or family business. Robert Tyson Grant was raised by an aunt in Ohio, where as a teen he got a job in warehousing. In his twenties he started his own warehousing business, and then began an export business after that, importing from the Far East just as China began a major manufacturing boom. He flooded the U.S. market with inexpensive goods, started his own chain of stores, and the economic expansion in the States took care of the rest. He took enormous investment risks, and nothing went wrong.

Unlike Paco's and Purity's parents, Fate had been a loving parent to Robert Tyson Grant.

Then the exposés discuss how this person is controversial, how some people feel he is doing harm in some way. Enemies of Robert Tyson Grant were those who felt he paid his workers poorly and bled the American market of manufacturing jobs by importing so heavily from China. On the other hand, the profiles explain, Grant gave a lot of money to cancer research because his wife died from this terrible affliction. He also gave to orphans and hospitals for children. So in the end, the article leaves it up to the reader to decide if the filthy rich person we have been reading about is a good guy or a bad guy.

Ah, but Robert Tyson Grant's exposés were different from those of other titans of industry in one important way.

Purity Grant.

As the topic of countless tabloid features for her many exploits—both with and without drugs and alcohol, both with and without the police, both with and without the various unworthy men—the exposés could not help but focus on her relationship with her father, and his inability to control his spoiled brat daughter.

On the flight to New York, I read a number of these magazine articles that I had printed out to while away the hours among the clouds. I also had some on Purity herself.

I have not fathered a child, so I could not fully appreciate the dismay Robert Tyson Grant felt over the misadventures of his stepdaughter. On the other hand, I could appreciate Purity's body and wanton ways. I'm sure this sounds bad of me, to speculate on what it would be like to actually meet Purity Grant, and whether she would appreciate my charms. Still, I must be brutally honest: While men have many noble qualities, they are first and foremost about charming women, even speculatively, even women far too famous and exquisite for them.

And by charm I do mean *charm*, to make a woman admire you. You do not get them naked unless you charm them first. Alas, this detail escapes many men.

Under the circumstances, there was a remote chance that I might actually meet Purity, so my speculation was not entirely pathetic. I make a good first impression. I am tall, tanned, practiced, and reasonably wealthy, not a disheveled janitor freshly emerged from a boiler room. Might God grant me this little diversion as a reward for pursuing my holy mission? I looked forward to finding out just how far on my side God might be.

I departed the jet with my smart new matching black luggage on wheels, following the herd toward Customs. Mexican officials scanned my luggage and let me pass; U.S. Customs singled me out for an inspection.

The plump little Customs woman pawed through my bag. She managed not to smirk when she felt up my freezer bag of condoms. Then she fished out the gilded box containing the finger of Hernando Martinez de Salvaterra. She held it out to me.

"Please reveal the contents."

I flashed an obliging smile, the back of my neck suddenly cool with sweat. "Of course."

The box lid creaked open, and the agent wrinkled her nose, the hairs on her lip bristling. "What is that?"

I could only guess, but my instinct was that if I told the truth, they would confiscate the mummified finger as contraband. Permits were probably required to transport human body parts. After all, I'm sure Paco would not have put a human head in his luggage and expected to pass unmolested, so why a finger, even if it was six or seven hundred years old?

"This is a cigar."

Her eyes met mine, looking for sincerity. "That's a cigar?"

I nodded slowly and blinked slowly, a gesture of integrity. "Yes, a cigar."

"Cuban?"

"Not at all. It is not even a smoking cigar."

Her eyes narrowed. "Cigars are tobacco products."

"Yes, of course, except this is a very old cigar, a collector's item, not for smoking. One would sooner smoke a cigar picked off the street than this one. It is hardly really a cigar at all if it cannot be smoked. Here, smell."

"Puh!" Her eyes crossed, and then focused on me unhappily for having made her smell something so repugnant. I feared the finger would be confiscated.

"It is the cigar of Hernando Martinez de Salvaterra, a conquistador from six hundred years ago."

"What is the declared value?"

"Value? I have no appraisal. It is really a family heirloom and nothing more. Besides, how much could such a smelly little cigar be worth? Who would buy such a thing? It smells more like a rotting finger than a cigar, yes?"

She had a moment of indecision, but I saw part of her face relax before she waved a hand at the door to the terminal. "You can go."

It is a beautiful thing when a bureaucrat who could make your life miserable realizes you are not worth her time.

New York. It had been a long time. You would think I would head for East Brooklyn, my old stomping ground, where I grew up. That was the last place on earth I would have gone. Brooklyn was securely part of my past, and I intended to keep it that way. No, I was going to stay in Manhattan, that shining citadel of commerce and glitz. I will tell you that although I visited Manhattan a few times when I lived in New York, I felt like a tourist when I did. Yes, even in my own city, I felt like a tourist. Manhattan was a completely different place than East Brooklyn, sophisticated and fast. I always had the feeling that I had to pretend like I knew what I was doing when I didn't. Hailing a cab: I didn't know if I needed to whistle or shout, and when I did I felt people look at me like I was doing it wrong. Restaurants: There was an awkward moment when I ordered tap water instead of the expensive Italian water. Sidewalks: I often felt like I was in the way, not walking fast enough, or standing in the wrong place. Revolving doors: Timing is everything.

Ah, but those apprehensive days were before the East Brooklyn caterpillar blossomed into a La Paz moth of gentry. People with money like me have special license in New York to be foreign. You get points for being exotic. So I was both excited and a little nervous about being newly exotic and back in my hometown, even if it really was my hometown only on paper.

Even I knew Manhattan hotels were mostly in midtown, in the Times Square area. If there is any place in Manhattan that makes even an exotic person nervous and out of place, it is Times Square. I do not even think I have to explain why—most people have seen this place on TV. Standing in this flickering, blinking canyon of a thousand billboards, one cannot help but feel intimidated by the prospect of having to actually read them all.

My research said nice hotels had begun to appear in many places around town, so I had reservations at a swank boutique hotel in a nice quiet neighborhood on Second Avenue in the twenties.

The lobby was exactly as it had been pictured on the Web, with frosted glass columns, plants, and free coffee service. The room was also as pictured on the Web, only much smaller. That was OK. I didn't need a suite, even if I could afford one if I wanted to. Believe me, even though I banked a couple million just before leaving Brooklyn, it somehow did not seem like that much once I bought the hacienda in La Paz and began sinking money into fixing it up. If you throw money around at fancy hotels, next thing you know there are casinos, limos, and pricey women. Spend money like that and ill winds will blow you into desperate circumstances. I was careful with my wealth. You never know when you're going to need it.

It was late afternoon. My plan was to go to the Grant Industries headquarters on Sixth Avenue in the Forties the next morning. You are probably wondering how I came to get an appointment with the great Robert Tyson Grant, yes? Ah. Well, I did not. I knew that if I were to try to make an appointment, a complete stranger, he would never see me. Were I Donald Trump, yes, I am sure Grant would have invited me into his palatial offices and offered me a glass of champagne and a fine cigar. I was not an idiot—I know a man like Grant only sees important people like himself. First, I would try just dropping by to see him, leave my card with a note on the back about the finger of Hernando Martinez de Salvaterra. After that, I would call and ask for an appointment. If that did not work, I would wait for him to leave his offices and intercept him on his way to his limousine.

So how would I fill the rest of the day? There was a Spanish restaurant on Twenty-third Street, El Quixote, where I felt sure I could sip a glass of Valle de Guadalupe nebbiolo.

CHAPTER

SIX

EVEN AS I WAS CHARMING a girl named Nancy at the El
Quixote bar, Robert and Dixie were on a date in Greenwich Village, a part of Manhattan that is a little more freewheeling than
the Upper East Side where Grant lived. Greenwich Village was
not a place where all the headwaiters and wine stewards knew
him. It was not a place where men wore blazers to dinner, and
women pearls. Subways were not an afterthought in Greenwich
Village. "The Village" had jazz clubs, students, quaint restaurants,
porn shops, and off-off-off-Broadway shows. It was a bastion of
smiles, not smirks.

The birds and the bees were chirping and buzzing about Robert and Dixie's romance. Thus they were given to youthful impulse, to the kind of abandon that would take them out of their
lofty uptown circles down to where nobody knew them. To the
realm of the unexpected.

Grant took Dixie to a French bistro on Waverly for dinner, and
then to an Italian place on MacDougal for cappuccino and pastry.
He was in gray slacks and a pullover crew with a sweater around
his shoulders; she was in a festive print tiered halter dress. They
were walking the streets afterward, enjoying the warm spring

night and sights, when on Spring Street they passed a shop with a
neon sign: READER.

"Let's get our palms read, Robbie!" Dixie yanked on his arm
excitedly.

Robert smiled but rolled his eyes. "Come on, Dix. They're phony
as a three-dollar bill, these gypsies."

"Poo." She pouted playfully. "Where's your sense of adventure? It'll take our minds off of Purity. We were supposed to blow
off some steam and relax tonight."

"Darling, it's a carnival act. You do not believe somebody who
sits in a shop window can tell you the future, do you? If they really could tell the future, don't you think they would work their
magic on Wall Street?"

"I try to be open-minded, and so should you, you old fuddy-
duddy. Relax for a change."

"Fuddy-duddy?" He pulled her close for a kiss, but she pushed
him away.

"That's what I said: *fuddy-duddy*. Robert Tyson Grant, you are
stuck in your ways."

"Just because I do not want to pay someone money to tell us
lies—"

"*Oh ho.* So it's the money you're worried about?" She dodged
another of his attempts to kiss her.

"Come on, let's walk up to Washington Square."

She laughed and moved to the door of the shop. "So Robert
Tyson Grant, the tycoon, is a cheap fuddy-duddy."

"If you say so. Come on, let's go . . . oh, great, here she is."

There was a disapproving woman with dark circles under her
eyes standing at the window, shaking her head at Dixie, saying
something that they could not hear. The palmist was dressed in a
plain olive dress, her graying hair pulled back into a bun.

She crooked a finger, beckoning them to enter her lair.

"Oh, come on, Robbie! Do something fun for a change." Dixie pulled him into the palmist's storefront.

"Welcome." The palmist smiled weakly and motioned behind a curtain. "Please, come in, there is much to tell you, and little time. There is danger."

"Danger! What danger?" Dixie looked alarmed but snuck a wink at Grant.

"Please, sit." The palmist steadied herself on the wall, hand over her eyes. "I must feel for a better picture of what has unfolded, and what will be."

Grant rolled his eyes. "Dix, come on, let's go!"

The palmist grabbed his hand. "My name is Helena, and I know why that ring is so important to you." He stared down into Helena's pale eyes nesting under dark eyebrows: *How on earth did she know about the ring?*

She did not, of course, know anything more than that the ring was the only piece of jewelry he wore, and that men only wear rings that mean something to them. It was clearly not a class ring from his college, and the design did not look new, so it must be old. When she clasped his hand she took the opportunity to inspect the ring as closely as possible. Now by the look on Grant's face she knew the ring was very important to him indeed. This is what gypsies call a "hit"—they examine their client's clothes, habits, face, jewelry, age, marital status. Then they make educated guesses and ask questions in the form of statements, trying to pin down something important about a subject's life. They often do not find that something right away. The better ones do. Helena was better. This was why she had a shop on Spring Street and not on Flatbush Avenue.

As soon as her subjects said to themselves *How could she possibly know that?* they were hooked. Magicians are not magic: They succeed because people, down deep, want to be fooled, even skeptics. I am not sure why this is so. Perhaps it explains hypnotism, and maybe gambling. You know what they say: There is an idiot born every moment.

Helena drew the lovebirds into the dark séance parlor, a grotto humming with the green glow of the crystal ball. They sat across the mystical orb from Helena, her lined face on one side, Grant's chiseled jaw and silver hair on the other.

Mysterious violins whined from a hidden speaker as Helena stared at his ring. Well, she could see very plainly it had a cross on it, and that it was solid gold. From Grant's clothing, manicure, teeth, and haircut, she knew he was wealthy. The gold ring was old. It was unlikely that a man would wear an old ring unless it was a family ring of some sort. It was not from Cartier or Tiffany.

Helena took his hand. "This ring is very old, and it carries a spirit."

Dixie clutched Grant's arm. "I knew there was something about that ring!"

"Silence!" Helena hissed at Dixie but kept her eyes on Grant. "You were married, but she is gone now." She read his face, the glint of extra wetness in his eyes, the tightening of his jaw. "She is no longer with us, here on this earth. You loved her very much. I am sorry."

Again, any rich man of this age has likely been married if he is not gay, and just as likely he will be divorced at least once. Of course, it was easy to see that Dixie was not his wife—they were too playful.

Grant was now doubly hooked, his eyes fixed on hers so she could detect how his pupils dilated when she guessed correctly.

"It was very difficult . . . a long illness . . . the doctors did not prevail." Helena knew the odds were in favor of illness over accidental death. That was an easy one—the more hits she could rack up, the more she could explore other areas and risk guessing wrong.

She tightened her grip on his hand. "There is a child!"

Helena could have guessed wrongly, even though the odds were that a rich man who was married had created heirs. If so, she would have seen a dulling in his eyes and could reverse herself: *No, not a child, but someone you care for very much, and sometimes see as a child. Perhaps not a young person but an old person.* What were the chances that someone like Grant had no children or any elderly relatives?

Grant's eyes tightened: *There is a child.*

"You are very concerned about this child. It is a boy!" He blinked, and Helena covered her eyes. "No! The child is willful like a boy. A girl, blond, very pretty. She is troubled."

Show me a rich girl that is not willful, and a father who does not think his daughter is pretty.

Based on Grant's age, she knew the girl had to be at least a teenager, a tender age of unfortunate choices and equally unfortunate consequences. Blond? Grant's hair still had a hint of light brown in it, so it was just a matter of guessing that his daughter had light brown hair also. By extension, Helena guessed that a rich man's daughter would likely have her brown hair dyed blond, or streaked so that blond was not far off the mark.

"Damn!" Grant was amazed.

"You have argued. Bitterly." What parent does not argue with his teenager? "You worry about this child, about what will become of her. She is of great worry to you. Sometimes to the exclusion of all else."

Grant suppressed a wince, remembering his impotence episode with Dixie.

Helena figured she had banked enough hits with Grant to go

out on a limb, so she held up his ring hand in the glow of the crystal ball. "There is much danger here. The ring!"

Grant and Dixie were wide-eyed in the green glow of the orb.

"This ring has spirits, ancient spirits from your family." Oops. "From a very old and religious family, from far away. You are not religious, but bear the ring for a different purpose. It was given to you under important circumstances, and you wear it as a badge . . . you feel it brings you good fortune . . . but this ring does not belong to you, and the spirits in the ring will bring you misfortune. The ring has helped you this far only to make you fail at the worst possible moment. You will soon be making important decisions, choices that will be influenced by the ring, by its history. There is much danger."

"Holy cow!" Dixie gasped.

"This woman!" Helena's eyes were ablaze, a trembling finger crooked at Dixie. "She is part of this danger, but also the solution. You must keep her close. But not too close. Do not tell her all or you will lose all." Of course, what had she said other than the girlfriend might or might not have something to do with whatever it was that might or might not happen? Theater, palmist style.

Helena smiled gently, pleased with herself. Was she a smokin' hot palmist or what? These two were about ready to keel over. She'd earned her fee. Best not to risk a repeat visit from these customers. With a gasp and a low moan, Helena slumped and fell from her chair to the soft carpet.

Dixie lurched to Helena's side. "My goodness! Robbie, call 911!"

Helena awoke suddenly. "No! No! I will be all right. It is you who must beware! The vibrations, they were very strong . . . the child . . . the ring . . . I cannot see any more tonight. You must go! That will be sixty dollars, please."

Robert and Dixie paid and left.

In the cab, Dixie was beside herself.

RINGER 39

"Robbie, where did you get that ring?"

"I told you, it is a family ring. I don't know its history."

"Like Helena said, I do not think you're telling me everything." Of course, this was true. What man actually tells a woman *all*? "You have to get rid of it!"

Grant laughed, unconvincingly. "She was very good, that palmist woman—but Dixie, darling, that was acting. You do not really think . . ."

"She knew about Purity, about what a thorn she is in your side. How did she know about that?"

"Dix, she could have guessed, I do not know, but it's an act. A good one . . . but that's how they stay in business. Believe me, you're getting too worked up about this."

Grant did not manage to bed Dixie that night; she was too upset by Helena. He went home and drank Scotch from a decanter, and then slept . . . but not well.

NO, I DID NOT BRING Nancy back to my hotel. She brought me back to her apartment. To be brutally honest, the evening was not all that I had hoped. Believe it or not, once I was naked, all she wanted to do was pose me. Yes, like a statue, and while I stood there naked she danced to flute music. This unsatisfactory perversion was new to me. Perhaps worse, even when I did kiss her, she did so with her teeth closed. Have you ever heard of anything so infuriating? Nancy was one of these overly coy women you hear about that frustrate men to the brink of insanity. She kept calling me her muse. I am not even sure what "muse" means. Anyway, I came up with the idea of her posing naked with me so I could have a better shot at moving things along toward the bed. No success. I finally succumbed to the nebbiolo, dove into her bed, and slept. The new day found Nancy still dancing to flute music in the living room. I think she may have been on drugs of some sort, but I cannot say for sure. Her muse managed to slip out unnoticed.

Which was why I was late the next morning in my holy mission. I had to go back to my hotel first and put on a fresh suit and, of course, pick up the humidor with the finger inside.

I entered the glass tower of Grant Industries on Sixth Avenue at 11:30 A.M. I left at 11:40 A.M. The large guard told me nobody is even allowed beyond the lobby without an appointment. So he lent me his phone, and I called up to the offices and was told that Mr. Grant was in meetings all day. When they asked my business, I told them I was La Paz gentry, and that I came at the behest of the Catholic Diocese of Guadalupe, on business of a personal nature. She said that I should call back later and they would see if they could schedule me.

My first attempt had not gone as well as I hoped it might.

On the street, I turned the corner and went into an inexpensive restaurant called the Red Flame. At 11:45 in the morning you would think such a place would be empty. You would be mistaken. I had to go all the way around the side to what looked like an open booth at the end next to the wall, but there was a placard there that read: RESERVED. Exasperated by my sexual misadventure, by my failed attempt to meet Grant, and now by finding reserved seating in a diner—of all things—I straddled a stool at the counter and ordered a coffee and grilled cheese.

I resolved to shake off my encounter with Nancy—I could not stumble over such things in my holy march toward reuniting the ring with the finger of my ancestor. How could I have known that Nancy would be so relentlessly coy?

So I would call Grant Industries that afternoon and see. Perhaps Grant would see me, thinking I was there for a charity of some sort. I was an idiot to think that he would handle charitable institutions himself, but I did not know at that time about the rich and their chummy charities. Nor had I any reason to believe that Grant knew the ring came from La Paz, much less that it belonged to my ancestor, much less that it came from a desecrated relic and holy shrine.

The grilled cheese was excellent. You know, they do not make

"Is something wrong, señor?" My focus shifted to his r
and the buttery gold ring bearing the cross of Caravaca.

"You called my secretary?" His eyes blinked rapidly. "But
were to meet here."

"Yes, so we have, which is good fortune as we have a very important matter to discuss."

"Look," he began in a whisper. "I'm not used to this sort . . .
this sort of thing. My reputation . . . this is very delicate. In fact,
call this number; ask for Dixie, she'll arrange everything."

With that he jumped to his feet.

"Señor, please, stay and enjoy your salad."

"Not at this time, thank you." He strode from the table and
out the front of the restaurant.

I said to myself, "That went well."

Except that the rich guy stuck me with the tab for his Caesar
salad and iced tea. Even so, the second grilled cheese was actually
better than the first.

good grilled cheese in La Paz, or anywhere that I have b
Baja Sur. A quesadilla is not the same thing.

I heard someone sit at the reserved table behind me. Thi:
to see: What kind of man reserves a table at the Red Flame l
Some rich, entitled bastard, no doubt.

Sure enough, he looked the part: steel gray hair, wid
three-piece suit.

I turned back to my grilled cheese and took a bite.

The crunch of the toasted bread became the strum of hai
my head. I looked again. Yes, it was Robert Tyson Grant a
table behind me, inspecting the menu nervously. I stood.

"Señor?"

He glanced up at me, then back to his menu. "I'll have the
sar salad, hold the anchovies. And an iced tea."

"Señor Grant, I am not your waiter. My name is Martin
have been sent from Mexico."

You could have stuck an anchovy in his ear and he would
have looked more surprised. He gulped and said, "You're her

"Yes, as you can see. I left a message with your secretary th
was here. I do not know if she gave you the message, but—"

"Gentlemen?" A rather pretty blonde stood over us waiting
our order. An actress, I thought.

Grant just stared at her, unable to speak, so I spoke for hi:
"He will have the Caesar salad plate, no anchovies, and an ic
tea. My food is on the counter, there, I was waiting for my frier
here and did not know this was his table. Just the same, I wi
have another grilled cheese, rye and American this time, and an
other coffee."

The waitress left us, and Grant was staring at me like I would
surely burst into flame. Helena's insights into his curse from the
previous night had made him jumpy.

EIGHT

DIXIE WAS RIGHT. PACO WAS not punctual. In fact, even as I sat in the Red Flame enjoying my second grilled cheese, the Headhunter was still in Texas. He was lucky to have even been that close to New York.

The border crossing had gone wrong when the pickup truck stalled in the desert. Border patrols spotted their flashlights as Paco, the driver, and four other men tried to coax the truck back to life. They were rounded up and put into a school bus with fifty other illegals. Paco had tossed his bag of guns into the scrub, but when he was patted down the gringos missed the hatchet in the small of his back. That is how the Honduran farmers he grew up with carried their hatchets home, tucked into the back of their pants, blade nestled between their shoulder blades, where scar tissue and calluses formed to protect them from the edges.

At a transfer point near the border, Paco ducked back under the bus and scuttled behind a portapotty. As his countrymen were being herded by flashlights into a set of new buses, Paco skipped off across the dark desert, headed for a parking lot. He had to climb a fence to get there, but he found haven in the bed of a pickup truck next to some roofing supplies under a bed cover.

He awoke hours later when the owner of the truck drove out

of the parking lot. Paco had no idea where he would end up, but when the truck stopped, it was at a convenience store. The driver was inside buying coffee when Paco crept from under the cover. The amber glow of a Texas dawn warmed him as he headed east along the highway.

After an hour's walk, the sun high, he heard a truck pulling onto the shoulder behind him. He expected the border patrol, but saw it was a van packed with migrant workers. The driver motioned to him. Paco knew he could not walk to New York. He needed to get to Houston, soon, to catch that bus. Since he'd ditched his bag with the guns in the desert before the border patrol grabbed him, he had no weapons and did not know what he would do to kill his target.

So Paco shambled over to the car window, where the driver's round scarred face shone darkly like a hammered brass plate. They spoke in Spanish, naturally, so you will want to use subtitles.

"Work?" the driver said.

"I am headed to Houston."

"My crew is a man short."

"I need transport to Houston. I have work in New York."

The mention of New York seemed to impress Plate Face. "That is a long way. You have money?"

"Can you get me to Houston?"

"You come across last night?"

"I need a ride."

"I know friends who can help. If you have money."

"How far can you take me?"

"Not to Houston, but in that direction. And like I said . . ."

"Is there room in there?"

"There's always room for another countryman."

The passengers slid open the side door and helped Paco squeeze inside.

Lurching forward, the van rattled back onto the highway, heading east.

Paco was back on his way to New York.

Slowly.

THE GRILLED CHEESE SANDWICHES WERE still fresh on my mind when I exited the subway at Lexington and East Seventy-seventh Street and walked east. I had made the call to this woman Dixie and had arranged an appointment immediately. God was still on my side. Better to get this business with the ring completed as soon as possible.

The meeting location was near an esplanade, a raised pedestrian boulevard perched over the FDR Drive and the East River. The access to this esplanade was five long crosstown blocks east of the subway, at an East Eighty-first Street cul-de-sac. It was a nice day so I did not mind the exercise, but it was warm so my jacket was thumbed over my shoulder. When I reached the esplanade, a panoramic view of the East River lay before me. Fat power yachts and tour boats plowed the turgid green river, and glassy green apartment buildings across the channel on Roosevelt Island twinkled in the afternoon sun. I laid a course north along the esplanade through a steady stream of Rollerbladers and dog walkers. Benches faced the water to my right and were strewn with sunbathers.

Sturdy stone apartment buildings on my left soon parted to reveal a leafy park. As instructed, I exited into this park and curled down toward where the path encircled a statue. It was the statue of Peter Pan, a bad one. It didn't look anything like Robin Williams.

I spotted her immediately, and she me.

With a thin waist and compact behind, she was in black slacks and a white wraparound halter that cradled her implants to wonderful effect. Her raven hair curled at her temples like little devil horns.

By the way her blue eyes inspected mine, I knew she was not displeased by my appearance. A little surprised, in fact.

I raised an eyebrow and took her hand. "I am Morty."

"No you're not."

"No?"

She shook her head. "You're cute."

I cocked the other eyebrow, favoring her with a knowing smile. That was my way of disguising the displeasure of being called cute.

"Perhaps this is so," was my reply, "but I can also be dangerous."

I am so charming sometimes I can hardly stand it.

She shifted her weight to the other hip and curled her hand around my bicep. "I would hope so." We began to walk slowly around the bad Robin Williams statue. "So you first. I have to be careful."

"Very well. May I call you Dixie?"

"Mmm."

"Well, Dixie, I have come from La Paz, Mexico, on a quest. Of course, I had no idea I would have the pleasure of expediting this quest with someone as fascinating as yourself."

If Antonio Banderas is not available for this movie, I implore you to see if Benjamin Bratt or Jimmy Smits is still around. I suppose by now Erik Estrada is up on blocks in Pasadena.

She smiled to herself. "Go on."

"This quest of mine is to make things right, to correct an intolerable situation that has gone on for far too long. I am not here to assign blame, let me be clear. That is not my place. Only God can judge men."

"I see you are being careful, too. Let's do be clear, though. How much do you want?"

"It is not money Father Gomez seeks."

She knit her brow. "Gomez?"

"*Father* Gomez. He is the one who sent me, from the orphanage Nuestra Señora de Cortez. I know Robert Tyson Grant is a very generous and charitable man, but it is not charity I seek."

"Ah, OK. So what will it take to make things right with *Father Gomez*?"

"Do you not even want to know the details of my quest?"

"Less I know the better. So we're talking about a *donation*? Is there a size donation you had in mind?"

I took from my side pocket the box containing the finger and creaked it open. "This is the finger of a conquistador. Hernando Martinez de Salvaterra. It is very old, a religious relic, and it is very powerful. Yet it has been desecrated."

Dixie wrinkled her adorable little nose, and her eyes betrayed concern, but she held her tongue. I continued.

"Somehow this finger has become separated from the gold Hapsburg ring bearing the cross of Caravaca. That ring is now on Robert Tyson Grant's finger instead of this one. I seek to return the ring to the desiccated finger of my ancestor, Hernando Martinez de Salvaterra."

Dixie released my arm and turned to me. "You mean to say all you want to complete your quest is that ring? The one Bobbie wears?"

"God willing. That is why I am here."

"You're here to right a wrong, to correct a *situation* that has gone on far too long?"

"You are as perceptive as you are beautiful."

She stepped back from me. "You *are* cute and dangerous, aren't you?"

"You will discuss this with Robert Tyson Grant?"

"Over dinner."

"Ah, I see. My misfortune."

"How so?"

"I have come all the way from La Paz and am a stranger here in New York. It would have been an honor to buy you dinner and discuss matters more pleasant than desiccated relics."

"Slow down, cowboy." She wagged a finger at me, but she was smiling. "Rope another calf, I'm spoken for."

I shrugged. Never let a woman think you care.

"My error, then. As you are not wearing a ring, I would have been an idiot not to seek your company for dinner. Yes?"

Dixie laughed and began a retreat toward East End Avenue. "Enough, Morty! Save those charms for someone else. Where can I reach you?"

"I will call you tomorrow morning."

I watched her retreat with interest, and sighed. How could I compete with Grant, a tycoon? Still, I would have to do better than Nancy.

CHAPTER
TEN

A PIZZA DELIVERY VAN IN Midland, Texas, went missing, and was later found in Fort Worth, Texas.

The same day in Fort Worth, a man was robbed of one hundred and eighty dollars by a Hispanic male wielding a hatchet. This occurred in a Waffle House bathroom.

Paco was on his way to Memphis.

ELEVEN

THE PICTURE WINDOWS AT MR. LEE'S on Mott Street are filled with large fish tanks glowing with goggle-eyed carp and eels ripe for the menu. You might want to have your cameras focused on the fish and then pull out to see Grant navigating the rain-slicked narrow sidewalk, his golf umbrella towering over the Asian people crowding his way. June had just begun to heat up, which brings late-day thunderstorms to New York.

Mr. Lee's was an ideal setting for a conversation about murdering Purity. It was a noisy restaurant, and most of the Asian patrons would not understand English well enough to understand what Robert and Dixie were plotting.

We find Dixie in a booth in the corner, her shapeliness packed into a blue silk Chinese tunic and her hair piled in place with chopsticks. She was the very image of intrigue. The booth was padded in red vinyl, and lit by a single plastic Chinese lantern rigged with gold plastic dragons. She kissed Grant on the cheek as he slid into the booth across from her.

"You look gorgeous," he said, hoping she would keep that outfit on later until he could get her alone.

Dixie merely smiled and bowed to her man like she'd seen geishas do on TV. Tokyo and Beijing were all the same to her.

The waiter appeared. "Howyoo?"

"Very good, thanks. What wine do you have?"

"Wine? All kind."

"What do you have in a white?"

"White? Vergood. For man?"

"What Scotch do you have?"

"Scotch? Vergood."

The waiter vanished.

Robert clasped Dixie's hands across the table. "So you met the Mexican, the one in the white suit?"

"I did indeed."

"He wasn't at all what I expected."

"I know, Robbie, he's so . . . gentlemanly."

"I would have thought that he would have looked rougher, a little more like my gardener or something. He doesn't exactly fly under the radar, does he?"

"Well, you know, maybe he finds it easier to dress down for what he has to do, so that nobody will recognize him."

"But he's our man?"

"Definitely."

"Wine!" The waiter thunked a tumbler of white in front of Dixie and thunked a tumbler of amber in front of Robert. "Scotch! Take order?"

Dixie patted her menu. "Give us a few moments, sweetie."

The waiter vanished.

"Are you sure this is a good idea, Dix?"

"Chinese?"

"No. The Mexican."

She patted him sympathetically on the cheek. "Buttercup, we discussed this over and over. Unless Purity happens to get herself killed—and Lord knows she's tried—there really is no other way out of your predicament. It's intolerable. You've tried your best, Lord knows. She's a disgrace and besmirches your good name."

"Let's not forget every time she pulls a stunt Grant Industries stocks dip."

"How many times has she been arrested?"

"Twelve in this country. Four in Europe."

"Rehab?"

"Six."

"Worst of all, she's besmirching the memory of her mother. Does such a soulless being, bereft of remorse or conscience, have a place in God's world?"

"When people hear the name Grant, they think of Purity Grant first, not Robert Tyson Grant. Makes me look like a fool."

"Well, it just has to be done, for you, for the stockholders, for us. I love you, Bobbie-kins, but there have been nights when you've been too angry about Purity to make love to me."

Grant's face went red at the thought of the temporary impotence he'd suffered due to Purity. "Does the Mexican know it has to look like an accident of some kind?"

"We didn't discuss details. Yet."

Robert replied with a confused cock of his head.

"Robbie, we only got as far as the donation."

"Donation?"

"He's using a charity as a dodge to make the fee look like a donation, which of course is perfect for us—the fee would look like any number of our other donations to orphanages. Only he doesn't want money."

Robert paled as his mind flicked through possible alternatives.

"Robbie, it's nothing bad." Dixie squeezed his hand, and turned it so that the buttery cross of Caravaca glimmered in the cheap Chinese lamplight. "He wants your ring."

Grant pulled his hand away, thumbing the ring of my ancestor. "Why?"

Dixie laughed, briefly. "Robbie, who cares? You know how much money he could ask for? To take out Purity?"

"He must have said something about why he wanted it."

"Well, darling, he had that story about an orphanage, in Mexico, and some sort of relic."

Lightning flickered in the carp tank, the thrum of thunder in the distance.

Grant drifted back from the lamplight, his eyes glassy. "La Paz."

At this point, our camera zooms dreamily into Grant's eyes: *La Paz, La Paz, La Paz* . . .

From the dark mists and murk of Grant's memory emerges the chapel tower of Nuestra Señora de Cortez against the night sky, a flash of lightning in the distance, the bells chiming midnight.

OK, so in reality the Nuestra Señora de Cortez bells stop chiming at nine, but only people in La Paz would know this. It's much spookier with the bells chiming midnight, I think.

Inside, the chapel is alight with dripping candles, lightning flickering across the stained glass windows, illuminating the visages of dour and pious saints.

The camera looks slowly down to a heavy wooden door in the corner, which slowly croaks open to reveal eyes. The door croaks wider open, and we see that the eyes belong to two boys, one blond and thin, the other black-haired and of Spanish descent, their faces orange in the candlelight.

"Pasqual, I do not think we should do this," the blond gulps. "Let's get back to the room before we are discovered."

"We are on a quest, Bobbie—do you not remember?" says the Spaniard.

"*You* are on a quest."

"Yes, I am on a quest, and you said you would come to help fulfill my destiny."

"This destiny you speak of is in your head."

Pasqual winked at Bobbie. "You have to earn your destiny, Bobbie. Does it matter where it comes from? Come on."

The two rascals slipped out of the doorway and ducked between two pews. Reappearing in the center aisle, the boys scampered to the altar, at the base of the pulpit.

"This is crazy, Pasqual. We'll go to hell for this!"

"What does the church need it for? The ring will help me find my destiny, and I will help you find yours."

Bobbie watched as the Spaniard crept up through a gauntlet of candles, toward the altar, and to the carpeted sacramental steps.

Flickering stained glass saints loomed above the boys. Candlesticks and chalices on the altar rattled from a boom of thunder as the Spaniard crept toward the sepulchral cabinet in the altar's base.

His fingers curled into the iron rings of the cabinet door and pulled.

The cabinet doors rattled but did not budge.

Back at the base of the pulpit, Bobbie was so frightened he fought back tears.

With a bent piece of wire, Pasqual's trembling fingers worked the ancient iron lock.

Metal clanked, and the sepulchral cabinet doors jarred open.

Thunder boomed in the distance.

Candlelight wobbled into the dark recess of the cabinet to reveal a golden box, a shimmering reliquary.

Yes, it was the humidor.

Pasqual's face glistened with sweat. His thumb hesitantly lifted the latch on the gold box and squeaked open the reliquary.

There in the golden light of the chapel of Nuestra Señora de Cortez, the boy beheld the stinky brown finger of Hernando Martinez de Salvaterra with the golden Hapsburg ring of Caravaca nestled in the humidor.

"*Destino ganado!*" Pasqual whispered.

Subtitle: "Earn destiny."

In the distance, there was a creak, a clang, and then footsteps.

Pasqual's eyes went wide.

"Someone's coming!" Bobbie squeaked, his face white as a sacramental cassock. "Hurry!"

Pasqual tossed the box back into the cabinet, folded the sepulchral cabinet doors closed, and scuttled back to his blond friend.

Footsteps approached, growing louder.

The boys darted out the door through which they had come.

On the opposite side of the chapel, a similar door opened. An old, stooped friar entered, closed the door behind him, and with obvious pain knelt to pray at the altar steps.

Thunder boomed.

A wind blew through the chapel, the candles flickering.

The unlocked doors to the sepulchral cabinet creaked slowly open.

The friar raised his gaze from his clasped hands to the sepulchral cabinet, eyes widening.

The golden reliquary humidor slid from its shelf, hit the carpet, and bounced down the altar ledge. At the marble floor, it popped open.

The shriveled brown finger of Hernando Martinez de Salvaterra skittered across the marble and rolled to a stop in front of the friar.

Without the Hapsburg Caravaca ring.

So how's that for screenwriting? I believe the screenwriting manual has assisted me in providing cinematic drama to my story.

To be brutally honest, if I weren't dying soon, I would head to Hollywood, lock, stock, and barrel. Now get a load of this transition; I seriously doubt Sergio Leone could have done it better.

The amazed eyes of the friar, alight with chapel candles and flickering lightning, become the eyes of Robert Tyson Grant by the light of the cheap Chinese lantern in Mr. Lee's on Mott Street, the flicker of lightning in the carp tank behind him.

"Robbie, are you all right?"

Grant's eyes focus on Dixie. "I won't give the Mexican my ring."

Her mouth moved, but she had no words.

"Dix, find out how much he wants, but he cannot have the ring."

Her blue eyes were fixed on his, and they narrowed. "So now it's my turn. Why?"

"Because the ring is mine. *I earned it.*"

CHAPTER

TWELVE

THE FORTUNE-TELLER HELENA WAS GLUED to *Let's See if You Can Dance* on TV when there was a rap at her door. She had been so engrossed by her program, so titillated with the anticipation of Jocy and Marissa's pending tango routine, that she had forgotten to pull the shades on the shop windows. Normally she closed early for *Let's See if You Can Dance*. She pushed a button on an ancient VCR, and it began to record her show.

Parting the beaded curtain into the foyer, she beheld Robert Tyson Grant and his golf umbrella at the shop door, rain pounding the sidewalk around him.

Helena flashed a wise smile and went to unlock the door.

"I was expecting you," she said as he passed by her into the room. She sniffed. "But you stayed longer than you wanted to at the Chinese restaurant."

Grant's jaw dropped. "How can you know such things?"

She could know such things because the aroma of a Chinese restaurant is unmistakable, and it was on his clothing. Helena answered with a sad smile and gestured toward her parlor. "Please."

Grant rested his umbrella against the wall and followed her through the beaded curtain. "Someone has come for the ring, Helena. I must know more about him."

Ah, yes, this was the rich man with the ring and the Kewpie doll girlfriend.

She sat at the table, palms down on the red tablecloth. "I warned of danger. It is here. Sit."

He sat.

"Give me your hands."

He gave her his hands.

She clasped them between hers, eyes closed.

"Someone has come for the ring."

"Yes!"

Often, once a customer was hooked, all she had to do was repeat what people told her in order to amaze them.

"It is important to this person, this man, and he comes from the north. No, the south. Yes, he comes from the south." She peeked at the ring. "He has history with the ring . . . but you do not want him to have this ring." Obviously whoever it was had a history with the ring, or why would he have come?

"Yes!"

"The ring, the ring . . . you have had it many years . . . and it came to you under dark circumstances." She figured that someone, a relative perhaps, died and bequeathed it.

"Can you tell me who he is? How he knows about the ring?"

"There is a dark history with this ring. This man is part of that history, a member of your family."

"Well . . ."

"No, not your family, but a place where you once lived."

"Yes, the orphanage."

He had just given Helena a wealth of information to build on. "You do not know this man." If he did, he would know why he had come for the ring, wouldn't he? "But you must know someone who does know him. At the orphanage. Yes, the orphanage!"

"Yes, the orphanage! But who? Pasqual? I haven't seen him since La Paz."

"The man who has come is Bolivian." Helena watched *Jeopardy!* so knew some geography.

"Bolivian?"

"Yes, he is from the south, from La Paz."

"Mexico. La Paz, Mexico."

"Yes, of course, how silly, I am very tired . . . he has come from Mexico . . . but you knew he would come, did you not?"

"Yes! But when I asked him to come, I didn't think he was going to ask for the ring."

He asked the Mexican to come? "You had a business arrangement with this man. He is a contractor of some kind, a specialist . . ." Helena figured anybody from Mexico summoned by a rich white person had to be in the trades, maybe to stucco this rich guy's house or something.

Grant pulled his hands away.

Aha. There was part of the story he didn't want her to know. Must be something illegal. Drugs, maybe.

Helena smiled sadly. "The ring, which was taken under dark purpose, has brought this upon you. The ring is cursed, and now so are you. This curse has been a great burden to you."

"A curse? You mean Purity?" Grant blinked hard a few times. "Should I give him the ring? Will that lift the curse?"

"The curse is upon you, not the ring." Helena did not understand that Purity was a name, so was a little confused.

"So if I give him the ring, the curse will not go away? My burden will remain?"

Helena jumped from her chair, eyes wild, and loosed a shriek that toppled Grant right out of his chair. Then she sank slowly to her knees, sobbing.

Grant scuttled next to her. "Helena, what happened? Are you all right? Are you OK?"

Helena's sister, Abbie, appeared in the doorway, a behemoth in a tracksuit. She held up some dried leaves in her hand. "Stand back! Back, I say!"

Grant lurched backward and found his chair.

Abbie strode forward and crumpled the leaves over her sister, chanting as the shredded bay leaves rained onto the sobbing palmist. She paused and furrowed her brow at Grant. "Have you paid?"

"No, I—"

"You must come back tomorrow. She will be better then. Pay and go."

Grant slapped a hundred-dollar bill on the table, grabbed his umbrella, and pushed out the front door.

Helena abruptly stopped crying. "Lock the door, Abbie."

Abbie waddled over to the door and flipped the latch. When she returned to the séance parlor, Helena was at the table lighting a cigarette. "He's a live one."

"So I figured. What's the deal?"

"He's in some sort of shady business."

"Him? He looks rich."

"He is, but he is also up to something and has things to hide."

"Ah. Cursed, is he?"

"Cursed real bad." Helena grinned.

"Like I seen him before. Famous?"

"Not TV famous. Rich famous."

"I think I seen him on TV, Lena."

"That would be a help if you could ID him. When I mentioned the curse, he said something about the curse being purity. That make any sense?"

"No. So if I find out who he is, I get a cut of the cure, right?"

"I always need you when someone's got a curse, don't I?"

"Just checking. When?"

"No date yet. I figured I play him for another office visit before we cure him."

"Not like you to leave the afflicted strung out."

"He'll be back tomorrow. For sure. Like I said, he's got it bad. See if you can figure out who he is. Maybe check the Web."

"I was just on Facebook when you had your attack."

"OK, then."

"If I find out who he is, what do I get? I should get more than a small piece of the cure."

"Why?"

"If it's important and we find out all kinds of stuff, it could be worth a lot of money."

"Let's see who he is first, then we'll talk."

"No way, Lena. Remember that other time?"

"What other time?"

"That woman. The model."

"Seventy-five, twenty-five."

"Fifty, fifty."

"Seventy, thirty. Going, going . . ."

"Sixty, forty."

"Sixty-five, thirty-five. Done?"

"Done."

THIRTEEN

LET US CUT AWAY FROM the smoky confines of the palm-ist's inner sanctum to the briny exuberance of the sea crashing white froth on the dark sandy shores of East Hampton. The party lights of a lounge called El Rolo are visible beyond the dune. Lightning flutters on the west horizon.

El Rolo was a velvet rope place. If you were a man, you could only get in if you were accompanied by several beautiful girls or if you were famous and preferably both. Beautiful girls could get in even if they were not famous as long as their shoes were of the Prada equivalent.

You think I'm kidding, but Wilmer was the bouncer, and he had to know his shoes. Not only could he tell you the manufac-turer of almost any woman's upscale shoe, but he knew them by type: pump, mule, thong flat, espadrille, and even peep-toe sling-back. He could even tell the cheap knock-offs, the Canal Street Specials sold in Chinatown back rooms. His job was as much as anything to keep out the riffraff and the paparazzi, so being able to tell a pair of Gucci cork wedges from Payless cork wedges was an important part of his job. That and being large enough to in-timidate anybody on the planet. It's a fact: Mike Tyson came there one night and got drunk. Wilmer threw him out. And I mean that literally. After taking a punch to the chest from the heavyweight champion of the world, Wilmer picked up Tyson and flung him out the back door into the dune.

It was closing time this particular night. Wilmer had provided drivers for about ten people so far. El Rolo provided drivers and follow cars to get people home safely and help keep them out of the tabloids for DUI. This pleased the customers and the local police, who did not like having to arrest their meal tickets but could not turn a blind eye to their crashing into trees, either.

Wilmer drew the chain across the driveway so nobody else could try to come in. The sign by the road was turned off, but that didn't always stop Billy Joel from trying to come in for a nightcap. There were only four cars left. His drivers were all back now, and looking sleepy. So Wilmer went inside to assess who else was there that needed a nudge toward the door and a drive home.

There was a blond Dolce & Gabbana crisscross sandal with two brunettes, one a Ferragamo leopard-print platform sling-back, the other a turquoise Christian Dior slide. No men.

"Excuse me, ladies, hate to bother you, but it's that time."

The turquoise Christian Dior slide looked sleepily up at him. "Thanks, Wilmer. Any drivers still here?"

"Sure, sweetheart. All three of you girls need drivers?"

"Not me," said the Dolce & Gabbana. "I've been on smoothies all night. Can't be puffy tomorrow for the shoot."

"I'm OK," yawned the Ferragamo, "but you better check on Purity."

"Where's she?"

"Oceanside."

Wilmer squeezed out the back door to the patio. Nobody there, but he could see Purity with her blond pigtails sitting down near where the waves were breaking. So he made tracks—big tracks—down the beach.

"Purity?"

She turned, a bottle of tequila at her side and Prada ankle-strap thongs behind her in the sand. She was in cutoff jeans and a sleeveless man's oxford shirt, open in front and exposing a yellow bikini top.

"Purity, it's time to go home, sweetheart. I'll get a driver for you."

"Yeah. I have to get up tomorrow. Have to be in court in Manhattan."

"Not for that joyride the other night."

"No, another joyride, through Central Park, on a borrowed horse. Wilmer?"

"Yes, sweetheart?"

"Come here."

He stepped up next to her.

"Sit down, Wilmer."

"No games tonight, Purity. We got to close up. I'll carry you if you want."

"Wilmer, what would you do if you wanted to kill someone?"

He shrugged and held out his hands. "I'd just kill them with these."

"No. I mean kill them and not get caught, make it look like an accident."

"That depends."

"On what?"

"Who do you want to kill, Purity?"

"I'm just like saying. Nobody."

"Depends. Can't kill nobody in a car wreck if they don't drive. Come on, sweetheart. Let's get you off to bed."

"So you're saying that it, like, depends. Like, if they drive a car?" She staggered to her feet.

"That's right." Wilmer picked up her shoes, then picked up

Purity. She sat in the crook of his arm, reclining against his chest, and they started back to El Rolo.

"Would you hire a hit man?"

"Nah. Do not do that, Purity. Do not even talk about it. People who try that route always end up in jail. You want bad enough to kill somebody you do it yourself. That's the rules."

"There are rules?"

"There are always rules."

"I don't like rules."

"Just the same. You're a smart girl. You want to kill someone you do it yourself. But listen to me. I'm your friend, right? Your friend Wilmer is telling you not to kill anybody tonight. Go home, sleep, have some breakfast, take a swim, you'll feel better."

The lights in El Rolo began to go off, and Wilmer stepped sideways through the patio doorway into the darkened bar.

"You're a good friend, Wilmer."

"That's what they pay me for."

FOURTEEN

A NEON SIGN SIZZLES: ACE PAWNBROKER—OPEN 24/7. That's what our camera sees before drifting down into the confines of a narrow hallway encased in bulletproof thick-as-your-wrist Lucite. This seemingly glass hallway separated the customers from the used merchandise, which included almost anything you could think of that was of any value: guitars, drum sets, barbecue grills, fishing poles, hockey sticks, microwaves, taxidermy, silver sets, jewelry . . . and guns. Ceiling fans turned lazily under fluorescent tubes.

The pawnshop smelled of Lysol. Perhaps scratch-and-sniff cards could be given to the audience in the lobby before the movie. There could be a cross-promotion with Lysol.

While Purity was drinking rum on the beach, Paco was arriving in Memphis by Greyhound, and it probably would not surprise anybody to learn that the bus station in Memphis is not too far from some unsavory neighborhoods. The kind that have pawnshops.

Behind the Lucite, at the counter, was a compact Bangladeshi man. He had sideburns that went all the way to his chin, and a cutoff T-shirt bearing the Rebel flag. He didn't seem to like the looks of Paco even though he had not yet met him.

"Can I help you with something?" The southern lilt of the Bangladeshi's voice echoed from the other side of the Lucite barrier.

Paco spotted the gun case and stood before it, looking.

"You think I'm going to sell a gun to a greaser in the middle of the night you're crazy, Sanchez."

Paco wasn't entirely sure what the clerk had said—he was a little out of practice speaking English—but he got the gist. He wasn't so easily offended, and he knew that if this pawnshop was anything like the pawnshops back in Juárez, who you were and where you came from did not matter. Only money mattered.

He also knew pawnshops had guns on display, and then they had other guns. The kinds they kept around for greasers who shopped in the middle of the night.

Paco smiled at the clerk. "Very funny," he said in English. "We stop the bullshit. What pistols you have for me?"

The clerk knit his brow. "Who you think you're talking to, Sanchez?"

"You want my business? I have money. I go to the shop down the street. OK?" Paco strode toward the door.

"Now hold on, son. What exactly are you looking for?"

Paco stopped in the doorway, looked up at the security camera. "Turn that off, yes?"

The clerk hesitated, then reached behind him and depressed a button on a black digital recorder. "Now you wanna tell me?"

"Nine millimeter or bigger."

"What you see in the case. But . . ."

"No, señor." Paco was smiling, mostly with his eyes. "The other ones. The ones not in the case."

"Look, son—"

"*Por favor,* señor, you are wasting my time, and your time. Do you have nine-millimeter pistols or do you not?" Paco was looking for the ones that would fly under the radar, ones that there were no records of and that didn't require any paperwork.

The clerk squinted at him. "I have a police issue."

"*Bueno.* May I see it?"

The clerk unlocked a metal drawer behind him, glanced at the front door, and then held up the black automatic.

"Work the action, please."

Paco watched as the clerk cocked the gun.

"Now pull the trigger."

"That's not good for the—"

"You think I buy a gun with no firing pin? Show me the real thing, man, stop joking."

"You have cash? Serious cash?"

Paco fished a thick wad of greenbacks from his black jeans and held it up. The robbery in the Dallas bus station wasn't his only robbery along the way.

With a glance at the front door, the clerk motioned Paco to the back of the store. At the end of the Lucite hallway was a display case of watches. The clerk detached the top of the display case and set it aside. Below was another display case, lighted. In it were a variety of pistols, the serial numbers ground off of them.

Paco's face shone in the light of the display case, his yellow eyes aglow. "This is what I talk about."

FIFTEEN

WHERE HAD I BEEN WHILE Grant was falling under the spell of a palmist? While Purity was getting drunk and while Paco was cruising skid-row Memphis for guns?

There was no way I was cruising the bar at El Quixote again.

I asked the bald concierge in the red tie at my hotel where one could find a place where singles mingle. In case you do not know—and you might not if you are not gentry—a concierge is someone at a nicer hotel who can arrange things for hotel guests. Things like theater tickets, sporting events, and restaurant reservations. I only say this because you will not find a concierge at most Red Roof Inns. This one had a name tag that read ROGER.

The concierge leaned in across his desk and whispered, "You looking to pay for it or just to try your luck?"

"Pay?" I scoffed. "No."

"You looking for women or men?"

"Women, of course."

He nodded. "I have to ask. Some foxes like grapes." He jotted a destination onto a pad, tore the sheet off, and handed it to me. "Can I give you some advice?"

"You are the concierge, it is what you do."

"Do bottle service."

"Bottle service?"

"Find an empty lounge area, and ask the waitress for a bottle of Grey Goose, mixers, and ice. It will cost you, but you gotta break eggs to cook omelets."

"I do not drink vodka."

"The ladies do. If you hang around the bar you look cheap; the ladies will steer clear. If you stake out a lounge area for yourself, with a bottle and no guests, the ladies will come sit near you hoping you'll offer them a drink while you wait for your friends. Catch flies with honey."

"Ah, this is clever, Roger. We do not have bottle service in La Paz."

"When in Rome. So order whatever it is you're drinking, by the glass if you want. But do the bottle service and they'll come to you. Do not pay cash, just give the waitress your credit card." Roger looked at his watch. "It shouldn't be too busy there now, it's early, you'll get the after-work crowd. Girls headed out to celebrate a birthday, like that. Birds of a feather."

So I did exactly as Roger had instructed. I went to the West Side swanky bar on the note, I sat at a plush couch with a coffee table and flanking chairs, and I ordered a bottle of Grey Goose, and a glass of burgundy for myself. Just as Roger had said, two girls named Stephanie and Elissa sat across from me, and I offered them a drink. More girls arrived, friends of theirs, Cami, Meg, Grace, Mim, and Vim. Dena was late. I ordered another bottle, setting my sights on Vim. She was closer to my age than the others, slightly larger, so I calculated that she would be more susceptible to my charms. I'm not saying that she was a dog or fat or anything. She was just more full-figured than the others, and I know men these days lean toward skinny and insubstantial women. Vim had long blond crinkly hair, a short print dress, and platform shoes.

We struck up a conversation. Vim was a legal secretary, and I found that fascinating. I guessed her astrological sign, was wrong, but that never matters. If you show an interest in astrology, women think you are spiritual somehow, and I have found being spiritual is always a turn-on for the fair sex. Religious not so much.

I lured her away from the others by sharing an interest in wine. We went to the bar, had a glass of something expensive, and I regaled her with stories of La Paz and the life of gentry. While I spoke, she crossed her legs and her eyes were bright. She ran her fingers through her hair three times. Then she touched my arm and said she had to go.

I hope the men in the audience will pay attention to the little details, as they are crucial. Details of what scientists call "body language." If you are speaking with a woman in a dress and she crosses her legs, the body language tells you she is testing to see if you are attracted to her legs. You must sneak a look and let her catch you. Conversely—and this I find both fascinating and infuriating—do not let a woman catch you staring at her breasts, no matter how magnificent those parts may be. I cannot say why this is so, but it is OK to look at a woman's legs but not her tits. You will just have to trust me on this.

Unless she *speaks* of her breasts, of course. You think I am making a joke, but I am not. A woman with implants will often come right out and ask you what you think of her enhancements. Then you must tell her what marvelous cleavage she has purchased. Though a friend of mine once doubted they were better than real breasts, and played that line of conversation out to the extent that the woman showed him the breasts and let him handle them for quality. Do not try this at home, kids.

I think even the dullards in the audience will know that a woman who strokes her hair as she is talking with you wants a compliment to test your level of interest. You may compliment her hair, or better still her jewelry, because that opens a whole other line of ridiculous conversation about where she got it and what it is made of. You might even say something about how turquoise goes well with her skin, or that you prefer sterling silver to gold. It suggests that you know jewelry and more importantly might therefore be disposed to purchasing it, possibly for her sometime in the future.

If you compliment her shoes she will like it but think you are gay.

When a woman touches your arm as you are charming her, her body language translates a green light. She is telling you to ask for her number, and even perhaps more.

"I have to go as well. I really must eat. Would you care to join me?"

"I'd love to, Morty, but I have to get home to feed and walk my dog."

"As I am from out of town on business and really have nothing to do but go back to the room and watch television, I would gladly accompany you on the walk so that we might continue our stimulating conversation."

She smiled and laughed gently. "You have a very cute way of speaking, Morty, you really do."

Two insults in one—but I knew she did not mean it that way.

"You like dogs, Morty?"

"Dogs? But of course. Who among us does not like a dog?"

I signaled for the bill. It came.

"Excuse me a moment, Vim."

I found the waiter at the end of the bar.

"You mean to tell me each of those bottles was three hundred dollars?"

"Yes, sir."

"I thought you said thirty."

"No, sir."

"Are you sure?"

"Tip is included."

"At thirty dollars a drink I would hope that a four-course meal and a box of condoms would be included."

"There are free condoms in the bathroom."

"Yes, thank you, I already prevailed myself of some."

I went back to Vim.

"Anything wrong, Morty?"

"Of course not, *querida*. The waiter, he only charged me for one of the bottles, not both."

She stood and smoothed her dress around her delightful behind. "And you told him? I'm not sure I would have at three hundred dollars a bottle."

"Well, I would hate to see him get in trouble." Might as well take the opportunity to look flush in front of the girl.

Six hundred simolions! Ay-yi-yi! Plus for the wine. I was in for almost seven hundred. To be fair, the concierge told me it was expensive, and he gave me the choice of paying for the sex outright. I reminded myself about the millions I had in Banco Cortez and kept my smile.

Outside, I hailed a cab, but Vim said we could walk. The June night was warm and breezy, so we walked.

It was a fine night, and as we walked, I inhaled the sweet fragrance of her fruity shampoo and felt her arm brush mine. I told her about Sparky, the mutt I had as a kid, about how I trained him, how he would try to climb trees after squirrels, how he was afraid of cats. "Yes, I loved that dog dearly."

"That's so nice."

"As fate would have it, he was hit by a train."

"A train!"

"We were poor and lived near the subway where it was depressed into the ground. Sparky and I were playing fetch. I threw the Frisbee, the wind caught it, and Sparky leaped after it."

"Oh, no!" Vim grasped my arm. "That's horrible."

I nodded sadly, flexing my jaw muscle to make it look like I might cry. "And you know, as he fell he caught that Frisbee, mid-air. Just before the Q train hit him."

Now Vim was stroking the back of my neck and kissed my cheek. "Morty, that is so horrible, you must have been devastated."

"I of course blame myself. Had I only thrown the Frisbee the other way . . ."

Now Vim hugged me.

I'm not trying to turn this into an instructional video, but I hope the men will see the logic of my fiction. I never had a dog, Sparky or otherwise. I do not consider this fiction a lie. People tell stories all the time. The way I look at it, this is all part of the game. It is all enhancement. Women wear makeup, they wear push-up bras, they wear perfume, and high heels improve the curve of their legs. And let us not forget about the implants. Is this all a lie? Men are entitled to enhance themselves as well. So they suck in their gut, they puff out their chests, they act like money is not important, they shave and make their jobs sound more important. Some tell stories that may or may not have a basis in anything that actually happened to them. I will bet you a hundred dollars that someone out there had a dog named Sparky that chased a Frisbee onto the railroad tracks and was killed. So the story is likely true. Inasmuch as it did not happen to me—that's just lipstick.

Anyway, my tale had the desired result—Vim's sympathetic hands all over me—and we walked on back to her place hand in hand.

It seemed at that moment like the seven hundred dollars was worth it.

She lived in a large apartment building near the river.

"I'll go up and get Ralphie." She kissed my cheek and vanished into the building. I hoped this little dog would not hump my leg as I was humping Vim later. That once happened, and it was very disconcerting, let me tell you.

With Vim's dog it would have been very disconcerting indeed.

Vim emerged.

In tow, behind Ralphie.

A Great Dane.

I will let the filmmakers imagine exactly how to portray my dismay, not only with the size of this animal, but with the size of this animal's excrement. Watching Vim wrestle Ralphie's loafs into a bag and then heave them in the trash can was less than appealing. As was the loss of Vim's sweet shampoo fragrance, replaced by the stench of dog poo. Slobber cascaded from this beast's maw, and the monster's yellow eyes looked at me like I was its next meal.

"I'd invite you up, only Ralphie needs to know you better. He's pretty protective of me."

"Yes, I can imagine that he would be." My smile was growing weary. "Could he be otherwise of someone so charming?"

"Call me?" She handed me her card.

"Of course, *querida*. Perhaps tomorrow? I am not sure how much longer I am in town."

She kissed me on the lips. "Tomorrow."

Ralphie's stomach gurgled, a four-foot strand of drool connecting him to the sidewalk.

SIXTEEN

I FELT PERHAPS CALLING DIXIE slightly before nine the next morning was too early, but she picked up on the first ring and immediately asked to meet for breakfast. She even insisted on coming downtown to meet me in a booth at the Lyric Diner on Third Avenue. Our coffee was set next to us, and the rotund waiter trundled back to the kitchen.

Dixie was in a V-strap halter-top dress, one in a white and black tropical print. Quite ravishing.

"Morty, I'm afraid we need a little more information."

"I am as always humbled to be of assistance in any way that I can." Her breasts were glorious. They were packed into the halter top.

"Why the ring?" she asked.

I smiled the beneficent smile of anyone who is doing God's work. "As I explained, the Caravaca ring must be reunited with the finger of Hernando Martinez de Salvaterra."

Dixie tucked a curl of dark hair behind her ear and leaned in. "I still don't understand, though, Morty. Why do you want the ring instead of money?"

I blinked, not understanding her meaning at first, then realizing that as a secular person, she may not have understood how the Lord does business. I tried to put it in terms she would understand.

"Dixie, I agree, this is certainly no ordinary business transaction, and yet, if you think of it that way, it may help. Who am I but my boss's emissary dispatched to perform a task? From where we sit it may look simple, but there are wheels turning up there. I have to assume that my boss knows what He's doing when He instructs me on the terms of the deal. Isn't the important thing at the end of the day that things are set right? We are not concerned with how Grant came across this ring, but it does not belong to him. My boss only wants the ring returned. After all, for Grant this is only a modest gold ring. Am I mistaken, or could Robert Tyson Grant afford to purchase just about any ring he wanted?"

Our breakfasts arrived. Mine: grilled American cheese. Dixie's: grapefruit.

"Morty, I completely agree. Whatever the reason, I think Grant should give you guys the ring. Frankly, the less we know about how you and your boss work, the better. But I have a problem." She reached out and put her tender, warm hand on mine. "Robert doesn't want to give up the ring."

I thumbed her forefinger, nodding with concern. "Has he told you why he would not surrender the ring?"

"Robert is *my* boss. Like you, I don't pretend to understand why he does everything that he does. So you're saying there is no way we can offer you money instead?" Her small fingers rolled in my palm.

"Were it up to me, an entreaty from someone as lovely as yourself would be impossible to refuse. However, when it comes to such matters, my boss is uncompromising. I think perhaps you should make sure that Grant understands that my boss is

God. You do not want to cross Him, do you? When it comes to rewards or punishments, He does not care if someone is rich or poor."

Dixie looked a little pale, I thought, and pulled her hand away. "I'll try again, but I don't think this is going to work, Morty."

"Yes, but I am already here. My boss knows where the ring is."

It is interesting to observe certain women, especially those who have made a man their meal ticket. While I did not understand this at the time, Dixie was becoming convinced that they had made a pact with the devil, that I was with a Mexican cartel. Her understanding was that if they did not volunteer the ring, Grant might himself be killed and the ring taken from him. She had climbed one rich philanthropist after another in order to reach this one. Once head of his foundations and apple of his eye, she needed to rid him of Purity, to unburden him for even more riches that would undoubtedly be hers. There could only be one woman in his life. One possible heir.

Looking back, I don't think Dixie was necessarily as calculating as I suggest. Like many women, though, she sought security, she sought the best match she could make for herself. If this is not so, why do women swoon over doctors and lawyers? It is not because one probes smelly human crevices and the other composes tedious tracts.

A complication had arisen, one that could undo Dixie's entire business plan and all her ambitions. As with women of this type, she determined to marshal her resources.

Dixie's hand was on mine again, her dark eyes crafty, her breasts somehow more inviting than ever. "Morty, I'll get you that ring, but we have to do it my way, and it may take some time. Can you do me a favor, and give me a little time, darlin'?"

"I will do what I can. If you will." There was the spark of

mischief in her eyes, and I grinned. "Dinner? So we can discuss details of my wait."

She stood and handed me a card with her address on it.

"Be there at eight."

As she walked out, the sway of her behind promised as much as the front.

SEVENTEEN

MY HEART DANCED A RUMBA in my chest as I left the Lyric Diner. After my two unfulfilling dates it looked like the third might be a charm. I had all day to prepare. Perhaps a mani-cure was in order, or a massage, or both.

At a newsstand, I bought a newspaper and began walking. I glanced at the cover. Then I looked again.

In a box in the corner of the front page was a file photo of Pu-rity Grant surprised by the flash of a photographer's camera on the streets of Manhattan as she emerged from a police station. Below it read: GODIVA GOES TO COURT, PAGE 6.

I turned to page 6 and read:

Purrrity Grant's day in court for stealing a horse in Central Park is slated for this morning, and sources say it is likely the judge will say "neigh" to a simple fine. Court watchers anticipate the catty heiress will get more than her claws clipped.

I stopped in my tracks and hailed a cab, and in the time it took to read the funnies, horoscopes, and advice columns, the driver had delivered me to Centre Street. I didn't know for sure where Purity's hearing would be, but I knew where the courts were, and thought perhaps the paparazzi would mark the spot somehow. If not, I would simply ask.

What was my object? To be brutally honest, I wanted to gawk at Purity the way everybody else did. I had spent a considerable amount of time reading up on Robert Tyson Grant and Purity, so it had become a hobby to study them. I could hardly be expected to spend all day preparing for my date with Dixie, so why not?

The paparazzi were in force in front of One Centre Street, so I climbed the stairs and went in. Police were inside checking bags, but I had none, so walked through the scanners and then up to a cop standing by the elevators.

"Can you tell me where the Purity Grant hearing would be?"

"You'll never get in now," he snorted. "Upstairs, third floor, look for the crowds."

I went upstairs anyway and found a crowd that contained a very mixed bag of people. Of course, there were reporters and court artists, who were easily identified among the rest because of their sketch pads. They all spoke to each other in low tones and checked their watches.

Then there were people who looked like a collection of people you'd find in a bus station, not very well dressed ones, who didn't look like they knew each other. Their eyes were turned expectantly in my direction and beyond, like they were expecting a Greyhound bus. I had not known this at the time, but there are crime gawkers who spend all their time haunting the courthouses. They entertain themselves at the expense of other people's problems and feed off the fleeting fame of the infamous. Obviously, attending a court hearing featuring Purity Grant was not to be missed.

I approached one of the gawkers, an older woman in a worn sweater whose only makeup was bright red lipstick.

"Excuse me, miss, but could you tell me if this is the courtroom where the Purity Grant hearing is taking place?"

"You shoulda got here earlier. All full up."

"Ah, so this is the right place, then?"

"All full up."

One of the reporter types was at my elbow. He wore a suede jacket, cowboy boots, close-cropped ginger hair, and a smile on one side of his face. His eyes inspected my white suit carefully.

"You don't look like one of these *scumtators*." He waved a hand at the woman, who snarled at him. "And you're not press. Who are you?"

I put out my hand. "Morty."

He clasped my hand. "Skip Baker. I'm with the *Daily Post*. Who are you with? Not just a spectator?"

"I am an interested party."

Skip cocked a blond eyebrow at me. "Legal expert of some kind? No, you'd have been here earlier. You know Purity? Her father?"

I grinned. "Who does not know the Grants?"

He laughed softly. "Cagey, aren't we? You want me to get you in?"

"How much would I have to pay?"

"You don't pay, you get here early."

"Then how would you get me in?"

"I have a press card. Only they know me, I don't have to flash it. You take mine, stick close to me, flash it, and they won't think anything about it. Done it before."

I folded my arms. I am from East Brooklyn and do not so easily trust helpful strangers. "Skip, why would you do this for me?"

He chuckled, his eyes sweeping the other reporters. "Hey, I'm guessing you're a friend of the family, connected somehow. I get you in, I'm a nice guy, maybe you do me a favor in return sometime, give me a little inside info. Anything you want to tell me. Or not. No skin off me. Doesn't hurt to be a nice guy and not get anything in return."

Now it was my turn to laugh. "You are quite a character, Skip. I will accept your offer, and if I have any information that I feel would be useful, I will pass it along. I will tell you this much right now: I am sympathetic to the Grants, so have no wish to say anything that would do them harm." Certainly nothing that would have interfered with obtaining the Caravaca ring. Besides, all I knew about Robert Tyson Grant, really, was what he ate for lunch.

"Morty, if you want to go off record and tell me that Purity is secretly a nun, that's OK with me. Every little bit helps."

The bus people all went to their tiptoes. There was some commotion by the elevators down the hall. A gang of men in wire-rim glasses and pinstripe suits marched toward us, briefcases in full swing, a flash of blond hair just visible behind them. Court officers pushed our crowd apart, and the lawyers marched into the courtroom, Purity a half step behind them, and then three harried legal assistants a half step behind her.

Purity was smaller than I thought she would be, or maybe she just looked smaller because she had her head down and shoulders folded in, as though she hoped to vanish into her trench coat entirely like a snail into its shell. Remarkably, she was proportioned very much like Dixie, which is not to take anything away from either woman.

Our crowd of reporters folded in behind Purity's gang. Skip put his arm around my shoulder and greeted the court officer by name as I flashed his ID. He guided me to the spectators' gallery, fifth row.

It was pretty much like on TV—that is to say that the doors were closed, the session was called to order. A slim blond judge seated herself behind a placard that bore her name: CAROLYN GEHMAN. She tapped her gavel and said something to the prosecutor—it was hard to hear in that room as there were many hard surfaces and a high ceiling. The prosecutor stood and said that a deal had been worked out so that Purity would accept a guilty plea to a list of violations such as public nudity and disorderly conduct rather than a felony conviction for theft of the horse. Judge Gehman looked over her glasses at the defense table and asked them if the arrangement was correct. They said yes, but with about two dozen words, most of which meant nothing to me. I guess when you're being paid what that legal team was being paid, the client didn't get his money's worth if the lawyers simply said "yes."

Judge Gehman's eyes shifted to Purity, rested there a moment, and then drooped to a document on the bench. "Will the defendant please rise."

Purity stood, letting the trench coat fall to her chair. The pros had been at work on her, and the pigtails had been combined into a contrite French braid. The makeup was slight, and she wore a gray skirt suit with a white blouse. Her eyes were on the floor.

"Will the defendant please look the judge in the eye."

Purity looked up, and there was no defiance, simply the eyes of a girl who was in trouble. I couldn't tell by looking if it was an act.

"Purity Grant, I don't have to review your record aloud, do I?" The judge held the thick document up for everybody to see.

"No, ma'am."

"And this doesn't even contain your juvie record. You're getting a little old to be rebelling like this. There's a clear and continuing pattern of misdemeanors and petty crimes, none with any apparent malice except the disregard you show for the efforts the police have to expend parenting you. I'm seriously tempted to say no to this arrangement, send this to the grand jury for indictment on felony charges, and throw the book at you."

One of Purity's lawyers stepped forward, finger raised. I can't even come close to repeating what the lawyer said, because like before, the words were expensive. The gist of it was that Purity had been diagnosed with ADD, and that various documents submitted on the defendant's behalf showed that Purity had had problems with the dosage and adverse reactions, and that the doctors were busy trying to adjust her medications in order to alleviate some of the symptoms, which apparently included stealing horses and riding through Central Park topless. He finished by saying that inasmuch as Purity clearly did not mean to steal the horse and sell it for gain, this was more or less a prank that a person with a disorder might commit, so the violation arrangement was more fitting with the crime.

Judge Gehman's eyes were dull over her glasses.

"If I had a buck for every kid who stands before me because of ADD medications I'd be retired. Got anything else?"

The lawyer took a deep breath and launched into another explanation, this one attributing Purity's behavior to her psychological profile, punctuated by the death of her mother when she was sixteen, and pointing out that subsequently she'd been diagnosed with kleptomania, for which she also had a prescription, and had been under psychiatric care for many years. There was some thought among the doctors that the prescription for the ADD was adversely reacting with that for the kleptomania, but that the medical team was hard at work trying to straighten it all out, which they hoped to do very soon, at which point Purity would surely be a model citizen.

The judge's eyes were on the document. "What about the substance abuse?"

Another lawyer stood as the former took his seat. Although this one looked almost identical to the other, I guessed that this one was the legal defense expert for those suffering from substance abuse.

I was correct. He explained that Purity's depression and

subsequent substance abuse had been treated effectively before, as evidenced by court documents corresponding to a lack of any episodes around the time of her detox and recovery.

The judge pushed aside the documents before her, crossed her arms on the bench, and leaned forward. "This has to stop. I agree, Purity is a troubled girl who should be a competent woman by now. The exact nature and cause of her recidivism I'll leave to the doctors, though I reserve judgment on their opinions and assurances, as the court has heard them before. Purity? Tell me, when will this all stop?"

Purity's lawyers froze, only their eyes turning toward their client.

Purity cleared her throat and in a very small voice said, "Now."

"Why should the people of the State of New York believe what you just said?"

Her lawyers inhaled.

The small voice said, "My medications are better now, and I'm not drinking."

The prosecutor stood. "Your Honor, the people of New York State can only hope that Purity gets the help she needs so that their tax dollars can go toward policing crimes and preventing terrorism. However, it is a matter of public record that Purity Grant was arrested only last week in a DUI and car chase in Suffolk County. Clearly—"

Purity's lawyer objected, and Judge Gehman asked all the lawyers to come back into her chambers.

A low murmur settled in among the spectators.

Purity slumped in her chair. Seeing her this way sapped any desire I may have had for taking advantage of her wanton behavior. When you boiled the soup down, these were the bones at the bottom of the pot: a girl emotionally scarred by the loss of her mother and resentment of her stepfather who was on a trajectory for ever more trouble and strife. Sad. It made me want to comfort her. I wondered if the right man might make it all right somehow. Not me, of course. Then again, her scars might run too deep for even the most ardent love to heal.

Skip elbowed me gently. "So what do you think?"

"I feel sorry for her."

"With all that money?"

"My friend, there is an old Spanish saying: Love makes better armor than gold."

"She's a looker to boot. Purity could have any guy she wants."

"Beauty is more curse than commodity."

"Where did you say you were from?"

"East Brooklyn."

Skip's blond eyebrows shot up. "No shit?"

"Well, I have made my fortune, and now live outside the country."

"Spain?"

"I'd rather not say."

"Cagey, Morty, very cagey. You're here on business?"

"Of course."

"Staying in Times Square?"

"While I am a man of means, I do not choose to squander my fortune on hotels where I will only sleep. I'm staying in a charming hotel on the East Side."

To the side of the courtroom, three sketch artists were busy scratching away at their pads, eyes flicking up intently at Purity to capture the celebrity in her moment of humility.

The door behind the bench opened, and the lawyers and judge spilled back into the courtroom. There was a lot of throat clearing all around, and then the audience slipped into silence.

Judge Gehman tapped her gavel. "Will the defendant please rise."

Purity stood and looked the judge in the eyes.

"Purity, I see all these doctor reports, and while I'm not a doctor, it is pretty easy to see that all the medications and rehab haven't and won't treat what's really bothering you to make you act out this way. If it were in my power I would remand you to the custody of loving, attentive, and engaged parents back when you were fifteen. Inasmuch as the court does not have a time machine, the alternatives available to me are prison, rehab, probation, fines, and community service. The only ones with a chance of working seem to be the first and the last. Which do you think would work best?"

Purity straightened up, her dull eyes now shining. "Prison."

The room gasped. The defense lawyers tensed, and you could see they wanted to jump up and say something but that they could not.

The judge smiled, shaking her head. "The court sentences you to three hundred hours community service, a fine of fifty thousand dollars to defray the cost of all the police and courts necessary to babysit you, and a week of in-patient rehab for good luck. Court adjourned."

Outside the courtroom, I handed the reporter his press pass. "Many thanks, Skip, that was interesting. You have enough for a story?"

"You kidding? She asked to go to jail, and the judge refused. That's big. The courts keep pampering her, even though she knows she deserves to be locked up."

"Do you believe that?"

Skip chuckled, scratching his scalp. "Since when did anything I believe have anything to do with anything?"

"I think it was Abraham Lincoln who said, '*I only know what I read in the papers.*'"

"Outrage and fear. The best news stories are about one or the other. For example, '*Lincoln Burial Costs Taxpayers One Million Dollars.*' Or '*Is There a John Wilkes Booth After Your Kids?*'"

A wave of pin-striped lawyers parted the crowd outside of the courtroom, Purity once again in their wake. She had drifted back two steps, and some of the spectators like that woman with the lipstick furtively reached out to try to touch her.

"See?" Skip pointed with his chin. "The scumtators come here to try to touch fame, to get some sort of spark of divine light in their dark lives."

I cocked an eye at Skip. "Divine light in their dark lives. You should put that in your article."

"That's writing, not journalism."

"Why don't the spectators take pictures of the celebrities?"

"Cameras aren't allowed in the building, but sometimes they take photos on the sly. Sometimes we buy them."

I noted that Purity's step seemed uneven as her legal pack lurched toward where Skip and I were standing. Like a school of fish, they suddenly wheeled together, toward the elevator. Only one little blond fish slipped out of the school, stumbled, and fell.

Into my arms.

I could feel her rib cage with one hand, and her upper arm with the other, and I felt the divine light leave her body as she went completely limp. Funny what occurs to a man at moments like that: I thought to myself that she probably weighed about the same as Dixie.

The crowd and lawyers gasped, and at least one person loosed a whinny of surprise.

Purity buckled at the waist, so it was necessary for me to kneel to cushion her fall. I lowered her to the floor, and the hallway grew dark with the crush of gawkers. Somewhere around me were shouts, commands, jostling. I felt alone at the bottom of the pit of commotion, Purity in my arms. At that moment, she did not look like a rich troubled sexpot. Did such a person have the tiniest of freckles on her nose like the spots on a tiger lily? Did her unconscious lips part like the petals of a blooming rosebud? Did the gentle curl of her ear have a layer of small blond hair like the fuzz on a petunia? A fragrance arose from her hair, one born of sun and sand and sea. I brushed the hair from her face.

A pinstripe suit on one side and a court officer on the other pinched in and squeezed me away from Purity, taking her into their arms. As I stood, there was a hand on my arm pulling me back. It was Skip.

"I knew it paid to be a nice guy to my man Morty. Nice catch, bro. Now you have to tell me who you are, for the story."

I was still in the moment with the gentle flower Purity.

I was not falling in love, so make sure that this scene doesn't get all fuzzy and warm with yellow light. Every once in a while, a man rises above his baser nature and feels genuine tenderness. Were Purity's sea green eyes batting furtively at me over a martini glass, her legs recrossing, I would of course feel differently. But the girl I held was just a child, a tragic one. The tenderness I felt filled my heart with something like what my holy quest for the ring did, the feeling that this was not something trivial, but a wrong to be set right. I felt protective of her; I felt that the senseless self-destruction of this innocent must end, and that if it didn't, mankind would lose a part of itself for allowing it to happen. At the same time, I knew this was not my mission, that this was something I could not accomplish because I did not have access or a personal relationship. Tragedy was on my tongue like a strong mint.

I looked at Skip and sighed. He had his pen poised.

"I am merely like a guardian angel who just happened to be passing by and made the catch, that is all."

There was more commotion as more court security arrived and began pushing the crowd back, and in the process, me away from Skip. The stairwell was open, and the crowd was being guided into it, down the stairs.

So I went.

EIGHTEEN

SOMEWHERE ON A LONELY STRETCH of South Carolina interstate there towers a mighty Mexican named Pedro. Approximately a hundred feet tall and lit with neon, he wears a sombrero, poncho, mustache, and toothy smile beaming out from his brown face. In his arms there is a festive sign that reads: SOUTH OF THE BORDER. Pedro straddles a roadway next to a restaurant.

Pedro is the patron saint of the mother of all tourist traps. Gracing the highway's edge for hundreds of miles in either direction, billboards trumpet fireworks, a two-hundred-foot-high sombrero-topped space needle, an RV park, a motel, a spa, a wedding chapel, a porn shop, chili, steak, fried chicken, a kiddie park, and diesel fuel. South of the Border's festive if fading buildings straddle I-95 and sprawl over a dozen acres cleared of scrub pine in a shallow valley.

When you first see this vacationland oasis, you can hardly believe it is actually there before your eyes. When you drive away and are again in the pine barrens, you are not sure you didn't dream it somehow.

Panning down from the giant Pedro and an overcast sky, our camera finds the yellow-eyed El Cabezador, sleepily surveying his surroundings. A small red backpack dangled from his hand.

In the other was a Waffle House place mat. On the place mat was a map of Waffle House franchises dotting the East Coast. This had become Paco's map to help guide him to New York.

Tractor-trailers gurgle and whine off-camera.

Paco headed for a souvenir shop. Inside, he made his way past the mildly humorous bumper stickers, jerky, pecan logs, baby cactuses, saltwater taffy, ashtrays, pinecone art, sombreros, and Mylar balloons to the racks of sport shirts, windbreakers, and sweatpants.

He emerged from the souvenir shop wearing a black sport shirt and a yellow South of the Border windbreaker. His beaten and scarred black boots peeked from below new black sweatpants with white racing stripes. To look at him, you might have guessed he was from Bayonne. In his hand was a clump of clothing, the smelly stuff he'd had on upon arrival. That found a home in a trash can, with a thunk.

Little red backpack over his shoulder, Paco headed for the restaurant, though not for the front. He headed for the back, where he found what he was looking for. Fellow Mexicans, two dishwashers, illegals, on a break.

They spoke in Spanish, so here are the subtitles:

"Good morning, brothers. What's going on?"

"Not much."

"I'm passing through here, heading to New York, where I have work with my cousins, doing construction."

"Day labor?"

"Better than my previous job."

"Each job is both better and worse than the one before. We wish you luck, friend, but hope you are not looking for a handout. We cannot afford to risk our terrible jobs."

Paco laughed at the weak joke. "No, my friends, I am not looking for a handout. I have a little money to keep me going. Just wanted to speak with countrymen about the best way for me to continue north. Cheaply, of course."

"Nobody around here would pick up a Mexican hitchhiker."

"I am Honduran."

"Yes, you look like one. A Honduran from Mexico. Your last job was not what you thought it would be, either?"

"I was thinking about whether any of you travel north after work. Just another step closer to New York, you see? I can contribute to help pay for petrol."

The dishwashers exchanged a glance. "You might be able to get a ride with us to Culpville. There you might get a bus. But you would have to ask John."

"Who is John?"

"He runs our bunkhouse, provides transportation."

"I will ask John. Where is he?"

"He arrives after our shift, at eleven, and takes us all back to the bunkhouse for a meal and then sleep."

"Good. I will be back here to ask John."

"Don't come here. We meet in front of Pedro, at eleven."

"Many thanks. I will see you then."

Paco wandered off to look for a bathroom. His reaction to this place was similar to his reaction to most things American: bewilderment and resignation. Could he ever understand gringos and their excesses? He wondered if South of the Border was what Americans thought Mexico was like. He had to admit that the touristy parts of Juárez were at least a little like this, once. Even so, Paco had never seen anybody but a mariachi wear a sombrero, and yet there was this grinning statue of a peon at every turn.

Even a grinning Pedro in a bathrobe and slippers. The statue was standing in front of a public restroom that had showers.

Paco bathed, and was back at the road-straddling Pedro at close to eleven.

There was an aging white Econoline van there, and some of his countrymen were slouching outside. Including the dishwashers.

"What's going on, friends?"

"We spoke to John. Here he comes now."

Paco turned. Bald and buck-toothed, John was a large gringo who limped across the lot from the restaurant, a foam container of coffee in his hand.

When he drew near, the dishwashers gestured to Paco and stepped back. John's puffy red face looked down at Paco and grunted. His smile was large, but the teeth were small, and there seemed to be far too many of them. "You want work?" His Spanish was coarse, but understandable.

We're back to subtitles:

"No, Señor John. I am on my way to New York. My countrymen here said I might be able to get a ride with you to the nearest town where I can find a bus."

"A bus?" John laughed, but without humor.

"I can pay for the petrol it costs to get me there. I am not a hitchhiker."

"Why don't you want to work here? Hm?"

"I have work elsewhere."

John patted Paco on the shoulder. "Good for you. Sure, we'll give you a ride. Get in, boys. All of you."

The van was packed with illegals as John pushed the wheezing Econoline to highway speeds and onto I-95. Paco thought the van was very solemn for a bunch of Mexicans, who were usually talkative. They exited in North Carolina, and John brought the van down a dirt road through the pines and into a large clearing. In the center of the clearing on a rise was a cinder-block bunkhouse flanked by fading red tobacco barns. These in turn were flanked

by a few large trees and rusty threshers. Overgrown fields, color-less under the overcast, stretched away in all directions.

Paco felt eyes on him, those of his countrymen, as the van stopped next to a pile of construction debris and wood at the cinder-block bunkhouse. He looked into the rearview mirror at John. "Is town far from this place? I can walk."

John flashed those little teeth at Paco in the mirror. "You might as well come in and have some chow with the rest of them. You have traveled far and must be hungry." He shoved open his door and came around the side to open the van so the illegals could exit.

One by one the illegals climbed down from the van, but none would meet Paco's eyes.

Last from the van was Paco, and as soon as his feet landed on the dusty red dirt of the driveway, John clamped a hand on the back of his neck.

"You'll work here or you'll go to prison, pussy." The little teeth seemed more plentiful than ever.

The grip on Paco's neck was intense; his vision swam and dark-ened. John kicked the back of his knees and pushed him to the dirt.

Paco rolled onto his back, facing the big gringo. His little red backpack had fallen by the van, the nine-millimeter automatic out of reach.

One end of a length of bristled rope was in John's fist. The other end of the rope had a knot in it.

"You'll work here, sleep here, eat here."

The rope whistled through the air, and the knot caught Paco in the ribs, delivering a bolt of pain.

Then again in the thigh, then in his shoulder as Paco rolled and tried to scramble away from John's whip. The big man lurched

after him, red dust rising and stinging Paco's eyes, the other illegals clustered by the debris pile, watching in fear.

"And if you don't do as I say, you'll die here, pussy!"

The knot delivered another bolt of pain to Paco's ribs just as he rolled. The knot lodged momentarily between his side and the ground.

John cursed and yanked the rope clear, but Paco caught the rope above the knot and tried in vain to pull the bully down.

The fat man held fast, jerking Paco toward him and thrusting a foot at his head. The boot missed its mark. John staggered forward.

Paco let go of the rope and leaped to his feet behind his attacker, hatchet in hand.

John turned in time to see the hatchet, and in time to lean away from the rusty blade an inch before his bulging eyes. His weight pivoted on his limping leg, and the fat man could not move away quickly enough to avoid Paco's kick. It caught him in the knee, on the side, and the big man fell with a groan to the red earth.

Paco lunged into the cloud of dust, onto John's side, and the big man shrieked and bucked. To Paco it sounded like the shriek of a whore. He slashed backhanded at the fat man's neck with the hatchet, chopping off much of his chin instead of the jugular, so he angled the blade in on the forward thrust and drove the hatchet under John's ear and up to the hilt behind the jaw. He felt the blade crack through the nasal cavity and give, like hacking a pumpkin.

Paco rolled off John and onto his side next to the van. Next to his little red backpack.

In the cloud of red dust before him, John staggered to his feet. There did not seem any way to open the backpack quickly enough, so Paco felt for the pistol's grip and trigger guard.

From the red cloud John rushed toward him, the handle angled out from behind his ear, gore gushing from his nose, the little teeth

swimming in blood. Paco had found the shape of the gun in the backpack, but realized he was holding the gun upside down. He pointed it anyway. He fired.

You may want to film this next part in slow motion.

Flame shot from the bag, and the slug punched John just below the navel. He was staggering forward, so the wound didn't alter his course toward Paco. John's hands were raised in claws, a wounded beast intent to take El Cabezador with him beyond the mortal veil of tears.

A two-by-four swept out from the red cloud and cracked John square in the temple. The fat man rolled midair, blood arcing from his nostrils into the sky, his eyes rolling up into his head. With a low moan, he thundered to earth onto his back a foot from Paco. Like a mortally wounded bear, John lay on his back—huffing, bloody, and immobile.

One of the illegals stepped from the red cloud of dust with the two-by-four. He looked down at John with a curled lip of defiance and disgust. The other illegals had also picked up lumber from the woodpile.

Paco had heard it said that there's no more pissed-off person than a woman who has been done wrong, but he came to think otherwise as the illegals and their clubs finished off John, pounding him into the red earth long after Satan had taken his soul to its dubious reward.

NINETEEN

THE FORTUNE-TELLER HELENA WAS MAKING a liverwurst on rye in the pantry behind the séance room when she heard Abbie's heft thumping down the stairs. "Lena!"

"In here." Helena put the French's back in the fridge and picked up the paper plate with the sandwich on it. Who had time for washing plates?

"Lena!"

"In here, Abs." Helena took a bite of the sandwich over the sink and chewed thoughtfully. Wasn't the same without Miracle Whip.

You have to appreciate the contrast between this and the knife fight, am I right? Blood spewing in slow motion through the air versus the importance of Miracle Whip. There is irony in this, and they will love it at Cannes.

Abbie huffed and puffed into the séance room. "Lena, you won't believe it."

Helena walked through the beaded curtain and stopped, still chewing, eyebrows raised without too much genuine anticipation.

"Lena, I know who he is!"

"*Who* he?"

"The man."

"What man?"

"Last night."

"Oh."

"I was just watching *The View,* and at the break, there was one of them things where the news people tell you the headlines, you know, the way they do."

"Mmm."

"Anyways, they have this newsflash, and Purity Grant was in court this morning about that thing with the horse."

"*Horse* who?"

Abbie was trying to catch her breath. " 'Memmer when Purity Grant stole a horse and rode through Central Park with her top off?"

"Oh, yeah."

"Well, she was in court this morning about that, and when she was coming out, she fainted, and they took her to the hospital."

"Is she OK?" Yes, Miracle Whip would have made a better sandwich.

"They don't know."

"Was it something she ate?"

"I dunno, Lena, but—"

"Because there's been a lot of food poisoning lately. A lot. They talk about it on the news all the time."

"I dunno what it was, I don't know if they know. Anyways—"

"Could have been stress. That girl takes on a lot of stress."

"Anyways, they show her ambulance arriving at the hospital—"

"You can get sick just being at a hospital. *Germs.*"

"—and they show a picture of her father."

"I somehow feel sorry for that tramp. Rich people, they think they have it so good, but then you see this."

Abbie groaned as she settled into a chair at the crystal ball. The chair groaned back. "Her *father,* Lena."

"Hm?"

"That's him."

"*Who* him?"

"Aren't you listening? *Him* him. From last night."

Helena stopped chewing and swallowed. "That was Purity Grant's father?"

"That's what I'm saying, Lena. Robert Tyson Grant. He's a gazillionaire. And his stepdaughter is Purity Grant, the one who's in trouble all over the place."

"You're shitting me. Really?"

"Lena, would I run all the way down here like this in the middle of *The View* to tell you this if I was lying?"

"You sure?"

"Poztiv."

Helena sank into her chair at the dark crystal ball. "You *sure*?"

"*Poz*-tiv."

Helena shot a suspicious glance at her liverwurst sandwich and set the paper plate on the table. "He's very rich."

"Gazillionaire."

"A gazillionaire with a curse. Who's his girlfriend?"

"Whadda I know about a girlfriend? They didn't mention anything about that. Purity Grant fainted, not the girlfriend. They got no reason to mention the girlfriend."

The front door tinkled, and there was a rush of air. "Hello?"

Abbie and Helena stood and went to work, parting the beads out into the foyer where Dixie, in a smart turquoise pantsuit, stood anxiously.

Abbie clasped Helena's hands. "Thank you so much, Helena, you are so gifted, and have helped me so much, how can I ever repay you for all you've done for me and my family?"

Helena dished up her long-suffering smile, the one that betrayed sacrifice as its own reward. "Go, and be happy."

Abbie burst into tears of joy and pushed through the front door onto the street. Helena turned her eyes to Dixie, parting the curtain into the séance room. "Please, enter."

They eased down on either side of the table, and Helena moved her sandwich under it. "You have come about Robert. You are worried about him." Inasmuch as she came alone, Helena could only imagine Dixie wanted to know something about her boyfriend Robert Tyson Grant, who was probably acting strangely.

Dixie's lips parted, her eyes alight with wonder. True, Dixie had aimed to find out about the ring from me later that evening, and also to soften my loyalties, find some wiggle room, perhaps get me to kill Purity for money instead. Some women know the incredible power they hold over men, and Dixie was certainly one of them. Yet it occurred to her that the more information she had the better. So she had returned to Helena.

"How did you know that, Helena?"

"I feel this thing." The fortune-teller tapped her heart and squinted. "Is it that you want to know about his business? About Purity?"

"You do just *know* things, don't you?"

With the tip of her toe, Helena activated a switch under the carpet, and eerie violin music began to play softly, the room getting slightly darker, and the crystal ball glowing almost imperceptibly.

"It is my gift, and my curse." The palmist held a hand over the crystal ball, and it got brighter and blue, smoke swirling within. "To see, our minds must be one. Hold my hand and look deeply into the ball. Deeply!"

"I need to know more, Helena. Yes, about Robert. About Robert's past."

Sparkles appeared in the orb, the light inside flickering.

"Deeper! Look deeper!"

Dixie felt Helena's grip tighten and saw her eyes roll up into her head, just the whites showing. Lips trembling, the palmist hissed, "The ring!"

Heart pounding, Dixie's watery eyes gazed into the orb. "Yes, tell me about the ring!"

"The past is very distant, and holds many secrets. Secrets! They have lives, these secrets! Spirits! Something happened. Robert got the ring many years ago, under mysterious circumstances, I am trying to see . . . look deeper! Deeper!"

"I'm looking as deep as I can!"

"A thief! I see a thief!"

"Someone is going to steal the ring?"

"Deception!"

"What? Who is the thief? Who deceived who?"

"Look deeper, child! Deeper!" Helena was of course fishing for some sort of hint. "Robert will not tell you about the ring. He does not want you to know. He doesn't want you to know because of the deception!" All very obvious, of course. He would have told her about the ring otherwise, and a deception can be almost anything.

"Helena, why is the ring so important? Why won't he give it up?"

Ah ha, Helena thought—*finally, a clue.* Then she remembered something from the previous night. With her knees she started to vibrate the table.

"I see now!" the palmist gasped.

"What is it you see?" the girlfriend gasped.

"The man from Bolivia," the palmist hissed.

"Bolivia?"

"La Paz!"

"Mexico."

"Yes, of course, I see the man from Mexico!" the palmist whispered.

"Do you know . . . do you know why he is here?" the gazillion-aire's girlfriend whispered, afraid the palmist might know the man from Mexico was a hit man.

The music stopped.

The orb went black.

Helena jumped to her feet and pointed a trembling finger at Dixie.

"THIS MAN, HE HAS COME FOR THE RING!"

This time it was Dixie who nearly fainted. She gulped. "Should I give him the ring?"

"At your own peril if you do—*and if you don't*!" Helena collapsed into her chair, fanning herself with the hem of her skirt. Well, that answer covered her bases, anyway.

"What do I do?"

The palmist tipped her face forward into her hands. "I have seen all that can be seen for now. I must rest."

"But I must know."

Helena lifted her face. "I can only do so much at once. Follow your heart. Cash or charge?"

Dixie fished out four twenties from her purse. "Is it eighty?"

Helena took the twenties. "Want me to call you a car service?"

"I can catch a cab."

"Don't be silly." Helena pulled a cell phone from her skirt pocket and speed-dialed. "My nephew Tony works at a car service around the corner."

Occasionally Tony also worked for Helena when she needed more information.

TWENTY

CUT TO A SHOT LOOKING up at Grant International's Sixth Avenue headquarters, a shining glass hive of commerce on Manhattan's skyline. Floors thirty through forty were occupied with Grant Industries worker bees, and the business of making the honey was kept humming by spiral staircases linking each floor to the next. The king bee had not wanted the workers to be waiting around for elevators and degrading productivity. The directory for the floors included many divisions in support of the discount importer's retail operations, such as administration, accounting, research, promotions, and distribution. Robert had kept the company insulated and independent by maintaining various departments in-house that many other large companies would have shopped out, like advertising and auditing. Robert's guiding principle in business was to maintain a strong but simple centralized corporate identity. Translated, that meant "Don't pay other folks overhead and profit for what we can do in-house." Their customers and their success relied on clarity of message: value and variety. A recent media blitz by the marketing department relied solely on billboards and ten-second commercials in prime time that were black letters on white: Value. Variety. Grab-A-Lot. No contests or cross-promotions or product placements or scratch-offs or blimps or stadiums or celebrities.

A new department called Initiatives had recently launched Grant Industry's own discount products. Buy-It Electronics contracted with an off-brand manufacturer of third-tier CD, DVD, iPhone, and iPod devices, in an attempt to absorb that company's manufacturing and distribution. The other was a discount gourmet food concern and an obvious attempt to steal market share from Trader Joe's and Whole Foods. Within each Grab-A-Lot store Grant Industries had begun installing a store-within-a-store called Trade Winds, which sold everything from deluxe sugar cubes to exotic and supposedly healthy snack chips to frozen meals.

I read all this in the exposés on the plane, and lots more, of course. That was Robert Tyson Grant's company in a nutshell. I'm sure in the movie the audience could be shown various images of the company at work with the sound of typewriters and telephones in the background, snippets of conversation, interviews, business reports, what have you. Yes, I know nobody uses typewriters anymore, but I think they still use that sound effect in movies to make us think people are very busy at work, don't they? Of course, like with the penguins at the cocktail party, you could intercut images of bees with Grant's workers running to and fro with documents and charts, the hive in action. Yet the buzzing sounds may become annoying to a theater audience when mixed with the clacking of typewriters. That is up to you; I am just telling you what happened so you can make the movie in the best way. The point I am making is that the audience needs to understand Robert was actually a captain of industry and not just a millionaire with a conniving girlfriend with great tits, with a troublesome daughter also with great tits, and with the ring of Hernando Martinez de Salvaterra on his finger. All of which were becoming a distraction in his day-to-day at Grant Industries. Which was why on this given day, while the hive was buzzing and type-writers clacking, or what have you, our king bee was alone in his office, standing before a window with a commanding view of midtown Manhattan.

The sky had grown cloudy, another late-day storm brewing, New Jersey dark and foreboding in the distance.

How?

Grant was mystified, to be sure, because he could not figure out how an assassin picked at random had any connection to his own past, much less the ring. Was the Hapsburg/Hernando Martinez de Salvaterra ring somehow common knowledge in Mexico? Surely this ring was an obscure relic, and only a few would know of it, much less know its power. Grant held up his hand, admiring the simplicity, weight, and color of the gold ring bearing the double cross of Caravaca.

One part of him wanted to give up the ring. Were he to do so, he might find that his success was his own invention. He might find that his admittance to Princeton was not a fluke or mistake. Was investing in Chinese imports a shrewd business move or a roll of the dice? Was his unusual business model the product of his genius or the by-product of destiny? Would it be Robert Tyson Grant's armada of stores that sank the fleet of Walmart and Costco and Trader Joe's? Or would kismet rot their hulls before his advancing navy arrived? Was he a brilliant businessman and magnate who would be mentioned for eons to come in the same breath as Kroc and Gates? Or as a footnote?

Yet there was another part of Robert Tyson Grant—the fearful little boy.

There was hardly a day that passed when he did not recall those days in the orphanage, the stormy night in the chapel with Pasqual, the days when the orphans had to comb their hair and stand in line for inspection by prospective parents. It is one thing to not be picked for kickball teams at recess, then quite another to have your prayers rewarded by stinging hopelessness as couple after couple walked down the line of boys and picked someone else to be their son. A dark spot formed on Robert Tyson Grant's soul, a depraved yearning to finally be chosen. Which was why one afternoon Bobbie stole back to the dormitory and forced open Pasqual's footlocker with a butter knife. Hidden inside, he found a small clay donkey, one that Pasqual had made in art class. Grant smashed it on the edge of the locker—from inside glowed the gold ring of Hernando Martinez de Salvaterra, the cross of Caravaca flickering in the late-day sun.

Earn Destiny.

Did it matter how the destiny was earned?

Could Pasqual still be alive? Grant had tracked him down for years—a Brooklyn truck mechanic—and was assured that he had been killed by loan sharks. Who else would know he had the ring or what it was?

What if his current success—like finding parents to take him from the orphanage—did rely on the ring? Then his business model would result in bankruptcy. Buy-It Electronics would become an object of the *Wall Street Journal*'s derision and founder on the rocks of hubris. Trade Winds would be broadsided by a fusillade of foreign trade sanctions. Overleveraged and insolvent, the once strong and invincible Grant Industries armada would be sunk by the same hand of fate that floated it, the ships of BJ's and Sam's Club sailing triumphantly to port.

Where the mighty Grant's Industries once sailed, only the flotsam of lawsuits and the jetsam of ridicule would remain, the miserable orphan Robert Tyson Grant adrift in a lifeboat of failure with a paddle of regret.

Earn Destiny.

Did it matter how the destiny was earned?

Grant seriously had to wonder: Was Purity a curse, one that came with the success the ring had brought? There were other business magnates who suffered bratty daughters that did not seem as afflicted. Yet for Grant, Purity's evil was relentless, like he'd somehow earned this curse, as the palmist had suggested. Was this the price he had to pay for stealing the ring? For using it to build the Grab-A-Lot empire?

Relentless. Now there was this court scene Purity had pulled off, and it was all over the paper and the news. If he could just rid himself of her, of this curse . . .

Of course. How obvious. If he were to rid himself of the ring, he would rid himself of the curse that came with it, because Purity would be killed in exchange for the ring. Even if the result of relinquishing the ring was forfeiture of his continued success, was it worth such success at the price of Purity's persistent hatred and media humiliation? Perhaps it was possible to circumvent failure if he ceased to seek success. What if he were to relinquish the ring to the Mexican, and Purity were to be disposed of? Could he sell Grant Industries to the Chinese and retire with his money? He could wrap up his life in the States, and then he and Dixie could move down to his retreat in Cabo San Lucas. Would a hurricane then come and wash his life away? He didn't feel it should work that way.

Grant took a deep breath and let it out slowly. He had to take command of this situation. Dixie was a help, but he was not without his own resources and clever ways, especially when dealing with tricky business deals or situations. He felt like he was allowing himself to be frozen like a possum in the headlights because he could not understand their motives. How Asians did business and their priorities were still sometimes mysterious, yet he had always managed to deal with them, hadn't he? Robert decided it was essential to look at this like a business deal.

They want the ring in return for killing Purity. I want to give them money for this service. Is there a middle alternative? Making the deal is about finding alternatives.

There was a gentle rap at the door.

"Come!"

His pixie-like assistant Kathy stuck her head in. "I e-mailed you a link. Can I get you anything else?"

Grant nodded glumly. "Not at this time, thank you." The assistant vanished.

He sat at his giant desk, in his giant chair, and wiggled a computer mouse around until the video clip loaded. He did not shy away from Purity's debacles. He needed to know how bad it was, if only to confirm that the curse needed to be over, that hiring the Mexican was the right thing to do.

Chin in hand, he watched a TV reporter cheerily relate his stepdaughter's latest embarrassment.

"Purity Grant is back in the news, and back in court. You may recall her Lady Godiva stunt in which she stole a horse and rode bareback and bare-chested in Central Park. A guilty plea had been entered by her legal team, and now it was time to pay the piper. A sentencing was held this morning in downtown Manhattan. When Judge Carolyn Gehman asked Purity—yes, she did show up!—what her punishment should be, the wealthy heiress chose prison over community service! The judge declined Purity's choice, instead fining her fifty thousand dollars for all the trouble she caused the police and court system, three hundred hours community service, and rehab. But that wasn't the end of the excitement. On the way out of the courtroom, Purity Grant fainted."

They showed a film clip, taken with a phone.

"She was carried from the building to an ambulance, and was transported to Beth Israel Medical Center, where she apparently is recovering from what sources are telling us is a hangover."

Grant blinked hard and played the clip again.

He stood, leaned in, and played the clip again. This time he froze the film clip to a single image.

"Good Lord! Kathy!"

The pixie reappeared. "I have the lawyers on the phone."

"Forget the lawyers. Get me Ms. Faltreau at the Grant Foundation."

"Dixie?"

"Yes!"

The image on his screen was of Purity, fainted into the arms of his hit man.

Me.

TWENTY-ONE

WHAT MAKES A MAN IRRESISTIBLE to a woman?

It is not found in a bottle of aftershave; let us get that part straight right away.

It is not a chiseled physique, expensive clothes, or a flashy sports car—even though those may attract a woman's attention initially. Like a peacock flashing his immense and colorful tail, these do not ensure eggs in the nest.

What makes a man irresistible to a woman is *being* irresistible. You think I am playing games, but a man simply has to believe he is irresistible—if *he* does not believe it, *she* will not believe it. Now, I am not suggesting that a man swagger up to a woman and inflict a smoochie-faced embrace on her. I am asking the men out there to think! When a woman knows she is irresistible to a man, does she throw herself at him? Except with rare exceptions, the answer is no. Why? Because in order to be irresistible, you must create desire in the object of your passions. Desire is a tower built from the bricks of anticipation, and the bricks of anticipation are fired from the clay of waiting.

Think again: If a desirable woman *does* throw herself at men, what happens? The men very often recoil, because any woman who is truly desirable knows she has a commodity for which she must find the best buyer for her charms. Or they take her and toss her aside. People do not give away what is valuable. While she may seem an attractive package, men will know that what is given away freely is cheap, and perhaps burdened with a mental disorder or worse.

So let us review so there are no misunderstandings. To be irresistible you must be confident that you are desirable. You must make her anticipate an expression of desire in return. I think I said it before, but it is worth mentioning again: While being charming is essential, it is unwise to let a woman know you care too much, that she is a commodity you cannot live without. You must contain your passion, because if she thinks you desire her more than she desires you, well, my friend, I am afraid you are doomed. You are no longer a commodity at that point. She will cease to respect you, and like as not she will drive you out of your mind with games and shameless flirting with other men. Why? Because at the point she knows you are smitten, you can be used to affirm *her* irresistibility, which she is now free to use to attract other men whose desires are not so easily conquered, and are thus more valuable.

I am explaining this in the hopes that some men can be rehabilitated from shabby circumstance. So that when they watch the dark, handsome actor who plays me they will not say, "Well, of course he can charm women, he is Jimmy Smits or Benjamin Bratt, he is dark and handsome and La Paz gentry." It saddens me that so many men miss life's crucial details, and that so many pretty women must sit home waiting for their irresistible man. So I implore oafish men everywhere to get in the game, as I am only one man, and these legions of women need you.

And for the love of Jesus please go easy on the Old Spice.

Which brings me to my date with Dixie, an occasion for which containing my desire was as difficult as it was crucial.

Aside from the anticipation of being graced with Dixie's considerable charms, the women of the previous two nights had me in a state of sexual agitation.

So, what does a man bring to the apartment of a girlfriend of a millionaire? Even as a man of means, I certainly had no intention of trying to compete with the diamond tiaras, rare Parisian perfumes, and trips to Hawaii that Grant could ply her with. Yet flowers would have been too commonplace and romantic. I was not looking for love, only a lover—and what better suggests that than a fine bottle of sparkling wine?

I ventured down Second Avenue until I found a large spirits shop and went in.

The proprietor was a reedy woman pushing sixty with strawlike yellow hair, a purple sweater dress, and rhinestone glasses around her neck on a chain. She stood behind the register and looked over her glasses at me with a toothy smile.

"What can I do you for?"

"Are you a wine specialist?" I asked.

"Looking for something special, are yah?"

"I am. I don't suppose you have any cold duck?"

Her smile was frozen, and she blinked rapidly. "I believe we do. And you said you were looking for something special?"

"I am not from this country. It is difficult to locate cold duck in Mexico."

"Holy smokes, I'll bet it is!" She laughed softly. "So you're looking for a sparkling red wine?"

"I have always relied on the André vineyards for cold duck. Do you have it chilled?"

With small rapid steps the proprietor led me to the champagne aisle and plucked a bottle of André cold duck from the bottom shelf. She took a deep breath and blew on the bottle; a puff of dust swirled from the label. "Two thousand and one was a good year for cold duck, sport."

I eyed her suspiciously. "Are you suggesting there might be a better vintage in another brand?"

"That is the only cold duck we carry. In fact, it is the only cold duck made in the world. However, if I might be so bold, what special occasion is this wine for?"

"A beautiful woman."

"Her place or yours?"

"Hers."

"Is she expensive?"

"Expensive?"

"Wealthy. Or a working girl?"

"She works, but she is accustomed to the company of the wealthy, like myself."

She took the bottle of cold duck from my hands and put it back on the bottom shelf. "I like you, champ, so I'm going to do you a favor. You want to get lucky with this dame, am I right?"

I knit my brow. "I wish to be charming, if that is what you mean. I have always found ladies enchanted with a chilled glass of cold duck."

"Were these ladies—ahem—like this rich broad?"

"I'll grant you, they were more casual."

"Fine. I'll fix you up—but it'll cost you more than six ninety-nine. You, sport, need a trendy champagne."

My nose wrinkled. "But champagne is not red."

"*Ex*-actly."

I shook my head. "Really, I appreciate your advanced knowl-edge of wines, but red is more sultry than white."

"Captain, you show up with cold duck and you'll never charm her pants off."

"It must be red."

She laughed, scratching her head. Then she threw her hands in the air. "Eureka! Follow me."

She led me to the Italian wine section, went on tiptoes, pulled down a bottle, and displayed it for me. "At least this she'll never have heard of before and won't know it's only thirty a bottle. It's red, see? And it is naturally fizzy, not carbonated like the André."

I raised an eyebrow at her. "You say this is definitely superior to cold duck?"

"If it isn't, come back tomorrow and I'll give you a free bottle of cold duck, howzat?"

"The bottle is most elegant. As you say, perhaps something even more festive than cold duck is required."

She clapped her hands. "Goodie. Sorry, I don't have it cold, but do you want a fancy wrapping for it?"

"I think not. Do you sell champagne buckets?"

"Yessiree bob. Nothing in gold plate or anything. See here."

"Glasses, too?"

So it was that at eight that evening I rode the elevator up to the fifteenth floor of an Upper East Side doormanned apartment building holding a champagne bucket containing two glasses and an iced bottle of Banfi Rosa Regale. My suit was freshly dry-cleaned, my nails manicured, my hair rakishly brushed back so that a lone black curl tumbled onto my forehead. I knew I was looking good. Everybody in the lobby couldn't keep their eyes off me. In the elevator, an old man with a big cigar and a small dog asked me if I were Ricardo Montalban. Though I think he was joking (because Ricardo is, alas, dead), a resemblance to such a striking figure of a man is never a bad thing.

Dixie opened the door to her apartment and stared at the champagne bucket. "Did you come through the lobby like this?" Ah, but she was ravishing, dressed in black silk pants and silver brocade top, the zippered kind, I imagined for easy access. Her hair was up in a naughty tumble, those adorable ringlets at her temples.

I smiled secretively. "How else was I to deliver refreshments? In a plaid suitcase?"

She looked both ways down the hall. "Come in, come in."

I stepped past her, through a small vestibule and into her living room. There were paintings on mustard-colored walls, art not intended to look like any particular thing, just a patchwork of colors and shapes. I liked the colors but had no use for random shapes. The furniture was modern, no wood, angular and upholstered flat, without pleats. Again, not my style, but not offensive. The important part of the living room was a couch with many throw pillows. It was nicely placed by the window overlooking the lights of Manhattan, and in front of a flickering gas fireplace. Opposite that was a small, open kitchen and facing bar. The bar was arranged with place settings for two. *Excellent.*

I stepped over the glass coffee table in front of the couch, placed the bucket on the coffee table, set the two glasses aside, and slid the napkin-wrapped bottle from the ice. "I thought you might like this. While not wildly expensive, it is nonetheless difficult to find. Are you all right?"

Dixie's silver pumps seemed to step a little uncertainly toward me. "Yes, yes, of course, I'm just a little surprised by the, um, refreshment. That's very gallant, Morty."

"You cannot tell me that I am the first guest to bring wine into your home?"

"The first to bring it in the ice bucket with glasses. Through the lobby."

I favored her with a small laugh. "Where I come from, it is bad manners to be welcomed into another person's home without wine. Especially before dinner." I popped the cork into my hand and poured the fizzy red wine into the glasses on the table.

With a cautious smile, Dixie took the glass I held out to her. "What shall we drink to?"

"We have a quaint toast where I'm from: To old friends, new friends, and health of the chickens."

She clinked my glass, giggling. "Chickens?"

I made a slight bow. "Where would any of us be without chickens?"

"I don't get you, Morty." Sipping, she shook her head. "You're not anything like what I expected. I can't even imagine you doing what you do."

"God called. I cannot refuse Him. Ah, but you have a fine view, and I am admiring your art. Yes, you have a very cozy and charming home, Dixie. Shall we sit?"

I offered her the corner of the couch, and she slid past me, still somewhat cautiously, I thought. She seated herself facing me, and I sat with my arm on the back of the couch.

I thought perhaps we should film this scene in one long take. This will give the actors an opportunity for continuity in their mutual attraction and help sell the moment. A very slow circular tracking shot with us in silhouette against the fire and city lights might help to sex it up, too. That is all up to you, of course.

"Morty, I don't think I've ever had a sparkling red wine before. Well, except maybe cold duck when I was a kid." She sipped.

"Yes, cold duck is good, too."

Dixie slapped a hand over her mouth, and I sat forward.

"*Querida,* are you all right?"

She swallowed and laughed. "Don't do that!"

"What did I do?"

"Don't make me laugh while I'm drinking."

"My apologies." I clinked my glass to hers. "Well, I hope that if I am not what you expected that it is a pleasant surprise and that if I amuse you it is agreeable. You seem a little nervous in my company, which you should not be, as I am a very relaxed and social person."

"Morty?" She took a gulp of her wine and set it on the coffee table. "Why were you at Purity's hearing this morning?"

I was about to sip but didn't. "I am at a disadvantage. How did you know I was at Purity's hearing?"

"You were on TV with her in your arms."

Now I took a gulp of wine and set my glass aside. "But there were no cameras, they are forbidden."

"Someone took a video with their phone of Purity passing out and falling into your waiting arms."

"Remarkable. How did I look?"

"Morty, what were you doing at that courtroom? And to be seen with Purity. Don't you think that's a little . . ."

"*Querida,* there was time in my day to fill. I read in the paper that Purity Grant was going to be sentenced. I know these are public events, so out of curiosity, I went. And it was quite interesting. I met a reporter there who got me in."

"A *reporter*?" Her crystal blue eyes were wide.

"He asked all kinds of questions of me, but I said little. Especially after Purity fainted into my arms."

"How *little*?"

"So little I do not really remember what I said. This event—does it cause you concern, *querida*? Is it possible this is what is causing your anxiety for some reason? More wine?"

Dixie slumped back into the corner of the couch in dismay and drained her glass. I refilled both our glasses.

"You are one cool customer, Morty. You come here to 'make things right' and then you actually save Purity from being injured, and on TV. Doesn't that seem just a little bit ironic to you? I would think that it's best you stay out of sight and not be seen anywhere near Purity."

"Dixie, this seems to have caused you distress, and for that I am sorry. However, I am only God's instrument. If in the course of events I save Purity or anyone else from injury, perhaps that is only part of the grand plan."

She sat forward, peering into my eyes, her cleavage beckoning me. "So this is part of the plan? I mean, the less I know the better—but what you're saying is that . . ." Dixie put a hand on her forehead and looked at the fire. "Well, I suppose if you are seen on TV actually *saving* the monster, nobody would ever suspect you of . . ."

"*Querida,* you must learn to relax, drink, and trust in God." I patted her knee and clinked my glass against hers. "They tell me He moves in a mysterious way, and I am inclined to agree. You are wearing a most stunning top. It goes very well with the sapphires, which in turn are stunning with your eyes."

Dixie leaned in again, a hand on my knee. Her perfume was ambrosia. "So how often do you go on missions like this, Morty? For 'God.' "

I let the fire play on my eyes as I looked to the ceiling, one eyebrow cocked, the wisdom of the ages clearly mine. "Are we not all on God's mission? In one way or the other?"

She moved closer, her eyes moist and looking up at me.

"And the ring?"

"It bears the double-barred crucifix, the cross of Caravaca. It was cast from a golden Hapsburg trinket of some sort that encased a part of the true cross."

"You mean Jesus Christ's cross, that cross?'

"Of course. The conquistador Hernando Martinez de Salvaterra wore this ring, and he believed himself invincible as long as he wore it. Then there was an unfortunate occurrence. While in battle defending a monastery in Peru, the ring and finger were cut from the conquistador's hand, which separated him from his good luck charm and allowed his enemies to vanquish his soul back to heaven. The finger with the ring still on it was returned to his wife in La Paz. It was the conquistador's family fortune that helped establish an orphanage. This orphanage is still there in La Paz, though I believe it has been rebuilt many times. Hernando Martinez de Salvaterra was himself an orphan raised by the church. Thus these relics, the finger with the Caravaca ring, were stored in the altar at Nuestra Señora de Cortez. The finger remains, but the ring went missing under mysterious circumstances many years ago. The ring was recently identified as being one and the same as on Robert Tyson Grant's finger."

"So the ring is magic?"

"So they tell me."

Dixie swilled some wine, her eyes on the fire. "One thing I don't understand, Morty." Her hand was on mine. "When we needed help and sent for you, how did your people know it was Grant seeking help, with Purity, I mean? They must have known it was Grant to have asked for the ring."

I sipped my wine thoughtfully. "I am not sure I understand, *querida*."

"I sent for you."

"Really?" I placed my hand on hers and gave it a squeeze. "How charming."

"So how did you know about the ring if I sent for you anonymously?"

My brow was knit. She sent for me? She contacted Father Gomez? "We knew about the ring because it was in a picture on the cover of *Forbes* magazine. The one with Grant in yachting togs. So if it was you who sent for me to make things right and recover the ring . . ."

"I sent for you to make things right, but not about the ring."

To be brutally honest, at that moment, I was on the cusp of asking exactly what she meant. However, I was also becoming weary of the confusing conversation interfering with the sex. She was sitting very close, and I could see directly down her top to where the bra bridged the gap between her breasts. It was time for our meeting to turn more intimate, not less. A kiss on the lips was too forward and abrupt at that juncture, but not far off, either. So I smiled, brushed her ringlets aside, and placed a gentle kiss on her forehead. Instead of continuing the interrogation, I became mysterious. Pay attention, oafs. Being mysterious, holding back, is important; it creates bricks of anticipation. If they know everything, it leaves nothing to find out. Remember all that stuff I said about desire.

"Dixie, as you said before, perhaps it is better there are some things you don't know. At least not yet."

As if a divine light had parted the clouds, I had a eureka moment. *Of course.* Dixie saw me with Purity in my arms. This divine creature's inquiries all stemmed from a mild state of jealousy. No woman likes to set her sights on a man—however tentatively—and then see him in the company of another woman, especially a younger woman. I decided to stack my bricks deftly.

"You know, Dixie, when Purity fell into my arms, I felt how delicate life is, how easily it can be here one moment and then gone the next. To be brutally honest, I had been thinking about you all morning, since breakfast. At court, my mind was both places, you and what was going on around me. Then, in the moment Purity tripped, my left hand grabbed her here." I put a hand on Dixie's rib cage, below the breast. "My other hand held her here, on the upper arm. As she fell before me, and I eased her down to the floor, I noted that she has delicate little freckles on her nose. She seemed at peace, almost like she was dead."

Sometimes I think I am a genius when it comes to women, even if my reasoning is not entirely accurate. Dixie was getting turned on, but not through jealousy. It was established earlier in the film that she liked to be bad, in a sexual way. She was used to being on the giving end of being naughty, and led Grant around by his man parts. This type of woman likes to be the one in control during sex. There are times, however, when they encounter a man who dominates them, someone who is bad like themselves, verging on dangerous. Here she was drinking wine with what she thought was a hired killer, one so deft he was making public appearances with his victim, and then describing in detail how he saved her while at the same time thinking about killing her. It was the comment about the freckles that got her, though the hand on the rib cage probably helped.

Dixie's lips were on mine, and our tongues met.

As I sit here in my cell, it is quite pleasing to reflect on this salacious event.

Oafs: Pay attention. When you are seated on a couch with a woman, and you kiss, it is important to have her in the corner of the couch so she has no avenue of easy retreat. Some will retreat because they think they should, others because they genuinely did not want the kiss. The former will remain seated, the latter will stand. Forget about the latter.

Dixie seemed to catch herself, and began to move back, but I could feel her breathing heavily, excited, and she did not stand up.

I should really sell this next maneuver for more than the price of a movie deal.

With your left hand on her right flank, spin her away from the sofa corner, pivot, and lay her down. You may have to use your knee to help nudge her legs up. You spin with her, and continue the kiss, transforming it into a full-on embrace. Be careful. If you perform this swoop too abruptly you may smash your teeth into hers, which can ruin the evening and result in expensive visits to the orthodontist. The swoop must be done assertively yet gracefully, as if you were whirling her on a dance floor. The Martinez Swoop sweeps them off their feet.

At this point the camera should swing in on the gas fire, away from the passions on display on the sofa.

TWENTY-TWO

WE SWITCH FROM THE GLOW of the fire to the blue glow of a computer screen, one that sparks Purity's green eyes.

At the very moment I was enacting the Martinez Swoop, Purity was in her room at the Mandarin Hotel dressed in a plush bathrobe. She was watching the news video of herself fainting into my arms. Spilled on the bed next to her was a folder featuring details of various rehab centers the lawyers said she was to choose from. On a tray on the floor was a half-eaten room-service hamburger.

Released from the hospital midafternoon, she'd been escorted by a fearsome female nurse named Greta to the expensive Columbus Circle suite. This was temporary, an overnight. She was to be shipped back to East Hampton in the morning. Greta sat outside her door, more guard than nurse.

You may ask: How could she be imprisoned in this way at her age?

She had imprisoned herself. Purity had no money of her own, only that which her stepfather meted out to her from a trust fund. Her career as her stepfather's nemesis did not come with a salary. She had nowhere to stay except where he let her have an account, and that tended to be out in East Hampton. Grant felt keeping her out there limited the amount of embarrassment she could cause, so he had an open account she could use at local stores and of course at the local lounge, where she could drink herself silly. This did not mean that Purity could not effect the occasional escape.

The hotel room windows at the Mandarin did not open, and even if they did, Purity's suite was thirty or more flights up. It killed her that there was a bar on the top floor of the hotel and she couldn't get at it. So she'd logged on and reviewed the latest thorn she'd stuck into her stepfather's side.

The news reports from the morning's events had evolved beyond what I had been told, and even what Robert Tyson Grant had seen. The news report flashing in front of Purity's eyes went something like this:

Lady Godiva or Sleeping Beauty? You decide. Earlier today after her sentencing for stealing a horse and riding topless through Central Park, bad-girl Purity Grant fainted into the arms of a Prince Charming outside the courtroom. Who is this guardian angel, this dashing protector? Just a spectator? Rumor has it he's either a friend of the family or Purity's latest fling. Nobody seems to know for now. Stay tuned as there are sure to be further episodes.

Purity stared at me in the video on her screen, wondering if she knew me somehow, from somewhere. She watched the video in slow motion, and liked the way the stranger hovered over her and brushed the hair gently from her face. He looked like a nice guy, even if he was wearing a white suit. She didn't meet many nice guys. Most people who met her were interested in only three things: money, fame, and sex. She wasn't fixated on me or anything, just curious about me, not sure whether I was someone she actually wanted to know or someone she could use to outrage her stepfather. Perhaps both. Assuming the tabloids discovered who I was and she could reach out to me. Idle speculation.

Her cell vibrated, and she whispered into it.

"Hey . . . not yet, hopefully soon . . . I'll call you. Where? . . . OK, I'll meet you there."

She flicked off the call and looked at the door to her posh cell.

On the way to the hotel, she had asked Greta if they could stop at a pharmacy so that she could pick up some things for over-night. Originally, she was supposed to go back to East Hampton, but the hospital detour pushed that trip off to the next day. Which of course had been Purity's plan all along. The faint was an act, and when she saw me standing there, she more or less tossed her-self into my arms and hoped I'd catch her.

The nurse glumly supervised the pharmacy expedition: tooth-brush, toothpaste, deodorant, face wash, Tums, extra lip gloss, and eye drops. Of course, a nice hotel like the Mandarin has many of these things for its guests, but Greta wasn't familiar with these nice-ties. Purity didn't actually need any of these items, just the Nytol gel caps she shoplifted.

Logging off of her laptop and snapping it shut, Purity crept to the door to her room.

"Greta? Greta?"

She knocked on the door to her room. No response, so she gently turned the knob and cracked the door open. Greta was slumped in the easy chair next to the door like a deflated Thanksgiving Day Parade balloon, snoring loudly.

Shedding her bathrobe, Purity was already dressed in the skirt she wore to court and a sleeveless blouse. She quickly put up her hair in pigtails, slipped on some thigh-high moccasin boots, and unbuttoned her blouse to show the black bikini top she wore in-stead of a bra. Greta's purse contained eighty dollars. That was all

138 BRIAN M. WIPRUD

that was necessary for cabs and such, if even that, because where Purity would go men would pick up the tab for everything. She slid the cash into her own purse, which only contained makeup, cell phone, and lip gloss. Gently backing out of the hotel suite, the wayward Purity exited into Manhattan's open arms.

TWENTY-THREE

A CLOSE-UP OF THE GLOWING bus destination sign
RICHMOND pulls back to reveal a roaring silver Greyhound motor
coach. It sweeps like a flashing diesel sword into a passenger bay
next to a station, whines, and then gasps to a stop. You can add
the sound effect of a slashing sword if you think that would help
sell the menace of the bus's arrival.

The doors jolted open, revealing our cat-eyed killer, Paco, who
is in the act of kissing his Santa Muerte medallion. He hops to the
macadam, the medallion dropping back into his shirt.

Chin up, the man who came to kill Purity Grant strode with
renewed confidence as he moved toward the depot. Paco served
his mistress Santa Muerte that morning, and he felt particularly virtuous and rejuvenated about having killed and beheaded
John.

Yes, the beheading was a little unnecessary, but he was El Cabezador, and he felt that he should take pride in his craft and use
bloody goggling noggins to sign all his killings. He had decided
that leaving a head would be his own personal way of showing
respect to his beloved protector Santa Muerte. Certainly the she-
devil was there protecting him during his battle with the charging

bull John. There was no such thing as luck, only that which his God allowed. It was clear to Paco that it was Santa Muerte who inspired the other illegals to pick up clubs and pound John into a pulpy red meat pancake. Santa Muerte was giving Paco a sign, one of encouragement.

Once John was dispatched, the illegals felt it best that they all scatter, and the sooner the better. After burying John's body in a shallow grave under the pile of construction debris, Paco drove them all in John's van to the Greyhound bus station in Culpville. In a locker there, Paco placed a plastic Cinnabon bag containing John's head, which was wrapped in the yellow South of the Border windbreaker. No sense in cutting off a head if you do not leave the trophy where people will discover it and fear the killer. The other illegals all bought tickets taking them west, seemingly as far as they could go from where John met his just end, and close to border crossings where they might be able to slip back to Mexico should the police come looking for them.

Paco, of course, was still heading north to New York, with his Waffle House paper place mat showing the franchise locations across the eastern seaboard. At a Goodwill store near the Culpville bus station, he bought a cheap fringed leather jacket, black and lightweight. There was an inside pocket, and this was the perfect place to put his pistol.

It was late by the time Paco reached Richmond, and he needed sleep. He was fairly certain that finding a cheap room on his own might be a problem. He knew Hispanics were not entirely welcome everywhere in the United States. As in Memphis, he was easily able to find familiar surroundings near the bus station in which to operate.

A few blocks away he turned down a street that was lined with low brick commercial buildings catering to plumbers, masons, and janitorial supplies stores. The sidewalk in front of these buildings and loading platforms was sprinkled with women, and the curb in front of the women was dotted with the brake lights of the ladies' customers.

Striding down the block, Paco surveyed the prostitutes. Some asked if he was looking for a date; others turned their backs, not wanting to turn a trick with a Hispanic. He smiled at them all, but was looking for a south-of-the-border girl, and sure enough he found one. Cue the subtitles:

"Dear one, how are you tonight?"

"Looking for girlfriend?"

"I am looking not only for a girlfriend, I am looking for a *chica,* and it would seem I have found one. What is your name?"

"Firecracker. And yours?"

"Bob. So, Firecracker, what is the cost of a movie these days?"

"A hundred."

"Is that for the date or the movie?"

"Room is extra, darling." She came closer and batted her eyelashes. He could smell her coconut perfume, and by her proportions—tits in a tube top and hips in a tight skirt—he was certain he'd picked one that was not a man in disguise. She was a little on the heavy side, muffin-topping over the miniskirt, but there were no evident sores around her mouth or track marks on her arms. Also, her long black hair seemed thick and healthy, which was a generally accepted way that his Juárez compatriots would select a healthy hooker. The ones with STDs tended to have brittle-looking hair.

"Dear one, I am not in the mood to bargain, but shall we say eighty for the whole thing? I will be sleeping in until morning, so you can, too, if you want. It is late, and customers here are thinning."

"I hate to ask this of a compatriot, but I need to make sure you can afford a movie."

Paco pulled a wad of twenties from his pocket, just part of what he'd stolen from John's wallet.

She turned away, looking at the passing cars, and it seemed as if she were going to ignore him. Her hand reached out to his, and she led him down the block, past the other girls, who said things like "Chica, I'll see you for breakfast" and "Firecracker's fuse is lit."

They went down an alley and emerged on another, busier street with gas stations and fast-food restaurants. A few doors down was a sign: SOUTHERN BELLE MOTOR LODGE. It was bilevel, blue, with doors facing out toward the parking lot, the office at the end near the driveway entrance. There were rooms on both sides of the motel, front and back, those on the first floor with parking spaces in front of them, the second floor fronted by a continuous porch from which the rooms were accessed.

There was a corridor off the parking lot into the motel, and past the ice machine were steps up to the second level. Firecracker led Paco to the back and all the way to the end. She unlocked the door with a key on a bungee around her wrist and shoved the door open.

The room smelled faintly of cigarette smoke and sanitizer, but the bed was made. Except for beverage rings on the sparse furniture, the place looked clean. It was certainly the nicest place Paco had had to bunk since he left Juárez.

He handed Firecracker the eighty dollars. She pulled off her tube top, wrapped the money and her key in the spandex garment, and wedged it behind the TV. Cupping her breasts, she pointed the large brown nipples at Paco like they were weapons.

Subtitles, please:

"You want me from the front or the back, Bob?"

Paco pulled off his black fringed jacket and draped it over the TV. "I want you on the bed."

Not exactly as good as what I had going in Dixie's apartment, was it? Well, each man has to live within his means, yes? Just the same, Firecracker's tits should help cement our R rating and keep male audience members alert.

Let us cut to the outside of the motel room. From the porch we see the room window, and we see the interior light beyond the curtain go out. We fade from night to first light, the faintest of sunrise glowing pink in the darkened window of Paco's motel room.

The early morning calm was shattered by a scream. A skinny black woman with long blond hair stumbled and fell in front of Paco's door. A bald, hairy white man in white briefs rushed up to the prostitute, whipping her with a belt. The girl screamed for mercy.

The motel door swung open, and Paco stepped forward, dressed in just his track pants. He looked down at the victim, then at her tormentor.

The bald, hairy white man stopped thrashing the girl long enough to look Paco in the eye, and then resumed his punishment.

Paco shoved the tormentor, flipping the bald, hairy white man over the railing and down to the parking lot where he landed off-screen with a crunch.

Paco stepped calmly back into his motel room and closed the door.

Whimpering, the skinny black girl picked up her long blond wig and scurried out of frame.

Paco opened the door again, and he was dressed and in the act of donning his leather jacket. He walked down the porch to the exit, the sound of approaching sirens in the distance.

CHAPTER

TWENTY-FOUR

EVEN AS THE SUN'S ROSY orb glowed low over a seedy Virginia motel, it warmed the cold glass and steel of midtown Manhattan, the denizens stirring in the brightening murk of their bedrooms.

Some, like Robert Tyson Grant, awoke alone and troubled, and went immediately for a swim in the penthouse pool.

Others, like me, briefly awoke entwined and spent with Grant's girlfriend, with no thoughts of swimming pools.

Still others awoke entwined and spent, but with thoughts of swimming pools and East Hampton mansions.

One might well have surmised that Purity found herself that morning in the bed of a bartender, or of a punk rocker, or of a rave club Romeo or worse still.

The audience will be somewhat surprised when the camera pans from where Purity is curled up with a pillow to a vacant spot in the bed next to her. The apartment is modest but clean, the walls checkered with black-and-white photos of Manhattan. The bathroom door is open and provides the only light in the room. Who do we see emerge freshly showered with a towel around his waist?

Skip Baker, the reporter.

As I think Lincoln once said, publicity makes strange bedfellows.

Skip sauntered to the bed and sat in the vacant spot. Grabbing Purity's hip, he gave it a shake. "Up!"

She rolled over, the blond pigtails draped across green eyes shriveled by slumber. "Give me one good reason?"

"I can give you more reasons than that, babe, but I'll start with: I have to get to work."

"Work on what?"

"The continuing adventures of Purity Grant, of course."

Purity hugged a pillow and rubbed her nose in it. "What happens in this installment?"

"I have to track down your Prince Charming."

"And that's certainly not you."

"Certainly not. The guy in the white suit who caught you."

"Who was he?"

"If I knew, I might not have to kick you out of here so soon. Besides, I thought we had a deal. No questions."

"No *probing* questions. That was an *incidental* question."

"Why'd you pick him to faint on?"

"Would you have caught me?"

"Good point."

"Ass."

"If I find this guy, you want me to tell you where to find him?"

"Why would I want to find a strange man in a white suit, even if he did keep me from bashing my skull on the courthouse's marble floor?"

"Makes a nice story, that's why."

"Is that really all I am to you? A comic strip character?"

Skip patted her hip. "Not only."

"You suck, Skip, you know that?"

He smiled and cocked an eyebrow at her. "I'll bet you I'm one of the few people who treats you like a person and not a celebrity or a belt notch. Don't knock it. I may be the only friend you have."

Purity rolled to her back, hands over her face. "Yeah, that would be about the size of it."

"I don't lecture you, I don't tell you what to do, and yet I'm always here when you want me. So I *suck*? Jeez, Purity, I wish I had someone like that."

"You're just after Purity stories."

"And you, babe, are after stories, too, aren't you?"

Purity took her hands away from her face and glared at him. "We also said no headshrinking, remember?"

"That's merely an *incidental* statement of fact. Let's get you in the shower. That'll wake you up."

"Wake up for what? So they can ship me back to East Hampton? Then to rehab? I don't need rehab. That's just where they send anybody who doesn't play by the rules."

"Do I need to point out that you are legally an adult? Only the courts can imprison you, Purity. Well, one other person, but we said no headshrinking." Skip rolled to her side of the bed, took her hand, and lifted her to her feet, the sheets sliding off of her rumpled but fantastically lithe young body. "Let's go."

"Any time you want to take the gloves off, I'm ready, Baker. I might just tunnel under the wire yet. I have a meeting today with some people."

"People?"

"*People.*"

"People who want to pay you money to do something so that you won't have to rely on the trust fund Robert Tyson Grant's holding out on you?"

"Watch TN2.com, maybe you'll find out before the *Daily Post* does." Purity stumbled toward the bathroom, her little butt swaying behind those slim tanned hips, the pigtails licking her shoulders.

I bite my hand just thinking of it. It is not for me to speak for other men, but for me, women are at their most endearing in the morning, complete with sheet wrinkles on their behinds, mascara-smeared eyes, tangled hair, and breasts posed as God intended. I suppose that is partially because when I witness this it means there has been a night of adventure, but more so because you now see the woman and her body at ease. While this body may have been spectacular and enchanting beyond all distraction the night before in fancy panties and bra, carefully scented, and the eyes painted to allure, there is a deeper appreciation of the female form to be had when it is fresh from between the sheets and natural. I suppose it is like the beauty of a sunrise compared to the glitter of Times Square. Women have a different scent in the morning, too. This fragrance is at once gently yeasty and salty, like fresh-baked baguettes, especially behind the ears and along the nape of the neck and all the way down the back to that depression at the base of the spine where the aroma is slightly nutty, the spot on which the behind seems to pivot as they walk. Were I a poet, I could write volumes on that spot.

Excuse the digression. I would apologize, except that when it comes to women, it is clear that I have the soul of a tormented artist who devours with his mind.

Purity swayed to the bathroom door and grasped the door frame. She cocked a leg and looked back at Skip from under her hair. "So are you going to write a happy ending for me?" Her eye and tone were at once mocking and challenging.

Skip walked over to the bathroom door and kissed her on the head. "I *write* the stories. You *make* the stories. It's as simple as that."

"Is it?" Purity latched onto his towel at the waist and pulled him into the bathroom.

Skip closed the door behind them, the wedge of light collapsing and leaving us in the dark.

TWENTY-FIVE

IT WAS A NIGHT OF passions for the players of my small tragedy, beginning with the sublime and following through to the tawdry. Everybody except Grant got laid.

So let us come full circle.

Like Purity, I awoke to find my bedmate missing, so maybe the camera finds me in exactly the same position in the bed as she was, and moves the same way across the bed toward the bathroom. Ah, but when the camera pans to the bathroom door, it is open but dark.

I arose, with a sheet wrapped around me. Despite my body being worthy of display, I certainly cannot imagine we are showing anything more than a mere glimpse of my buttocks. This seems to be the convention in film, though perhaps you can explain to me at the premiere why this is so. Ah, of course, I won't be at the premiere, I will be dead—you would think I could not forget this regrettable state of affairs, yet I am immersed in telling this story as fast as I can and as completely as possible, with as few digressions as possible because I can little afford the time. I personally am not a connoisseur of the penis. Mine is just there attached to my front, magnificent and wily as he should be. Those belonging to other men are like some beast worm from Pluto that if you did not know what it was you would smash it with a broom and burn it in the leaf pile. Yet I am sure this is different for women, and perhaps the penis as a general form is as pleasing to them as the female delights are to me. So I am not sure why a good-looking penis like mine or perhaps Jimmy Smits's is not worthy for a screen debut.

Where was I? Ah. So with the sheet wrapped around me I left the bedroom and went hunting for Dixie—and I mean *hunting*. When you bed someone with a body like hers, you must make the most of the access you have to it. The glasses and bottles and undergarments and pants and shirts that had been strewn about the couch were missing.

There was, however, a note on the bar.

Morty—I will make arrangements for you to have access to Purity and to set things right ASAP with the ring. Will contact you at your hotel. Close the door behind you. XOD

PS: Cheers to the health of the chickens.

Alas, it was not the first time that I had arisen to find that a woman was, shall we say, somewhat doubtful of her choices the previous evening. Such is the nature of passion that reason finds itself shamefaced, yes? Yet this was a novel turn of events. Dixie, who had been jealous of Purity, was now relinquishing me to her? Perhaps Dixie was gaining some satisfaction knowing that she had me first? I marveled at the multifaceted gem that is a woman. Yet as I said, I no longer viewed Purity as the object of passion. While I was touched by this selfless gesture by Dixie, I had no intention of accepting it.

I found my clothing neatly hung in the bathroom. Dressed, I strode from the lobby, full of heart for having won the desire and passions of such a delicious woman as Dixie, emboldened with the knowledge that a new day might bring further delights. At the very least, a further delight in the form of a grilled cheese sandwich.

Speaking of grilled cheese sandwiches, Dixie was meeting with

Robert at the Red Flame Diner, in the same back booth in which
I had introduced myself to the Grab-A-Lot mogul.

Perhaps as a segue we could have a close-up of a grilled cheese
sandwich on one table and pan over to a close-up of a grapefruit
and black coffee being set on the Formica in front of Dixie, and
whole wheat toast and tomato juice being set in front of Grant.
Between the two breakfasts, Grant slaps down a tabloid. On its
front page is a picture of me in my white suit holding Purity Grant
in my arms. The headline read: GUARDIAN ANGEL?

We don't have to stay in a close-up of their breakfast. It is probably best that the camera pull back, and perhaps watch the conversation through the window of the diner, extras posing as pedestrians
passing briefly between us and our characters. If you used real
pedestrians they might linger and block our view.

Dixie was in yellow slacks and yellow and black polka-dot halter top. Grant was in a blue serge suit with an open-collar white
shirt.

"Well, our Mexican surely can't kill her now, can he?" Grant
stabbed his hand at the tabloid picture.

"Shh!"

Grant's voice lowered to a whisper. "He's worthless. He's less
than worthless. He's protecting her! What kind of hit man pro-
tects his victim?"

"Yesterday when I met him, before my night at the gym, he
told me it's all part of a plan of some kind. He's a fairly mysterious character, this Morty, and wouldn't say why he did that or
how he knew about the ring or any of that. He's a cool cucumber
for sure, because he said he considered killing her right then and
there. Can you imagine? I mean, if she'd hit her head, or he made
it look like she had . . ."

"He said that?"

"I think so."

"You think so?"

"Robert, keep your voice down, please. As I said, he's a fairly mysterious character."

"He said he was thinking of killing her there but didn't? Is this some sort of leverage for the ring?"

"Well, pookie, I think you need to try to weigh your priorities."

"I have weighed my priorities and my options." Grant folded his arms. "He can have the ring."

She gasped. "Bobbie, I think that's a very mature decision."

Grant chuckled, waving a finger. "I haven't built Grant Industries into the giant that it is today by letting people push me around. Robert Tyson Grant settles deals on *his* terms." He leaned back with a jaunty cock of his head. "I'll give him the ring, the ring that looks just like the one on my finger. I dropped in at a jeweler on Forty-seventh Street, they photographed the ring and sized it, and they'll have a copy for me by one o'clock."

"They can do it that fast?"

"For Robert Tyson Grant *they will*."

"Oh, sweetums, that is brilliant! Woo hoo! Well, that solves that problem." They clinked coffee mugs. "To old friends, new friends, and health of the chickens."

"Chickens?"

"Oh, that's just a toast I heard on TV or something, I thought it was funny."

"You look quite ravishing this morning, Dix." He was positively leering at her. Like a tomcat, he sensed his puss was in heat, only he had no idea it was as a result of me.

"Thank you, sweet Bobbie." Her smile was forced, and masked the shimmer of guilt she felt for having cuckolded him. "Look, we need to get this show on the road. I was awake early this morning, and I think I figured out the perfect opportunity for Morty to target Purity. On her way home today to East Hampton. The limo can be ambushed and he can pretend to kidnap her or something. These Mexicans do a lot of kidnapping. Anyway, I can suggest it, but it's up to our hit man how he does it. I think we have the right to say *when* he does it. She hasn't left yet, has she?"

"Of course not." Grant's mood darkened, his eyes hooded. "She drugged the escort, Greta, and slipped out last night, but this morning she called my assistant, Kathy, and said she was doing some shopping and would head back to the hotel in the afternoon. I was going to have her flown by chopper from the West Side heliport out to the estate to make sure she didn't give us the slip again. My stomach hurts just knowing she's loose out there in the city. Anything could happen. I need Grant Industries stocks stable now. What with Trade Winds coming down the pike, I need our bond rating rock solid—and I certainly don't need her interfering with, well, you know. I missed you last night."

"I missed you, too, babykins. Try to relax. It will all be over soon, and then we can fuck like bunnies all night long."

"Let's go back to your place right now!"

"First things first, punkin'. I have to make sure I don't drop the ball, and I can't be straddling you like a bronco while at the same time making sure the Mexican arrives at the right place at the right time."

Grant pouted. "Make sure he isn't seen by the security cameras at the house."

"I thought it would be a problem for Morty to make his move on the grounds of the estate. It would look suspicious if your security system somehow went on the blink. No, I think we should send her back by limo. He could ambush the car on the local roads on the way down to the beach."

He gripped his forehead. "Just make sure the Mexican doesn't kill or seriously hurt the driver. No reason anybody else should suffer for her sins."

"You poor darling." Dixie patted Robert's cheek. "I'll get Morty on board, you let me know when she's on the road."

"I wish you wouldn't keep calling him by his first name, Dix. It sounds so, well, familiar."

Dixie looked at him sidelong. "Robert Tyson Grant. You're not jealous, are you?"

"I don't like you meeting alone with a hit man. It's dangerous."

"I can handle myself, Robert."

"Yes, but he's a hit man, he has guns and things, and you're very, very attractive, he could get it into his head to force you to . . ."

"You sweet man." *If only he knew.* Her feeble conscience was assuaged by the notion that she had straddled my loins for Grant's sake. "He comes near me and—*bam*—a shot right to the testes."

"Really?"

She winked at Grant and stood. "I am a force to be reckoned with, or hadn't you noticed?"

As always, Grant watched her behind intently as she walked away, though he noted that it wasn't swaying the way it normally did.

That long trip to the gym last night must have left her sore.

We see Dixie leave the diner from outside and follow her yellow polka dot halter top as she crosses the street and walks past a swarthy, dark-haired man with heavy eyelids and dark circles under his eyes. He leans against a building, watches her pass, and speaks into his cell phone.

"Helena? It's Tony. Where you been?"

Let's do a split screen so we see the palmist making a bologna sandwich in her pantry on the right side, and see her nephew the car service driver on the left.

"Tony, I was up late with Abbie watching TV. I'm just up making breakfast. You get there early like I said?"

"Uhn huhn."

"You see her?"

"Uhn huhn."

"She leave with the fella you saw last night, the fella with the champagne bucket?"

"Nuh uhn."

"How late did you stay last night?" She spread Miracle Whip on the white bread.

"Ten. I hadda get home to Ginny."

"OK, so Mr. Champagne left sometime late last night, figures. So where did she go this morning?"

"Met a guy in a diner."

"What diner?"

"Red Flame, off Sixth."

"What's the fella look like?" Helena tore open a package of bologna and began slapping slices onto the bread.

"Older, sixty maybe, gray hair on the sides, nice blue suit, maybe six feet."

"Figures. So where's she going now?"

"Way down the block."

"Follow!"

"I gotta make money, Helena, you know that. I gotta get some driving done." We see Tony start to walk quickly in the direction he saw Dixie go, craning his neck. "I got the baby at home."

"This *will* make money."

"I don't know that."

She spread Miracle Whip on the top slice for her sandwich. "I'm your aunt."

"I know that."

"When I say you'll make money, you'll make money."

"How long am I supposed to follow this broad?"

"All day."

"All day?" Tony comes to the end of a block and looks in all directions, but does not see Dixie's yellow polka dots.

"You want me to call your cousin Gina?"

"Gina?"

"Yes, Gina. She's not doing much these days, not acting in any movies right now, she could use the money."

"What if, like, the yellow polka dots loses me?"

"Don't let her."

"I'm just saying." Pedestrians streamed all around him.

Helena paused while cutting her sandwich. "You lost her, didn't you, Tony?"

"Kinda."

"Abbie?" Helena yelled at the ceiling.

We hear faintly from upstairs, "Yeah?"

"Call Gina!"

The camera pans up from Tony standing on the sidewalk to a glass tower and zooms in on a high window in which Purity Grant stands smoking a cigarette and gazing out over midtown. She's dressed in her trademark pigtails, white man's Oxford shirt open at the front, bikini top, and thigh-high moccasin boots. Large dark glasses covered her calculating green eyes. A diet cola can is in her hand. Could there be a more perfect opportunity for a product placement?

We move up into the office where she is standing, and there are two men talking alternately, off-camera. One has a high, fast voice; the other is lower, older, deeper.

High: "So what we're saying is that you've created this marvelously kinetic image of troubled youth, of dissatisfaction."

Low: "In effect. It is safe to say, Purity, that you have branded yourself. In so doing, you have commodity potential across a wide range of markets."

High: "We're talking Gen P personified, rebel zeitgeist, the female James Dean of our times. Your ride through Central Park? Using it! We'll capture that untamed wench, that mustang spirit in a pair of torn jeans, and a fragrance called 'Fuck You, Dad!' with Bad Girl Purity Grant on billboards ten stories high, bareback, police cars with flashing lights blurred behind you, your nipples covered with electrical tape!"

Purity knit her brow and half-turned. "How much?"

Low: "Compensation will depend on many factors, Purity, and we suggest you have an agent negotiate that for you. Ultravibe Media can suggest some that are tightly woven into the business and can guide you sagely through this process so that your needs are amply met."

She took a drag and blew out smoke. "How much *up front* are you offering?"

Low: "Well, ahem, there will of course be a signing bonus, and we're thinking that a reasonable first offer that would fit industry standards for endorsements of this kind might be in the low six-figure range . . ."

High: "There are residuals, sweetie, and royalties and bonuses. We're talking about jeans, fragrances, handbags, jewelry—I mean, sky's the limit on this sort of thing. *Reality TV.* That knock your socks off? Hm? This is just the beginning, the ground floor."

Purity nodded at the carpet and then turned back to the window. "You must have some first offer? In writing?"

Low: "Yes, we at Ultravibe Media have draft contracts drawn up for you and your agent to look over. However, there is something you must know, Purity, and it is written into the contract. As I said, you have branded yourself for a particular young adult that we are trying to market to. You have a countercultural image that we are proposing you, in effect, use to sell a variety of retail goods. This is a lucrative deal, and we do not make it lightly, and we place a high value on the image that you have cultivated for yourself."

High: "An album! Do you sing? Doesn't matter. We have people."

Purity smirked but did not turn. "So what you're saying is that I'll be contractually obligated to continue to have the tabloids pissing off my stepfather. IOW, you're going to pay me to piss off my stepfather to sell clothes to other people who want to piss off *their* fathers? Spiffy."

Low: "I would say that you have characterized the launch of your brand accurately."

High: "Purity will be the bad girl that is *so* good!"

"What if I'm not pissing off my stepfather on a regular basis? What then?"

Low: "That, I'm afraid, would erode the brand."

"Breach of contract?" Purity turned to look at them off screen.

Low: "Most likely."

"What if my stepfather dies?"

High: "Oh my God! The funeral! *Hello?* Black is the new 'it' color, every pissed-off chick who hates her dad buys the Purity Grant veil! Black torn jeans and a veil that is also a sleeveless tee. Can't you see it! Is he sick? Is he dying? Bob, really, this could be *huge*!"

Low: "I don't think that the brand is entirely dependent on your stepfather, Purity. You fly in the face of all authority. The target market yearns to capture a piece of that for themselves by buying your products but without going to jail."

"MEGO." She turned back to the window, smiling to herself. "So as long as I'm arrested now and again, my 'brand' is maintained?"

Low: "I would think that would fall into the definition of the brand that the current contract stipulates."

"What about jail?"

High: "BE STILL MY HEART!"

Low: "Your agent would have to find some vehicle to ensure that any royalty distributions or profits you might reap directly as a result of a prison term met with state and federal laws."

"So, he might be able to stash it for me somewhere if I went to prison?"

Low: "That is between you, your agent, and your legal counsel. So, Purity, does this sound like a venture that would interest you?"

"What about a triple play?"

A pause as we hear Low and High exchange a whisper.

Low: "Triple play?"

"That's right. What if I have three major events in my life in a week?"

Low: "Define major event."

"Take this down, guys: A major event shall be defined for the purposes of this contract as any event whereby Purity Grant is in the *Daily Post* or tabloid with equivalent readership, both online and in print, to include but not limited to Purity's arrest, Purity's disappearance, a Purity sex tape released to the media, Robert Tyson Grant's death, Purity Grant's death, etc. A triple play shall be defined for the purposes of this contract as any three major events occurring within seven calendar days (one hundred and sixty-eight hours) and entitling Purity Grant to ten million dollars for each event, payable in a lump sum directly to Purity Grant within thirty calendar days. However, in the event that Purity Grant's reported death ends up false, that part of the triple play can occur within one year of the last major event to qualify. This contract is confidential, and any release of its contents by your company to any person outside your organization will result in a ten-million-dollar bonus to be paid to Purity Grant—in Ultravibe Media company stock or cash—within thirty calendar days from the day that that information is published either in print or online or reported in any media outlet."

Low cleared his throat. "Ultravibe Media will have to discuss this with your agent, Purity. This is highly irregular."

Purity dropped her cigarette into the Diet Pepsi or Coke can, and it hissed like a striking cobra. She turned. "There isn't going to be any agent, and there isn't going to be any fifteen percent. I'll take five hundred grand as a signing fee, with an annual salary of two hundred grand for two years, complete with standard percentages of all merchandising. Complete with full benefits, but you can keep your 401(k). Wouldn't look good for the brand if I had a 401(k), would it?"

High (*whispering*): "Bob, take it! That's less up front."

Low: "I really think you should reconsider, Purity. These contracts are complex."

We see Purity through the window as she shakes out a fresh cigarette and flames it.

"That's the deal. Send the contracts to Mike Miller, he's my attorney at Steptoe. Today, or it's no deal."

The camera turns away from the window and zooms into the distance, and cross-zooms all the way to the front of my hotel, through the glass doors, and into the modern lobby. In an angular chair next to a glass-block pillar sits Skip Baker in his suede jacket and cowboy boots. He's sipping coffee and distractedly reading the paper, his eyes flicking out the window and toward the front desk and hotel entrance.

I know, we're making the camera whip around the city, but a lot is happening all at once, and I think this technique will give us continuity of action and a cohesive timeline at this crucial juncture in my story. If you don't believe me, see page 114 of this fine book I have, *Screenwriting: Yes You Can!*

Imagine my surprise as I came into my hotel and was approached by Skip. My mind was in rapture with the previous night's romp, the notion of a hot shower, and the inevitability of a grilled cheese at the Lyric Diner.

"Morty!" Skip's smile was on the side of his face, the eyes under his blond eyebrows sparkling.

His hand was extended, and I shook it. "Skip? This is unexpected."

"Is unexpected bad? How about some breakfast?"

"To be brutally honest, I was about to bathe." I cocked an eyebrow at my inquisitive friend. "So am I to assume you've come as a reporter, sought me out, gone from East Side hotel to East Side hotel looking for the handsome Mexican who caught Purity Grant in his arms?"

He held up the tabloid with my picture. I had not seen this yet, and took it from him to hold to the light of the windows. "Taken by one of the scumtators?"

Skip shrugged and smiled.

"So this is your work, then, making this small incident a sensation of sorts?"

"That's what I do, Morty. That's what reporters do. Molehill? No such thing. Only mountains."

I was not sure at the time whether I should be offended by his intrusion into my privacy or flattered by being featured on the front page and dining on a fleeting morsel of fame. I had never been in the newspaper before, much less on the front page.

My lip curled at the photo as I held it this way and that. "I suppose I look heroic."

"The ladies will love it." He had my number, as they say.

I nodded. "Yes, I suppose they might, as you say." I handed the paper back to him. "So, Skip, your generosity in allowing me to accompany you into the courtroom paid off. You have your front-page story. What else can you possibly want of this molehill?"

"I want your story. For tomorrow's paper."

I shook my head. "I am afraid not, Skip. This kind of publicity might be adverse for the business I am conducting here in New York. It is not that interesting, anyway."

Skip made a big shrug, sighed, and hung his head. "I totally understand, Morty. But if you were me, you'd try, too, wouldn't you?"

I patted him on the shoulder. "As Lincoln used to say, nothing adventured, nothing gleaned. Now, if you'll excuse me. The 'guardian angel' needs a shower."

"Lincoln was a very smart guy." He followed me to the elevators. "Can I at least buy you breakfast? It is the least I can do for the guy that gave me that awesome story yesterday. To be honest, things have been a bit slow, and being there when you caught Purity helped save my job. Generosity pays, who knew? So how about it?"

I sighed because I knew I should say no but at the same time I liked Skip. He was what you might call an honest liar. Skip made only the slightest pretense of disguising his disingenuous nature. I recognized some of that in myself, so felt a certain kinship with this hustler.

"I am going to take a shower."

"Great. Take your time." He pointed with his newspaper to the seat in which he had been seated. "I'll be right there."

You see? Skip was making it look like I had a choice to have breakfast with him. Yet the other option would be that he would stalk me.

I boarded the elevator, and as the doors closed I saw Skip sink contentedly into his chair.

Ninety minutes later, when the elevator doors opened on the lobby, I saw Skip rise contentedly from his chair, folding his cell phone as he did so.

I had purposely taken my time to see if he would perhaps be discouraged. Yet at the same time, I was not about to be held captive in my room. I did take a long shower, and while doing so, I had a chance to do some thinking about my situation and the negotiations with Dixie and Grant. On my part, there was nothing really to fear from this reporter; he had merely made a tabloid story about me and Purity that would likely be forgotten as soon as something actually newsworthy happened. I did not see why this small incident should have any effect on my dealings with Robert Tyson Grant for recovering the ring. If nothing else, were he to imagine that I was somehow insinuating myself into Purity's life, he might want to give me the ring just to get me out of the picture. On the other hand, now that I had Skip's attention, what if I were to tell him the story of the Hernando Martinez de Salvaterra ring and that Grant would not return it to the church. I thought this story of the rich man hoarding a holy relic might be newsworthy, and a story in the paper about it might compel Grant to cough up the ring bearing the double cross of Caravaca. So Skip might actually be useful to my holy mission.

Who can say? Perhaps Purity fainting and Skip chasing me down were all part of His will in action.

Skip looked at his phone as I approached in my tan suit and walking stick. "Brunch?"

"Why not?"

So we strode together from the hotel, and he veered right, so we went uptown. It was another fine June day, warm and breezy, the remaining blossoms on the trees now white petals floating through the air. "Any particular kind of restaurant?"

I shrugged. "French?" To tell you the truth, I had not eaten at a French restaurant, but thought I might as well as it was on his dime.

"Sure." He pointed ahead to where tables were on the sidewalk, their tablecloths fluttering.

Soon enough we were seated at one such table, Skip with a cup of coffee, me with a glass of champagne. Hey, I know it was early to be drinking, but the day was my own, it wasn't like I had anything to do but enjoy a nice lunch and wait for Dixie to call—and to be brutally honest, the notion of a tasty champagne brunch and a nap was quite appealing. When is it not, I ask you? For me it was made more so as I was still enjoying the afterglow of my romp with Dixie and her implants.

I feel I must take a moment to defend implants, which come under a lot of scrutiny and derision, mainly by women who do not have them. Would I rather have a woman with delightful breasts that were not implants? Absolutely. Yet for a man, this is not an either-or proposition. We do not look at a woman and think, *Oh, I must have natural breasts at any cost, so I will go home and masturbate rather than have sex with this woman with the cleavage of Venus.* The truth is that men's standards just aren't that high, and if women really want to know the truth, most men are just as happy with small breasts as large breasts. Implants do not feel like natural breasts, but who said they have to? Natural A cups and D cups don't feel the same, either. I for one would say there is room in the world for all kinds of breasts and that they can exist in harmony, each with their own qualities. To eliminate the one or the other would make no more sense than to say one would only be charmed by natural blondes. How many natural blondes are there versus the number we see? Not many, let me tell you. *Oh, now that she is naked before me, I see that her pubic hair does not match the hair on her head—I must have natural blond hair at any cost, so I must leave Jessica Simpson, who wished to engage in actual sex with me, and return home, where I will masturbate instead.* I would no more endorse a woman moping around with mousey brown hair that makes her unhappy than I would a woman moping around with breasts that make her unhappy. Dye the hair, install the implants, whatever makes you feel good about yourself that isn't over the top or a fixation. Nose job: by all means. Tattooed eye liner or eyebrows: if you must. Face lifts, collagen lips, forehead injections: please do not. If you mess too much with the face, it becomes angry and rebels.

Tolerance in this and all matters, my friends, including but not limited to implants. Amen.

"How long are you in town, Morty?"

"Perhaps another few days."

"Returning to Mexico or are you traveling?"

I remembered slipping and mentioning that I was Mexican.

"Back to Mexico, but I have been enjoying myself here."

"I'll bet. Any man that returns home in the morning to take a shower has been enjoying himself. Been clubbing?"

"Not so much, no. This bottle service at lounges is terribly expensive. One might as well just pay for it."

"Pay for what?"

"So tell me something of yourself, Skip. You are a handsome man, successful in your field. You must be what they call a man-about-town here in New York."

"I have a full life."

"Do you spend all of your workday chasing down Purity Grant stories?"

"Some days, not all."

"She must know you by now."

"Mm, you could say that."

"Does she despise you?"

"Yes and no."

"Ah, I see. Yes because sometimes she *does not* want to be in the news, and no because sometimes she *does* want to be in the news."

That smile slid up one side of Skip's face. "You're slick, Morty."

"Let's just say that I have been around. Does Purity do the things she does to rebel against her stepfather or is she really a whore and an unwieldly bitch, what we used to call in East Brooklyn a hump slap?"

"Hump slap?"

"She allows the former, but follows up with the latter."

I am not usually so ribald, but wondered if in some small way Skip was attached to Purity, whether he had seen the small ember of innocence lost that I had. If this was so, I hoped my insult to her honor would annoy him and put him off balance. He felt he held all the cards when dealing with me, and I wanted to shuffle the cards a bit to even the stakes. Not that at that time I knew there were any stakes—it was just clear to me he thought he could hustle me.

He shifted in his chair. "I think it's mostly, you know, the stepfather. Robert Tyson Grant is her stepfather, and her mother died, so Robbie holds the purse strings on Purity's trust fund and tries to more or less imprison her out on Long Island to keep her from acting out and that of course makes her want to act out. You see?"

"I see. So does she truly *hate* her stepfather? Or is this just an excuse to be a brat?"

"*Hates*, and he hates her right back for making him look foolish and impacting his business. Grant Industries stocks fluctuate whenever she pulls a stunt, and speculators have begun working the market based on her behavior, sometimes pushing his S&P rating down right when Grant Industries is trying to expand."

"Purity is not head of Grant Industries. What do investors care what she does?"

"Robert Tyson Grant is seriously rattled when she gets arrested. He was so angry the time that she burned down their Adirondack retreat that they had to take him to the hospital with an irregular heartbeat. He missed a key meeting with some Japanese investors and a big deal fell through and the stock dipped. Since then, Wall

Street is convinced he's shaky and that Purity might just be the death of him. You know, I even heard that when Purity hits the tabloids, the poor old guy can't get a boner. How sad is that? Here he has this hot girlfriend with the implants he's publicly pawing and panting over and then Purity gives him a limp one."

I leaned back, saddened by what I had heard. "Hate is a dangerous, ugly thing."

"Hate blinds people to the rewards of happiness. Robbie would have to die for her to even have a shot at growing up. So you're not going to tell me anything more about yourself, Morty?"

The waiter placed what turned out to be a fantastic *fromage grillé* before me. Skip just had more coffee.

"Only that I am here at the behest of the church. It is a sensitive matter."

Skip slid his cap forward and leaned in. "Sensitive?"

"Yes, sensitive."

"Meaning?"

"That means there are people involved who would rather not have the matter made public. I must investigate this Gruyère cheese upon my return to La Paz."

"Well, if for some reason you ever wanted it made public, you'd ring me, right?"

"Perhaps." I shrugged. "Although that is unlikely. The negotiations are almost complete."

"I'm just guessing, but from what you've said, it seems like you're on a charitable mission for a Mexican parish. You're fishing for a contribution for the local padre's good works from Grant? If so, he's probably not tickled pink about you photographed holding his daughter in your arms."

"I am not at liberty to say. Do you think they would let me bring Gruyère back with me to Baja Sur? Or is that considered a farm product?"

"Tell me about the sensitive matter and I'll sign you up for a Gruyère of the Month Club."

"A generous offer. One I must decline."

"Just remember, Morty: Sometimes negotiations have a way of going sour." He finished his coffee and tucked a card behind the handkerchief in my jacket pocket. "Call me if things go sour. Or even if you just want to have some more Gruyère. I like your style. Gotta go." He dropped forty dollars on the table and made his way down the sidewalk.

I felt I'd handled Skip well, and ordered another glass of champagne.

"Make it two."

Purity Grant stepped from the sidewalk into the outdoor café, dressed as she was at the meeting with the merchandisers: pigtails, large sunglasses, white man's oxford shirt open at the front, bikini top, thigh-high moccasin boots.

I stood.

She sat opposite me, moccasin boots crossed.

Surprised, I mistakenly spoke Spanish. Subtitles, please:

"This is an unexpected surprise, señorita."

She replied in Spanish. "It was an unexpected surprise to fall outside the courtroom yesterday. It was my good fortune that you were there to keep me from injuring myself. I am grateful to you."

I sank back into my seat, and the champagne arrived. The waiter did a double take of Purity, but made no awkward comment regarding her celebrity status. In East Brooklyn and almost anywhere else except maybe L.A., the waiters would have liquefied into euphoria and fawning. Proximity to notoriety has that effect on many people. Manhattan waiters are cut from less flimsy cloth.

I switched to English. "Your Spanish is quite good."

"Six or seven years of high school does that to a person."

"I am tempted to ask how you came to find me here. However,

I fear that would be naive of me." Dixie no doubt had her follow me from the hotel.

She raised her glass. "What shall we drink to?"

I tilted my glass at hers. "We have a quaint toast where I'm from: To old friends, new friends, and health of the chickens."

That's when a photographer stepped from the passing crowd. I only saw a hulking figure approach in my peripheral vision before flashes blinded me. I could hear the camera motor whizzing, and murmurs from people at tables nearby.

"Enough!" Purity shouted. The flashes and whizzing ceased.

I rubbed my eyes. By the time I could see again, the photographer had vanished into the pedestrian flow, and only a few passersby gawked at Purity.

"Sorry about that." Purity shrugged and waved at the waiter to provide more champagne. "I'm not using you, ITWYT. Unlike what they say in the papers, I am not a monster CU next Tuesday. I asked Skip to find you for me, so I could say thanks for keeping me from smashing my head into the marble floor. This little photo op was Skip's price for delivering you. NHNF, you'll just be on the tabloid front page again tomorrow, is all. Spiffy toast. The part about the chickens. What's your name? Marty?"

"Morty Martinez, of La Paz." I had only heard Purity speak in court, which was mainly "yes" or "no." Even though she had sought me out to deliver heartfelt thanks, her tone was flat and perched on the twig of sarcasm, ready to take flight into mockery at the first sign of danger. She seemed tense.

"Mexico or Bolivia?"

"Baja Sur, of course."

"My stepfather, Robbie, has a villa in Cabo. You should come by sometime."

"That would be an honor." My vision was returning to normal, and my facial contortions easing. Could it be that Dixie did not arrange to have Purity visit me? Even though this child was inviting me to stay with them in Cabo? Or could it have been that Purity sitting before me was an absurd coincidence, and that Skip did arrange it? I could not be sure how this came to be. "Of course, if you are ever in La Paz, I would be humbled if you were to visit my hacienda overlooking the bay. If you have not been to La Paz, you will be much pleased. It is less touristy than Cabo."

"What brings you to New York? You're not a member of the press, are you? A professional Mexican court spectator or something?"

"I am here on behalf of my local parish. It is a sensitive matter, which I am not at liberty to discuss." The waiter refilled our glasses.

"On a secret mission from the pope? Spiffy! Ironic that you should find yourself drinking champagne with the devil."

"I see no irony in our sharing a glass of champagne. Besides, you are not the devil, believe me, I have seen him. Though you no doubt have your demons, just like the rest of us."

"Thanks for letting me off the hook."

"I hope that you have recovered from what ailed you and caused the fainting spell."

"Just one of the demons—they come and go." Purity took her sunglasses off and leaned in. Ah, what beautiful eyes she had, truly as green and blue as the Sea of Cortez. "What are your demons, Morty?"

"My love of women, of course."

"Why of course?"

"I would think it would be obvious."

"Just any woman?"

I laughed and sipped my champagne. "As with choosing food, one is selective when selecting the women that make up life's meal. To dedicate yourself to ham alone is foolish. Yes?"

She put her sunglasses back on and smirked. "So you're a womanizer."

"No, that would be unfair to the women."

"Unfair to women? How DYF?"

"I only select the women that interest me." I laughed. "Do they not select me in return? I like certain women, they like certain men; if we like each other, the arrangement is completely mutual. A womanizer doesn't care who he mates with or whether they wish to mate with him."

"If you're not a womanizer, what are you?" She finished another glass of champagne.

"What am I?" The waiter arrived with the champagne bottle and poured fresh glasses. "I am Morty Martinez, La Paz gentry, on a religious quest, in New York sharing a bottle of champagne with the charming Purity Grant on a summer day."

She leaned back in her chair, arms folded. "So you're not thinking about fucking me right now?"

I think her intent was to put me off balance with this remark.

I smiled wisely. "Like any man who sees you or any delectable woman, I have mated you, the instant I saw you, and for that instant only, like a spark that floats from a fire, an ember that flares briefly and dies. However, I must be brutally honest, Purity. Any thought of mating you in reality is no longer within me."

"Really?" The smirk returned. "Be more brutally honest: Why?"

"When I caught you, when you fell and I held you in my arms, I knew this was not meant to be. I no longer see you as a woman, more as a child, and one does not violate the young. It is a terrible sin that will curse man the whole of his days. I have charmed women of your age, and they me, but their souls were . . . hm, how shall I say this?" I put a finger to my lips and looked to the heavens for inspiration.

"I'm looking forward to finding out."

"Unobstructed?"

"So I have an obstructed soul?" Purity cocked her head. "Where do you get off headshrinking me? How the hell do you know anything about me except in the papers or when you're whacking off to me in magazines with the embers glowing and all that bullshit?"

People at neighboring tables could not help but steal glances our way.

"It is how I feel." Smiling, I shrugged. "Did you not ask me to be brutally honest? If there is one thing you must know, it is that I have nothing to hide, and no reason not to tell the truth. You certainly have feelings about who I am. Did you not assume I am a womanizer? Yet when you said so, I was not offended, because I cannot be offended by how someone may feel toward me, because that is their own business. I can only be offended by how someone acts toward me."

"So what exactly does 'obstructed' mean?"

"In this context?"

"Yes, in this context."

"It is difficult to describe, but let us put it this way: If you were *unobstructed,* you would not have been offended by my honesty."

Her cheeks became rosy, but I could see the anger and resentment begin to drain back down into the depths of her heart. "Is it possible I've met the only honest person on the planet?"

"Purity, I live right at the surface of the ocean and frolic in its waves. The depths are dark and cold and full of sharks." I laughed. "But enough of this. We are drinking champagne on a charming afternoon in New York. Would you care for something to eat? I have found it unwise to drink much wine on an empty belly. Waiter?"

"Maybe a salad. I forget to eat."

"Salad? I think not." I winked at her, then raised my finger to the waiter at my elbow. "*Garçon? Two fromage grillé, por favor.*"

Purity wrinkled her freckled nose. "*Grilled cheese?*" Her lips parted, and the whites of her teeth emerged. A melodious, cynical-free sound came from her mouth—laughter. "You've *got* to be kidding. I haven't had a grilled cheese since I was . . ."

"Since you were a child?"

The laughter made Purity more graceful and relaxed. Perhaps it was the champagne. Perhaps it was resignation. Perhaps it was both. She laughed again, and it was better with practice.

"Yeah." She smiled. "Since I was a child."

TWENTY-SIX

THE CAMERA IS BLINDED BY sunlight as it pans down through a flock of pigeons and a large Amtrak sign that reads: BALTIMORE. From a Manhattan sidewalk café, we have been transported through the miracle of the editing process into bustling Penn Station, where we see Paco and his small red pack marching under the ornate skylights and exiting to the train platform, the crumpled Waffle House place mat in his hand.

In addition to the black leather jacket, he wore a Yankee baseball hat and half-tint sunglasses. Over the thrum of idling diesel trains, loudspeakers nasally trumpeted departures and arrivals, and more specifically:

"All aboard the Crescent to Wilmington, Philadelphia, Trenton, Newark, and New York City, track twelve. All aboard!"

As Paco moves down the platform, I suggest we split the screen, and not just once, but multiple times, because as he was boarding the Baltimore train for New York, his trail of destruction was beginning to be uncovered.

In one screen, we see the pawnshop clerk with the muttonchops, only he has a black eye. He is in his shop talking to a detective.

"It was a wetback. I told that to the cops who showed up that night."

"Why did you open the partition?"

"The ski poles wouldn't fit in the safety box. I ain't prejudiced."

"He came in at three in the morning to buy ski poles? In June?"

"He did. And when I opened it just a little bit, he pushed the partition open and socked me in the eye."

"You have a carry permit, don't you?"

"I didn't have the gun on me. I was in the enclosure, didn't need to have my sidearm, there's a shotgun under the counter, fully loaded. It wasn't in reach."

"The list says he stole cash. Ten thousand dollars."

"That's right, ten thousand dollars, and be sure that's on the report, 'cause I need that for the insurance."

"He didn't take anything else? No guns?"

"No, sir."

Split screen of Paco passing a policeman on the train platform.

Next split-screen scene:

A hunter in a birder's vest and a ball cap is jogging across an overgrown field. A dead rabbit swings from one hand, a shotgun from the other. The sound of a baying hound can be heard.

"Charlie?" the hunter shouts as he draws near the tobacco barns and bunker where Paco fought John. We see on the hunter's vest a patch for CANINE SEARCH AND RESCUE.

Out of breath, the hunter stops in front of the pile of construction debris. The dog is sniffing around the edge and baying.

"Charlie, you ratter. Leave them rats alone."

The hound howls plaintively, scratching at the lumber. The hunter's eyes narrow, and then widen. "Charlie, what're you onto?"

Split screen of Paco hopping up the stairs into the Amtrak train.

Next screen:

A mother with a double stroller is parked at a bench outside the Culpville bus station, luggage at her side. As she struggles to calm two crying infants, her four-year-old boy pushes through the glass doors of the station yelling, "Raspberries!"

"Michael, please! The girls are in a state! Don't yell!"

"Mommy, I want raspberries!"

"Michael, we don't have any raspberries. Come sit down and I'll give you a juice box."

"Mommy, there's raspberries syrup in there!"

The mother had managed to pacify the infants and turned to her son. "Well, we can't afford to buy any."

"Raspberries!" The boy turned and ran back into the station.

"Michael!" The mother chased him, and when she caught up to him inside the bus station he was standing before the rental lockers, pointing. The mother stopped in her tracks, eyes wide.

"Look, Mommy. Raspberries!"

From the hinge of a locker, bright red blood from John's head seeped in a streak to the floor.

Split screen of Paco. We see him through the train window as he ducks into a window seat in front of us. The train lurches forward and begins to move out of the station.

Next split-screen scene:

We hear the sounds of a hospital, machines beeping, gurneys rattling. An aging doctor in a bow tie is standing in front of a white curtain, facing a police detective with a badge hanging from his top pocket.

"Detective, the hotel manager is still in a lot of pain, and only barely conscious."

"Longer we wait, the less likely we catch the guy who did it."

"I understand," the doctor said, pulling back the curtain to reveal the bald, hairy man, the one from the motel in Richmond who chased the skinny black prostitute with the blond wig. Propped up in a hospital bed, he was encased in a cast, his neck in a high brace, and his head and jaw in the grip of surgical steel lattice.

The detective stepped forward, doctor at his elbow. The tormentor's bloodshot eyes looked sleepily up at them. Through a wired jaw he hissed, "Was a yeller-eyed Mexican that did this to me."

With that, all our screens come back to one of Paco's train leaving the station, the platform cop looking at his cell phone in the foreground.

TWENTY-SEVEN

FROM A CLOSE-UP OF A smoky crystal ball, the camera pulls back to find Helena, Abbie, and Tony seated around the séance table.

Abbie: "Remember, it's thirty-five percent me, sixty-five percent you."

Tony: "Then what's my cut?"

Helena: "We each give him five."

Abbie: "Not outta my end you don't."

Helena: "It's only fair."

Abbie: "How is that fair? I'm still doing my thirty-five percent worth."

Helena: "How do you figure?"

Abbie: "Because we said thirty-five, sixty five. That means I'm doing thirty-five percent."

Tony: "How much money we talking about?"

Abbie: "We don't know."

Tony: "How about I get a thousand up front."

Abbie and Helena: "Up front?"

Tony: "I got expenses. You seen what a box of Huggies goes for these days?"

Helena rolled her eyes, knowing full well she would cheat them both on their percentages somehow. "OK, you'll get ten percent out of my take, how's that sound?"

Tony: "What about the thousand up front?"

Helena: "What thousand up front? There never was any. You just made that up. Can I now explain how this is going to go?"

Abbie: "Please."

"So Robert Tyson Grant is the mark. He believes that a gold ring on his finger is cursed. All we gotta do is convince him to give us the ring to end the curse."

Tony smiled. "Cool. How much we getting for the ring?"

"You seen the price of gold these days?" Abbie waved a tabloid that was in her lap. On the cover was the picture of me holding Purity. "That ring is three ounces, anyway."

"We'll also get a fee on top of that. We have to make it look like the ring is destroyed. So we'll need Oscar at the magic shop to get us one of them wax ones we can make go up in flames. And Gina, we need Gina. She's an actress, she can do the ring switch."

"I called her machine." Abbie set the paper on the table.

"I heard she's in Toronto doing stunt work." Helena shook her head. "Such a pretty girl, I can't figure out why she isn't a movie star."

"They call her last minute sometimes to come to L.A. to fill in. They called her in to stunt-double Angelina Jolie."

"I thought she stunt-doubled for Catherine Zeta-Jones?"

"Her, too. But the work is spotty, she can't make a living. I know she'll help us out, she needs the money."

Tony pointed at Abbie's newspaper. "That's the guy."

Abbie: "Who is what guy?"

Tony stabbed the paper. "That's the guy I seen at the broad's place. He's the guy with the champagne bucket."

Helena leaned in. "You sure?"

"Sure I'm sure."

Abbie put the paper on the table, and leaned in to look at my photo. "You think maybe this is the Mexican that Grant is so worried about?"

"Let's review." Helena leaned back, folding her arms. "A Mexican comes to town and makes time with Robert Tyson Grant's girlfriend and his daughter. Does that sound like trouble?"

The other two nodded.

Helena cocked her head, squinting. "We need to know more about this fella. I mean, why does he come all the way from Bolivia—"

"Mexico," Abbie added.

"—*Mexico* to bother Grant for a ring and then move in on his girl and his daughter?"

"Cartels, maybe?" Abbie shrugged.

Helena shrugged back. "What do drug cartels want with a ring?"

"If the Mexican is a criminal, which he must be if he's extorting Grant somehow, then it follows he's with one of the cartels, am I right?" Abbie looked pleased with her logic. "Are there any criminals in Mexico that aren't attached to a cartel?"

"Perhaps, but how is he extorting Grant? He wants the ring, but in exchange for what?"

Tony all this time was deep in thought, or looking for one. "Maybe . . . he didn't just come but they sent for him."

Abbie and Helena: "What?"

"You know, they asked him to come here, to bring some drugs or something, and then he said for that he wants the ring instead of cash."

Abbie and Helena: "Why?"

Tony's brain was struggling. "Maybe . . . maybe they don't know why, either. It doesn't make sense, I know, but maybe that's the point. They're confused. We're confused. Maybe the situation is confused. Somehow."

Abbie and Helena: *"You're* confused."

"I'm just saying."

Helena took a deep breath. "It doesn't matter. What matters is that we strike while the metal's hot, while I have my hooks in them. It is enough that we know the Mexican is a curse on them, and that we sell them a talisman to make it go away, and palm the ring when we go to destroy it in front of them, using Gina, if she calls. The important part of the con is proving that the talisman works. That's where Tony comes in. He needs to be a hit man. You try to kill—"

"Hold it." Tony sat forward. "I'm a hit man now? That's dangerous."

"I'm going to give Grant the talisman, as temporary protection, telling him if it doesn't work, he doesn't owe me anything, but that if it does work, he needs to pay me, and to dispel the curse we need to destroy the ring."

"I could get in trouble," Tony whined. "What if the cops somehow get involved?"

Helena rolled her eyes. "You think you're getting ten percent for nothing? I don't think Abbie could pretend to be a hit man, do you? And Gina, she doesn't look like a hit man, does she?"

Tony continued to whine. "Why does there have to be a hit man at all?"

"He has to believe the talisman is working. What better way for him to think the talisman is working than for him to think it kept him from getting killed? 'Course, you have to look Mexican. We want him to think that guy in the white suit has put a hit out on him. Then we get the Mexican out of the picture. He wants the ring, we have to get it before he does."

"How am I supposed to 'look' Mexican?"

"Go to Oscar's Magic Shop, he'll fix you up. Pick up a gold wax ring while you're at it."

Abbie had a hand to her chin. "Tony gonna have a gun?"

"No guns!" Tony blurted. "No knives."

"Of course not," Helena said with a wave of her hand. "Just gloves so he'll look like a strangler. There's no crime against wearing gloves. He pulls a stocking over his face and has black gloves on. That looks like a strangler."

Tony folded his arms. "How am I supposed to look Mexican under a stocking?"

"Speak Spanish." Abbie patted his arm.

"But I don't speak Spanish!"

His aunts replied in unison: "Sure you do. *You're a New Yorker.*"

"Say *Por favor, señor* when you go to kill him. Look, this couldn't be easier. I catch him when he leaves work, tell him he's in great danger, give him the talisman. Then we follow him around until we see an opening. Tony makes his move, Gina runs interference, sells Grant on the idea that the talisman worked. He should come running to me soon after. If not, we'll play it by ear from there."

"I gotta be a Mexican strangler?" Tony sank back into the depths of thought, pouting. "I dunno. Sounds like a problem in your gut after you eat too much nachos."

"When do we do this, Lena?" Abbie asked.

"When else? Tonight." Helena stood, jerking a thumb toward the beaded curtain that led to the pantry. "Anybody want a sammie? I got fresh olive loaf."

TWENTY-EIGHT

AN HOUR LATER I HAD sent Purity on her way and was entering my hotel lobby.

"Mr. Martinez?" A slightly plump but bountifully attractive midthirties brunette at the desk hailed me. "I took some messages for you."

"For me? Are you sure? And more than one?"

"Three. She says you should call her immediately upon your return, that it is urgent."

I stepped up to the desk, and she handed me the messages. Her spicy perfume washed over me when she ran a hand through her hair.

All three messages said the same thing: *Call me—D*, followed by a phone number I did not recognize. The calls were logged about half an hour apart.

"Your wife?" The brunette eyed me.

"Business associate." A gentle smile played upon my lips, and I held up my ring finger. "Like yourself, I am not a spouse."

She unconsciously thumbed her empty ring finger. "We hope you're enjoying your stay in New York."

"I will be brutally honest . . ." I read her name tag. "I will be brutally honest, Consuela. When you travel for business, you often find yourself dining alone, which is not as much fun as dining with someone and having lively and charming discussions."

"I am surprised, Mr. Martinez. I would think you would have no problem finding dinner partners." Consuela ran a hand through her hair again.

Ah, I must have been doing the Lord's work for Him to smile on me this way.

"Is it against hotel policy for the staff to take pity on guests and dine with them?"

She seemed slightly uncomfortable with my forwardness, even though she had clearly invited it. "Are you asking me to dinner, Mr. Martinez?"

"But of course—you are quite charming and obviously companionable. Why would I choose to eat alone rather than with you? And please, call me Morty."

"Well, I really can't, I'm working tonight and . . ."

I waved the messages. "I fear I cannot dine with you tonight, either. Business calls. Perhaps tomorrow?"

The phone rang, and she smiled coyly at me. "Try me tomorrow." She tossed her hair as she turned to answer the phone. I went on my way to my room. A fascinating woman.

In my room, I flopped on the bed and put the phone on my chest. As you might imagine, I was a little tired from the champagne, and a nap seemed the next logical course of action. Truly, a champagne nap is one of life's great luxuries, second only to a foot massage before a champagne nap.

Yet my duty to God trumped the nap. I assumed the messages were from Dixie because Consuela suggested she took them and the caller was female.

"Morty?"

"Good afternoon, *querida*!"

"Where have you been?"

"I was at lunch, of course. A most delightful day in New York. It would have been nice to have had lunch at the bistro with you."

"We have to move." Her tone was flat and urgent. "We can set things right this afternoon, but you have to drive to Long Island. Are you ready?"

This seemed to me a happy turn of events. I would acquire the ring and have my mission accomplished. God was clearly pleased with my progress, and more sensual rewards were likely at hand.

"I am *always* ready."

"There is an old green Toyota parked at a meter in front of your hotel, probably just about run out of time, so you'd better hurry before it gets towed. The keys are in a hide-a-key under the back right bumper. Directions are in the glove compartment."

"Yes, but if I may, why must we do this on Long Island? Why not right here in Manhattan?"

"It can be done in an isolated place, as shown on the map. No witnesses. Except the driver. Don't hurt him."

I knit my brow. "Hurt him? I am assuming he can remove the ring himself."

"The ring?"

"Yes, I assume Grant will remove the ring himself rather than me removing it and possibly hurting him."

"Yes, of course, you'll get the ring."

I sighed. "*Querida,* this all seems quite complicated. If you just brought the ring to me at my hotel, we could then perhaps have a little dinner and—"

"Morty, let's get this done, but it has to be the way we want it done."

"As you wish."

"Leave now. Bring your luggage and check out of the hotel; you may want to stay out there tonight. The limo should be there

at about three, but you need to be in place to intercept it. I don't
have to explain what to do next, do I? How it should look?"

"God's work is no easy thing, is it?"

"If it were easy, it would pay less. When you are done, drive the
car to the wrecking yard on the directions, and take the nearby
subway back to Manhattan. There is a MetroCard in with your
directions. You leaving now?"

"Yes, yes."

"Call this number when it is done to let me know how it went?"

"Yes, yes."

She hung up.

I sat on the edge of the bed, puzzling. I knew that the wealthy
had complex lives. They had private jets, employees, and banks
overseas. I had not known that they embraced complexity as a
commodity unto itself. Yet I could see a twisted logic to the complexity as well as the secrecy. What to me was a simple matter of
pulling a ring off a finger and handing it to me might to them have
the potential for unwanted publicity and scandal. Robert Tyson
Grant was in possession of a stolen holy relic. It made sense they
did not want the press to know this.

I splashed water on my face, packed, left the room, and made
myself a cup of coffee in the lobby.

I went to the desk.

"Regrettably, Consuela, I have been called away and must check
out."

Her lips formed a mock pout. "Perhaps next time?"

"I shall return to this hotel next time I am in town, and we
will tango until dawn."

She giggled at my lie and took my room card.

The green Toyota was quite old and faded, but it started, cata-
lytic converter rattling. I drove the ugly green car away from the
curb and headed for the Midtown Tunnel.

The camera swings from my retreating car to Tony in his town car. He is wearing a white suit, his hair black and slicked back.

A thin mustache was glued to his upper lip, and a small goatee glued to his lower lip. He swung his limo out from next to a hydrant and followed my car, a cell phone to his ear.

"That's what I'm telling you. I followed her here from a charity junk lot. She left the car. Now the guy in the white suit came out of a hotel on Second Avenue and is driving the car uptown. Yes, I'm following. Yes, I have the stocking and the gloves. Yes, I went to see Oscar. I look like an idiot."

I suggest a split screen so that we see Helena sitting on a low wall surrounding the fountain outside the Grant Industries building on Sixth Avenue, a cell phone at her ear.

"Tony, you look like a Mexican, that's all you have to be concerned with."

"What about coming to pick up Abbie so we can do the con with Grant?"

"Change of plans. Follow him. This Mexican is up to something with Grant's woman, and we need to know what it is. It may mean more money, a lot more money. If the Mexican stops soon, call me, but he must be going far if he's using a car. You and Gina can do your thing tomorrow morning when Grant comes to work."

"You heard from Gina yet?"

"She got back from L.A. today. We're waiting to hear from her."

"So what about you?"

"I'll give Grant the talisman as soon as I catch him leaving the building today, which, God willing, won't be five o'clock, because I gotta be here all afternoon because you never know when rich people will knock off."

"Looks like the Mexican is going to the Midtown Tunnel. Want me to follow him to Queens?"

"What did I say? Yes, follow him wherever he goes, and call me with updates."

"If I see Grant, maybe I should jump him like we planned."

"No! You need Gina to be there to shill, remember?"

"What about the Mexican?"

"What about him?"

"He could shill."

"Why would he do that?"

"He would see what I do and tell Grant—"

"Tony, you don't grift without a shill who will really sell it. Gina will sell it."

"I'm just saying. If I can get this done sooner, the better. I'm not comfortable waiting."

"Wait for Gina. You'll do it tomorrow. Call me when something happens."

"Uhn huhn."

They both snapped their phones shut and shook their heads with dismay.

TWENTY-NINE

I DON'T THINK ANYBODY REALLY likes Long Island
except Long Islanders. If the Northeast were Europe, Long Island
would be France. Of course, I have not been to France, but you
see what I'm saying. The hundred-mile peninsula is heavily pop-
ulated by people who wished you had not come, probably because
the roads are too narrow for their suburban sprawl, much less visi-
tors like you clogging up the mall parking lot. The western isth-
mus of the peninsula is attached to New York City, and thus all
traffic between the mainland and Long Island must pass through
even more congested roads. This is not to say Long Island itself
does not have major roads and highways. It does. For whatever reason, though, there just never seem to be enough roads to accommodate the beach traffic and the commuters. The sense is that there
never could be enough roads. A bridge to Connecticut across Long
Island Sound has been proposed now and again to relieve conges-
tion and allow traffic *out* of the peninsula. Long Islanders are mostly
against this proposal because from their perspective a bridge to
the mainland would allow more traffic *into* the peninsula.

I left the East Side of Manhattan by way of the Midtown Tunnel,
which took me to the other side of the East River and dumped me
unceremoniously on the Long Island Expressway. This highway

is notorious for epic traffic jams, but I was ahead of rush hour
and jostled fender to fender with other motorists hurtling out to
ever smaller winding roads.

Which is precisely where I found myself—on a snakelike road,
hedgerows on one side, a large stone wall on the other, with large
leafy trees forming a canopy overhead. Behind the hedgerow was
a golf course, behind the stone wall a forested estate of some kind.
Sunlight filtered through the canopy. Farther down the road, the
tang and whoosh of the ocean beckoned, around the bend, unseen.

The instructions from the glove box told me to park in a small
turnout by the wall. At about three o'clock a limo with the license
plate RTGRANT1 would come down the road toward the beach,
and then I "would know what to do."

I had not forgotten the reasoning for this rendezvous, but just
the same, I felt like an idiot. I had allowed myself to be pushed
around and made to drive out to Long Island when Robert Tyson
Grant could very well have just come down out of his glass tower
and handed me the ring. I was in France for no reason. I should
have held my ground. My consolation was that I would soon pos-
sess the ring, and I could then pursue more pleasant diversions
until flying home to La Paz. Would Father Gomez leap with joy
at the sight of the ring? Would he kiss my hand, a tear in his eye,
and simply say "Bless you"? If his reaction to having someone drop
off a hundred grand in cash was any indication, he would probably
drop the restored relic in a top desk drawer and point to the door.
I was not performing this holy mission for him, but for Him, and
my heart was full with that knowledge alone.

I heard a car winding down the road. A white town car appeared,
and I could see stickers indicating that this was a car service. It
slowed as it passed, and the driver shot me a reluctant glance. He
had a unibrow that sat low on his forehead like a sleeping weasel.

A thin mustache, slicked hair, and a white suit jacket made him look like a down-on-his-luck coffee plantationer. I watched the town car's brake lights vanish slowly around the corner.

Another half hour of disappointment followed. I would hear a car coming, I'd look and hope, only to be once again disappointed that a Mercedes or Porsche or Bentley was not Grant's limo. There were a few nice-looking women, though, who gave me the once-over. They looked like those flashy housewives you hear about who cheat on their rich husbands with the exterminator. A landscaper with a reptilian tan actually stopped to ask if I needed help.

Leaning against my green bomber, I began playing a game where I tried using my peripheral vision to see what kind of car came next, to see what I could actually make out in my side vision. If you concentrate, you can make out the color and size pretty well.

When the limo did come, I did a double take so strong I practically got whiplash. By God, the RTGRANT1 limo was finally rolling down the slope toward me. I pushed off of the green Toyota shit wagon, squared my stance at the side of the road, and waved an arm overhead. I watched my reflection waving in the darkened windows of the limo as it slid past. The limo brake lights slid around the corner just like all the Mercedes and Porsches and Bentleys did.

Hands on my hips, I believe I uttered an unconscionable curse about sex with a family member. I was seriously pissed. There I was all the way in France and that bastard Grant drives right by me, probably giving me the finger as he did so, the gold Hernando Martinez de Salvaterra ring glinting in the air-conditioned sunflecked recesses of his limousine.

A whirring from down the road was followed by the limo as it backed slowly uphill and around the bend toward where I was standing. My ill humor melted away.

OK, enough fun and games, let's get this over with.

As I watched the limo back slowly toward me, my eye latched onto some motion in the hedgerow on the opposite side of the road. I wasn't sure what I was seeing at first. Just as with my peripheral vision, I had to concentrate to make sense of the shapes I was seeing. Like the pieces to a jigsaw puzzle, the image of what moved beyond the hedgerow was broken into pieces by the leaves and branches of the bushes. My eye put one piece with another, trying to find a pattern.

The limo whirred toward me, exhaust puffing.

An eye. I saw an eye—and like with a jigsaw, once you have an important piece like an eye, you can quickly attach to it. It was the man with the weasel eyebrows, in a white suit, from the white town car that drove by, and he was crouching behind the hedgerow. My first thought was that he was some kind of pervert, one of those people who gets their jollies by spying on strangers and little girls' birthday parties. That idea was discarded and replaced with the notion that this weasel man was there for a reason. That perhaps he had been sent by Dixie or Grant. That this was a setup of some kind. It would better explain why they wanted me in a remote location. Instead of giving up the ring, they meant to kill me and keep the ring. Why else would Weasel Man wear such a ridiculous costume if not to disguise his identity? My gut wound into a knot, and my first impulse was to jump in the green heap and drive as fast away from that spot as possible. Or leap to the far side of my car and use it to protect me from a fusillade of bullets. No wonder they wanted me on the wall side; there was no escape.

I spun toward the rear of the Toyota just as the limo stopped between me and Weasel Man. The limo's far rear door opened.

Weasel Man struggled through the thick hedgerow, a stocking stretched over his head and black gloves on his hands. He was clearly clambering for the open limo door.

He was not after me but Robert Tyson Grant in the limo.

I paused, unsure of what I should do, or whether Grant would see Weasel Man's attack.

The open door and dark glass obscured the passenger's view.

Purity emerged, looking my way over the rear deck of the limo.

"Morty? WTF are you doing here?"

I just pointed at Weasel Man, unable to answer fast enough.

Weasel Man launched himself at the open door.

Screenwriting: Yes You Can! page 221 recommends the use of the cut-away to build dramatic tension, so we will cut from Tony leaping at the limo to Robert Tyson Grant biting a fingernail as he strides from his glass tower on Sixth Avenue.

His spunky assistant Kathy was trotting in his wake, her arms cradling a dozen contracts.

"Mr. Grant, we really need to sign these agreements today. You can do it on your limo ride to wherever it is that you're going."

"I'm just stepping out for lunch, Kathy, I'll be right back."

"Remember, you have a four o'clock with the Vietnamese."

"Mm hmm."

They passed the plaza fountain, and Helena darted from her seat and grabbed Grant's arm.

Grant wheeled, a fist in the air, ready to defend himself.

"Robert, I have come to warn you!" Her eyes were as wild as those of any garden variety glue huffer. "Grave danger!"

"Mr. Grant, shall I get security?" Kathy began backing away with the precious contracts.

"Helena?" Grant stared at the fortune-teller with dismay. "What? How did you find me here?"

"This is your building, is it not?" A coy twinkle sparked her eye.

"Yes, well . . ."

"Should I not know this is your building?"

"No, nothing like that, it's just—"

"Take this!" Helena shoved what appeared to be a miniature, mummified hand into his face. It would fit in the palm of your hand, and was brown and shiny with carefully cut black nails.

"Yah!" Grant recoiled. "What is that?"

Kathy yelped, scuttling back toward the building entrance. "Security!"

"It is the hand of a race of Australian pygmies, now extinct, but they had powers." Actually, it was a dried raccoon paw that was supposed to look like a monkey paw, the kind from the ghost stories. You think I'm kidding? Check it out on eBay. They look like small human hands.

Grant looked apologetically at some nearby Asians with a tourist map. They eyed him and Helena curiously.

"Helena, why are you giving me the—"

"Grave danger! Do you hear? This is a talisman, and it is called a calludaroo. It is my last one—but you need it." She held it out, and it dangled from a leather thong. "Within twenty-four hours there will be an attempt on your life. This will protect you from harm! Wear it around your neck."

The Asians aimed their cell phone cameras at the palmist, the tycoon, and the talisman.

"Kill me?" Grant lowered his voice. "Who? Who would kill *me*?"

Helena snatched his forearm and gripped it with both hands. "I cannot see . . . but he wears a white suit."

Ashen, Grant stammered, "The Mexican?"

Helena sank to her knees on the sidewalk. "I cannot see any more. I have had my vision. But please"—she grabbed his pant leg, sobbing—"I beg of you, wear the talisman for one day, just one day, and see if what I say is not true!"

"I'll wear it. I'll wear the claderoon."

"Calludaroo."

"Sorry, calludaroo."

"It is my last one and is very precious, worth your life."

"Well, I'll take good care of it."

Helena looked up coyly. "And what is your life worth?"

"Now I'd have to look into that—"

"I guarantee it will work and that your life will be saved by this talisman. Just promise me recompense."

"I'll consult with—"

"A hundred thousand for your life?"

"There are many factors involved in any negotiation—"

She stood suddenly, wiping a tear from her eyes. "I have a vision, and I rush here to help you, to save your life, and give to you my last calludaroo, perhaps the last calludaroo in the world. Why do I do this? To help, that is all. That is my passion . . . and my life's burden. Whether that means anything to you or not, whether that has any value to you who owns billions and a giant building, let that be up to your conscience. I know in here"—she tapped her chest—"that you are a worthy and honorable man."

Two uniformed security guards who looked like they'd just woken from a nap marched toward Grant, Kathy in their wake making two strides for each of theirs. One of them called out as they approached.

"Mr. Grant, can we assist you, sir?"

"No, that's all right. I know this woman."

Arrival of the fuzz clearly coaxed Helena to wrap up her pitch.

"Wear the calludaroo for one full day! You know where to find me . . . I must rest. Taxi!"

A yellow cab screeched to a halt, she dove in, and it zoomed off. Slack-jawed, the Asians stood next to Grant, as did the two security guards and Kathy, all watching Helena's cab disappear up Sixth Avenue.

Cut back to East Hampton.

Tony the Weasel Man sprang from the bushes at Purity. *"Por favor, señor!"*

Her back was to him.

A branch caught his pant cuff. His leg jerked tight, and so did the rest of him before he fell flat onto the road.

Purity heard Tony fall, but could not see around the door.

For Robert Tyson Grant, I would not leap to action. For a cute blonde? This is Morty Martinez you're talking to.

I vaulted across the road and reached Tony just as he was getting to his feet. He saw Purity peering wide-eyed around the car door at him. His eyebrow rippled with confusion because she was not Robert Tyson Grant as he'd hoped she would be. Then he saw me dashing around the back end of the limo.

He was bigger than I was, mostly in the midsection. Just the same, my plan would have been to kick him in the nuts. What did you expect: Fisticuffs? Judo? Where I come from in East Brooklyn you fought to win, period.

Tony had no reason to fight me; he just wanted to scare Robert Tyson Grant, not this little blond girl. Besides, he had just inhaled his mustache up into his sinuses, which by the looks of it seemed quite painful. A kick in the nuts truly would have been an assault to injury.

Tony pivoted and dove headlong back through the hedge, rolled once, and began running across the golf course.

I kicked the hedge and yelled after him, "You will pay dearly for this!" I had no reason to chase the scoundrel, much less ruin my suit by diving through the hedge. I turned to the limo.

Purity was still behind the back door to the limo, eyes wide.

An Asian chauffeur stood next to the open driver's door. "What happened?"

"A strange man attempted to ambush your vehicle." I straightened my jacket. "I have chased him off."

The chauffeur looked me over. "Who are you?"

"He's a friend of mine, Earl," Purity said. "He's OK."

"Wait a minute." Earl pointed at me. "You're the guy from the papers. The one who caught Purity when she fell in court?"

"One and the same." I bowed. "My name is Morty Martinez."

A Mercedes rolled down the road behind the limo and honked. Purity cocked her head at my green car. "That your ride?"

"It is not, but I drove it here."

"Follow us to the house. I owe you a cocktail, but NFN I want to know what you were doing here, and who that dude was that ran off across the country club."

The Mercedes honked again.

"As a matter of policy, I never refuse a drink from a beautiful lady."

Dixie was still in the yellow polka dots, a black coffee before her. Robert was in a three-piece worsted suit, a tea before him. They sat in the booth where I first met him, at the end.

"It itches." Robert twisted his neck. "The damn calludaroo itches. It is caught in my chest hair. Can't I put it in my pocket?"

"No. She said you must wear it around your neck. So you wear it around your neck, silly goose."

"You think this is for real? I mean, come on, a pygmy hand? A talisman? This is the twentieth century."

"*Twenty-first* century. Sweet cakes, the fortune-teller was right about the Mexican, about the anger, about all those things. How can she not be right about this?"

"She said a lot of stuff. She even said I should be afraid of you."

"The important thing is that she was right about most of what she said, and knew things she could not possibly have known. How did she find you, and know who you are?"

"Maybe she recognized me from the papers or magazines."

"So her grand scheme is to shake you down by making you wear a pygmy hand around your neck?"

"You saw it." Grant scratched at his chest. "Have you ever seen a pygmy that small?"

"Darling, I have never met a pygmy, but maybe this was a dwarf pygmy, or a child."

"Do pygmies have dwarfism? And if so, what kind of God allows such irony? We should have a charity for dwarf pygmies. The African charities are hot now."

Dixie shot him a stern look and wagged a finger. "Don't you dare blaspheme, Robert, not now of all times. We need Him on our side."

"Hmph." Grant sipped some tea, his foot tapping audibly under the table. "I'd rather we met at my place. I could take this thing off there, and we could be screwing instead of sitting in this lousy dive."

"We need the alibi, punkin'. We need to be in public doing something perfectly ordinary when it happens. Besides, I hear the grilled cheese is good here."

"I hope the Mexican didn't make a mess, that there's not a lot of blood. I hope Earl the chauffeur is OK."

"Well, darling, what with Purity *isn't* messy?" Dixie sipped her coffee, looking at the ceiling, her thoughts drifting briefly to the previous evening. "That said, our Mexican doesn't seem the messy type."

"You're sure he went?"

"The green car is gone from where I parked it. The hotel clerk said he checked out."

"That car can't be traced?"

"Officially, that car has been demolished, so the VIN number won't register with any database. I got it from the Grant Foundation donation lot. Nobody else was there."

"What about being seen with the Mexican?"

"I only met him in parks, in public places, and I've only been talking to him on this disposable cell phone. You only met him once here, the first time. Let me see the fake ring again?"

Grant checked his surroundings before pulling the ring from his vest pocket. Dixie took the ring and his hand and compared the rings. "It's damn good. Those Jewish people are amazing."

In a close-up, we see the original ring and the copy. The genuine item is a darker gold color.

"They're good business people." Grant puffed his chest and winked. "So when this is over, what do you say we go to Cabo and take the motor yacht out for a few weeks? We'd be grieving."

"Boo-bear, the press needs to *see* us grieve."

"Oh, they will. I was thinking that we should set up a separate charity: Purity Cares. A fund to rehabilitate injured dogs and cats."

"Brilliant! *Yes*, fixing broken puppies! I can see the promo now— I'll call that ad man Scott Conti and start him pulling the stock footage right away. We'll want that by the funeral. I'll put my assistant on this, figure out whose relatives to hire. Have you seen that video on the Web, the one where the dog has no front legs and has to walk on his hind legs, like a human?"

"I can't say as how—"

"We'll find his agent. He'd be the perfect spokesdog. Or maybe we can find a cat on wheels? What a tearjerker, simply perfect, Robbie! There's a reason you're a captain of industry."

"Sometimes the substance of a matter is all in appearances."
He grasped her hand. "I like it when you call me Robbie. You think
it's done, that I'm free of my curse, that we can move on?"

Dixie's cell phone rang (the tune it played was "Dixie"), and
she scrambled through her purse to find it. "Hello?"

It was me on the line, so let's make a split screen. Put me near to
the camera, aglow in the afternoon sun and standing on the upper
deck of Grant's beach mansion. In my hand is a glass of red wine
that I am clearly enjoying. At some distance and out of earshot
is Purity in a bikini on a lounger behind me, soaking up the
sun. She, too, is on the phone. Behind all that is the beach and
ocean.

"Dixie?"

"No names! How'd it go?"

"Fine."

Dixie gave Grant the thumbs-up across the table and winked.
Robert bit his lip and thumbed her back.

"Where is she now?"

"Right over there, on the lounger."

"On the lounger? Where are you?"

"At the East Hampton mansion."

Dixie switched ears. "I don't understand. You intercepted her
on the road?"

"Of course."

"Then why are you at the mansion?"

"I was invited. Just the same, the little green car's water pump
appears to have expired, and now I must stay here until tomorrow."

"Explain what happened when you intercepted the limo. I'm
a little confused."

"*Querida,* I think we are both a little confused. To be honest, I
am sometimes mystified by how the rich operate. I thought I was
to have the ring today. Instead I have Purity. I know you said she

would be delivered to me, but that confuses me as well. While she is quite pretty, she is a child—what am I to do with a child? I have my God to think of, I must restore the defiled relic of my ancestor and the integrity of Nuestra Señora de Cortez's inner sanctum."

"We have the ring and will give it to you when the job is complete, that's the deal."

Robert leaned across the table. "Did he do it or not?"

"I'm not sure," she whispered, brow knit.

"Job? Perhaps it is me. At heart, I am a simple Brooklyn boy upon whom fortune has seen fit to shine the warming rays of a life as La Paz gentry."

Dixie and Grant unconsciously slid their coffee cups to the edge of the table to a Mexican who sidled up to their table, presumably the busboy.

"Yes, *the job, the wrong to be set right. What we talked about?*" Dixie shot an annoyed glance at the busboy.

"We spoke of the ring," I said, sipping my wine.

"You'll get the ring when the job is done."

"The ring *is* the job. That is why Father Gomez sent me. Perhaps I have been in La Paz too long, but this seems perfectly simple."

Dixie held a hand over the phone and focused a scowl on the busboy. "Are you done?"

Robert looked exasperated and said to the bus boy, "What is it you want?"

The busboy said, "I come to this place."

"*And?*" Dixie spat.

"I come a long distance."

"Dix, I think he's retarded, they sometimes hire them at places like this. Look, Pedro, we need privacy, please go back to the kitchen."

"My name is Paco, and I have come from Mexico, to this very table in this restaurant. You have job for me. Are you not the ones who contacted me to kill?"

Dixie and Grant couldn't have looked more flash frozen if they'd been shrimps, shrimps with their mouths hanging open and their pupils extremely small. I suppose shrimps don't have mouths that hang open, or eyes with pupils, but you see what I'm saying, yes? They were stunned.

Seemingly without moving, Dixie snapped her cell phone shut.

A waitress appeared. "Is this man bothering you, sir? Sir? Ma'am?"

Grant finally mumbled, "Not at this time, no."

The Red Flame Diner side of our screen goes away, and now you see only me with my wine at the beach mansion looking at my phone.

"Hello? Hello?" I snapped my phone shut as well. "Bah, these cell phones and their *signals*. It is just as well. I think they need to realize it is time to stop playing games."

Purity lifted her head. "What was that?"

"Nothing. Just a bad connection."

Let's cut to comely Purity on the phone with Skip Baker, split screen, and the reporter is reclined at his cramped desk in a hectic newsroom. Purity is near the camera, and now I am standing out of earshot at the far railing of the deck looking out to sea.

"Skip, tell me you sent Morty out here, that you had that creep in the stocking attack the limo. Otherwise, it is just too freaky, something bizarre is going on."

"Babe, I can only say it so many times. This is not my doing. I didn't rig this. You're right, something is going on, and I can't wait to find out what it is because there is front page written all over it. Just the fact that the guardian angel saved you yet again is pure gold. Did you call the cops?"

"The cops? LMFAO, you must be kidding. And stand around waiting for them to fill in their little reports?"

"Did Morty say why he was standing on Hill Road when you just happened to drive by?"

"He says God sent him, and that he was there on a holy mission that he can't discuss."

Skip snorted. "That's the same thing he told me—more or less—at 100 Centre Street. You don't suppose he actually is your guardian angel, do you?"

"True, the white suit is what angels are wearing this year. Check this out: It seems he only eats grilled cheese sandwiches and is some sort of La Paz lothario. What kind of angel is that?"

"Previous life?"

"Morty speaks his mind, I'll give him that. He's as honest a person as I think I've ever met. At least he didn't lie about why he was on Hill Road; he just won't or can't tell me why. IMHO, he must have been there waiting for me, waiting for the limo to come along. He was waving his arms as we drove past, and it took me a second to realize who he was."

"How would he have known you would be driving that way?"

"Good question."

"Morty must have arranged for the attack."

"Or someone else knew he was going to be there."

"Like who?"

"If the creep tried to kill me with a machine gun I'd say it was Robbie who set it up, or that CU-next-Tuesday Dixie, but OMG the creep looked like he was in a Halloween costume, and he didn't even seem to have a weapon, just black gloves. I dunno, he was like a pro wrestler."

"That is just too good." Skip barked a laugh. "*If only* your dad would put a hit out on you. We'd run out of ink selling papers, and the Web site would jam."

Purity scowled. "Gee, thanks, Skip, and FYI Robbie is *not* my father."

"Sorry, babe, but can you imagine?"

"If anybody should be putting a hit out on anybody . . ." Purity lowered her sunglasses, her gaze fixing on me.

"Yeah? Hello?"

"It should be me on Robert."

Skip slapped his knee. "Now you're thinking! Perfect. You could put a hit out on each other. Let's get this rolling. Wait first, I'm sending a photographer out to Hill Road. Can you two go out and reenact the whole attack thing for him? I can also provide an actor to play the creep wrestler guy if you want."

Purity wasn't listening to him; she was transfixed by me.

"Spiffy." Her thumb disconnected Skip.

THIRTY

CUT TO THE GRANT INDUSTRIES tower on Sixth Avenue, and Robert's pixie-like assistant on the phone at her desk. Before her is a yellow legal pad on which she taps a pencil. Cue the subtitles—Kathy is speaking Spanish into the phone.

"Good morning, is this Nuestra Señora de Cortez? . . . I would like to speak with Father Gomez . . . I'm calling from Grant Industries in New York . . . It is a private matter about Morty Martinez . . . Yes, I'll hold . . ."

THIRTY-ONE

WE START WITH A CLOSE-UP of Helena's crooked, angry finger in Tony's face.

"Fool!"

When we pull back, we see Helena, Tony, and Abbie arrayed around a park bench in a secluded corner of Washington Square Park, the giant iconic archway in the background lit by the setting sun.

Tony had his arms folded across his chest. "I thought it was the right move."

"Idiot!" Helena stamped her foot. "I told you to wait! Why did you not wait?"

"I thought it was the right move. I thought it was Grant in the limo. It was his limo, so . . ."

"Yes, but I told you to wait for Gina, so she could shill!"

"To tell you the truth, I wanted to get it over with. I don't like dressing up and attacking people. I could get arrested. I got a wife and a kid."

Abbie slumped on the bench. "I think we need a new plan."

Helena growled at the heavens. "We cannot. *This* plan is in motion. Grant must be convinced the talisman works and saves his life. We cannot switch plans in the middle."

"So then Tony just goes and tries to kill Grant now, in front of his building, and I shill. We follow the plan like this didn't happen."

"Bah!" Helena spat. "Grant will now be expecting it. He will know that there was an attack on his daughter."

"Here comes Gina." Abbie jerked a thumb over her shoulder.

Tony sat straighter.

Helena stopped pacing and turned to observe her niece's approach.

OK, I think for this shot we need the gauzy, milky, slow-motion view of Gina's approach, because surely this woman was a goddess. A goddess? You think I am kidding, but I am not. Of course she had long, lustrous brown hair, ice blue eyes, elegant ears, sumptuous lips, noble cheekbones, perfect teeth, killer tits, narrow waist, swaying hips, curvaceous legs, and dainty feet. However, her qualities were even in the minute details. Even her slim arched eyebrows were natural and required no plucking. She was hairless everywhere but where there was supposed to be hair. Her olive skin had a natural glow that required no maintenance, with a gentle muscle tone that was born to her and not manufactured in a gym. She could eat anything she wanted and not gain an ounce. Deodorant was a stranger to her, and her breath was always sweet and fragrant as a pear. Gina was female perfection, right out of the box. If she did not have to cut and shape her nails, her mortality would surely be in question.

As Gina approached, glowing archway behind her, men stopped in their tracks and stared at the goddess in blue jeans and tank top, their expressions pained with the knowledge that this sort of perfection could never be theirs, or possibly that anybody could possibly be worthy of this woman's charms.

The women in Gina's wake stopped and stared also, their expressions pained with the knowledge that the sort of standard set by women like Gina placed the bar unfairly high for them, and that only a pint of ice cream could erase the memory of this living totem of feminine quintessence.

One would think that Gina's life was as perfect as her packaging, yes? Not so. Her entire teen and adult life, men had stammered and fumbled around her, tongue-tied and fawning. Those brave enough to make a play for her sometimes succumbed to their passions and needed to be physically repelled. Which was why Gina was a student of Shui Ping, a martial art. Women immediately despised her for obvious reasons. As a result, she often had a hard time being understood when she spoke. She had wanted to capitalize on her looks and become a model. She was considered too "fat" to be a model because she had discernible hips and breasts. She wanted to become an actress, but despite continued auditions and a few screen credits in martial arts films, she was generally deemed "over-kinetic" for speaking roles on camera and a "distraction" onstage. In almost any workplace you can imagine her very presence was disruptive. Alas, she was relegated to stunt double work in martial arts films.

It is ironic that women this beautiful are truly cursed, not blessed, yes?

"Hi, Aunt Abbie, Aunt Helena." Gina's jewel-like eyes shot a look at her cousin, whose mouth was hanging open. "How you doing, Tony?"

He didn't say anything.

"So good to see you, child." Helena smiled like a crocodile and reached out to Gina. "Please sit a moment. We have a problem I think you can help us with."

Gina swiveled, and her exquisite bottom settled onto the unworthy wood of the park bench next to her lumpy, pale Aunt Abbie. Side by side you would not have known they were the same sex, much less the same variety of animal.

"Is it illegal?"

"Only if you think about it that way."

Gina's shoulders rolled, and she brushed her mane of silken brown hair from her face. "Do tell?"

"A billionaire has a curse, and it centers around a valuable ring. You must get the ring from him, switch it out with a fake, and make him think it has been destroyed. We want the ring, mainly to convince him that the curse is as I have described it, but it seems to have a value unto itself."

"We using one of those exploding rings from Oscar's Magic Shop?"

"Sharp girl."

"Complications?"

"There's a Mexican."

"Do tell?"

"There is a Mexican who has come to town, and he is after the ring. We are not sure who he is or why he is after it. Part of our plan is to sideline this intruder through suspicion, by making our billionaire think this Mexican may have sent another Mexican to intimidate him. Tony is posing as a Mexican hit man. No gun, just gloves, a strangler."

"A Mexican strangler? Sounds like a vine." Gina recrossed her legs. "I like the part about no guns. Does this Mexican have guns? Is he dangerous?"

"It doesn't look like it. He would have pulled one earlier when Tony showed himself. We're not sure exactly how the Mexican fits in or what he wants, but you may encounter him and have to derail him or sucker him into the curse scenario."

"What's my cut?"

"Five hundred dollars."

"A thousand."

Abbie sat forward. "That's not coming out of my thirty-five percent."

Helena crouched in front of Abbie and Gina like a football coach trying to explain a complicated play. "Here's the deal. Abbie can have the thirty-five percent, but like Tony, Gina's end comes out of both of ours. Fair?"

"Then the thousand should come out of Tony's end," Abbie harrumphed.

Tony seemed to wake up. "Hey, I'm only *getting* a thousand!"

"We still need Tony. Now we need a shill, but a beautiful one. If you and Abbie cannot come to terms I will ask my niece Petulia."

Abbie and Gina spoke as one. "Petulia?"

Tony just snorted.

"She cleans up nice and could be the shill. A push-up bra, perfume, a wig, shoes." Helena stood, arms akimbo. "So what's it going to be, eh?"

"I don't like it." Abbie slapped her hands on her knees. "But I'll do it. Gina, you'll have to wait for your cut, though. We don't have it. None of us do until we get it from the mark."

"The mark being male, of course?"

Helena nodded. "A rich man."

Gina's luscious pink lips curved into a catty smile. "We'll get it."

Helena turned to Tony. "Put on the white suit, and call your friends to find out who does Grant's limo service. Also we need a chauffeur's uniform for Gina. A tight uniform! Abbie? Brief her."

Tony began fiddling with his cell phone.

"Here." Abbie handed Gina a piece of lined notepaper. "That's the mark's address. His name is Grant. You're his limo driver. You go pick Grant up, and Tony will attack him as he gets into the limo. You save Grant—but he's wearing the calludaroo, so make him think that saved him. Then you two drive out to the Hamptons and go to a bar called El Rolo. That's where his daughter hangs out. Her name is Purity. Tony tells us—"

"Hold the phone." Gina held up a hand. "We're scamming Purity Grant?"

Helen patted her shoulder. "Not Purity, but her father. Tony was just out in the Hamptons and saw Purity go off with a Mexican, one who wants the ring Grant is wearing. The one we want. Purity goes to this bar every night, and we think she will go with this Mexican. You must convince the Mexican that the ring is cursed, too, so that he will no longer want it."

"So I'm saving Grant and then driving all the way out to the Hamptons to run interference with a Mexican, all so I can pull a switch with Grant?"

Helena nodded.

So did Gina. "I see. All this for a lousy thousand bucks? I just got off a plane."

Tony snapped his phone shut. "Got the limo, but we gotta hurry. Grant is expecting the car within the hour."

"Go!" Helena shooed with her hands. "We can discuss anything you like later, on your drive out there."

Gina stood reluctantly. "Aunt Abbie, is this going to work?"

Abbie and Helena exchanged a cautious glance, then spoke in unison.

"It's worth a shot."

THIRTY-TWO

THE CAMERA PANS DOWN ROBERT Tyson Grant's East Side town house to the front door just as the master of the house is exiting, a bag and briefcase over his shoulder, a limo idling at the curb. Grant has his phone to one ear.

"Hey, Dix. Kathy sent a car for you. See you at the heliport in fifteen? Great."

Grant thumbed the call dead, tucked the phone into his inside pocket, and hustled toward the limo. The limo trunk popped open. He dropped his bags in the trunk and slammed the lid shut. When he did he saw Tony next to the limo.

In a white suit.

With a thin mustache.

With a stocking pulled over his head and wearing black gloves, hands raised.

Grant's jaw just had a chance to drop when the white-suited menace was thrown past Grant onto the hood of a parked car. In his wake was Gina in a snug female chauffeur's outfit and cap.

"Aiee-hah!" Gina shrieked, throwing herself at Tony and punching a fist into his gut.

"Ooof!" Tony jackknifed forward.

Gina whooshed a backhanded chop to his neck, then kicked him so that he rolled off the car hood onto the sidewalk.

"Stand back, sir!" Gina called over her shoulder to Grant. "Aiee-hah!" She leaped onto the sidewalk and stood over the White-Suited Menace, fists of fury at the ready.

Grant fumbled for his phone.

"Run!" Gina whispered to Tony.

"That hurt, Gina!" he whimpered.

"Run, you idiot! If you don't I'll kick the ever-living crap out of you!"

Tony rolled to his side, got to his feet, and lumbered away down the sidewalk.

Gina held her spot but looked back at Grant. "Are you in a hurry?"

Grant poked furiously at his phone. "Damn these things, they do a million things, but when you just want to make a call . . ."

Gina broke from her pose and stepped from the sidewalk. She placed her hand over his phone. "Forget it. By the time the cops get here he'll be long gone, and it will take hours to explain and fill in paperwork. I am your driver. My name is Gina."

"Who?" Grant stammered, pointing where Tony had vanished around the corner. "Who was that? He was trying to, he was . . ."

"Excuse me." Gina took off her cap, and her gorgeous hair cascaded down around her shoulders like brown satin. She fluffed it. "I hope you don't mind. I broke a sweat."

Grant focused on her, his alarm from the attack eroding. "Well, of course, you don't have to keep your hair up, I mean, hell, that was amazing, you beat up that big guy."

Gina dipped her head in a slight, courtly bow, one sapphire eye looking up at him from under the dark locks. "A good chauffeur looks out for her passengers. If the Mexican had killed you, I would have been derelict."

"Mexican?" Grant blinked rapidly.

"Are you all right?" Gina put a hand to his face, and another on his chest, pressing the calludaroo.

"Ow!" The raccoon paw dug into his breast.

Gina jumped back. "You are injured?"

"No, it's just . . ." He unbuttoned his shirt and pulled out the talisman.

"Calludaroo!" she gasped, pointing.

Grant was being pulled—expertly, as we see—in three directions at once, his eyes flitting from where the Mexican Menace had gone to Gina's charms to the calludaroo and the realization that Helena's prophecy had come true. Just the same, it was evident by Grant's gaze that all but Gina were unwanted distractions.

"You actually know what this is?" Grant held out the talisman.

She unbuttoned her jacket, revealing a form-fitting red top. "Please, sir, get into the car. We must leave here. There may be more danger and the power of the calludaroo may be fleeting."

She hustled him into the back of the limo, climbed into the driver's seat, and zoomed the limo down the block. "The heliport?"

"Yes." Grant breathed deeply, Gina's scent intoxicating him. "Driver, what is your name?"

Their eyes met in the rearview mirror.

"Gina."

"Are you new?"

"Yes."

"Where did a pretty girl like you learn to fight like that?"

"I'm also an actress. I've done some stunt double work in martial arts movies."

"Man, you sure took on that Mexican. What made you say he was Mexican, anyway?"

"Wasn't it obvious?"

"Actually, I've never . . . well, I've only met one Mexican who looked anything like that."

"I lived in L.A. for a while and was a cocktail hostess. You see things. He was dressed the way the cartels dress. The ones from Baja."

"Really? In white suits?"

"And thin mustaches." Their eyes met again in the mirror. "Yes, really. That was a Mexican hit man, and he meant to kill you. These Baja hit men kill with their bare hands."

"Well, if that's the case you saved my life."

"No."

"No?"

"The calludaroo saved your life, sir. That is a very powerful talisman."

"How do you know that?"

"Perhaps where you come from, sir, people are not as superstitious as mine. My family, my grandmother, my aunts and uncles, they all believe in the power contained in objects, and the calludaroo is the most powerful."

"I respect what you're saying, Gina, but—"

"Then why are you wearing the calludaroo if you don't believe?"

"Well, my . . . this friend of mine thought I should wear it, ridiculous . . ."

"You knew someone was going to try to kill you then?"

"I saw a palmist, and she seemed to know an awful lot about my life and situation, so it seemed maybe there was something to the psychic predictions. The more I thought about these predictions, the more I thought maybe it was just coincidence."

"Do tell? Did coincidence assign me to this detail at the last minute over another driver? A driver who could save you from the attacker? How many coincidences can you stack one atop the other before they collapse like cards and reveal the truth?"

"This is all a little fantastic. There's no denying, though, that you saved my bacon back there. I think I owe you something for that."

"It was my duty as a driver. I cannot accept a reward. You should pay handsomely for the use of the calludaroo—that is what saved you."

Grant leaned forward and inhaled her sweet scent. "You think the calludaroo would mind if I took you to dinner? It would offend me if you didn't accept some small gesture like that. If for no other reason than having you explain more to me about yourself and the superstitions. It's a real education."

Amazing, is it not? We certainly see it in the papers all the time. The hubris of powerful men to have too many women seems boundless, if not sadly predictable. Grant had Dixie—a stunning sex toy if ever there was one—and yet he thought he should have this one, too.

Gina favored him with her sapphire eyes under her mane of hair. "I'm flattered, sir, that you would even consider being at the same table with me."

"Nonsense," Grant chortled. "How can I get in touch with you?" He pulled out his phone, and she recited her number.

"Gina, I'll be out in East Hampton for a little bit but will call when I get back, how's that sound?"

"Again, sir—"

"My name is Robert. My friends call me Bobbie."

"OK, Robbie." Her eyelashes fluttered, and so did his heart.

The limo swung into the heliport drop-off, the sunset reflecting orange on Manhattan's skyline above. Dixie was standing at the curb in a lavender pleated bustier and matching jungle print pants, lavender luggage at her side. She raised her large sunglasses and peered into the limo at the driver as Grant climbed out. Wind from an idling chopper lashed his jacket and hair.

"Pretty driver," Dixie shouted over the whine and roar of the helicopter engine. She kissed Grant on the cheek.

"Hm? Oh, yeah, well, have I got a story. You won't believe it."

"What?"

He turned Dixie away from the limo. She shot a glance back at the driver before he hustled her toward the heliport. "A Mexican hit man just tried to kill me."

"No!"

Cut briefly to Gina, with Grant and Dixie in her rearview mirror, a cell phone to her ear.

"Tony? I'll pick you up—where are you? No time for food, we'll grab something along the way. No way we're beating the helicopter out there, but we have to make tracks if we want to make sure to catch Purity and the Mexican at that bar later."

Dixie gasped. "What happened?"

"The driver kicked his ass."

"*Her?*"

"You bet!"

Dixie gasped. "Then it all came true, just as Helena said!"

"Worse. There are now three Mexican hit men on our hands, not two."

"Ours is around the side where we can slip him into the chopper pretty much unseen. I think he's nervous about flying. He's praying to a little statue that hangs around his neck."

They paused before going into the heliport, and Grant looked to the sky, as if to God. "Great. We finally get the real hit man and he's both phobic and religious."

"The little statue is a grim reaper about this big."

"Then let's all pray to our talismans that we get this over and done with. Soon."

A flight controller in a headset stuck his head out the door.

"Sorry, Mr. Grant, but the mechanic has to check the rotor, so there's a delay."

"How long?" Dixie groaned.

"We're working on it. Maybe an hour or two. Sorry, but your safety comes first."

He disappeared back into the heliport.

Grant shrugged. "Maybe not as soon as we wanted."

THIRTY-THREE

THE CAMERA JUMP-CUTS FROM THE heliport to a close-up of a tiki torch flame at night. Panning left, the camera sees Purity and me drinking wine on loungers on the East Hampton mansion's upper deck. Purity is in a robe; I am in my tan suit. Between us is a table with two small plates and crumpled napkins. The ocean crashing on the beach roars off-camera.

"That was a most excellent meal, Purity, and the wine, while not carbonated, is quite nice. I thank you for your hospitality."

"No worries, Morty. The staff may be at a wedding tonight, but I'm not a bad chef. I've had a lot of time imprisoned out here at the mansion, time I sometimes spend cooking. It's about the only thing to do around here other than try to drink down the wine cellar."

"I will say again that I hope I am not imposing by staying the night. The little green car was not mine, and I must say, at a hundred and ninety-seven thousand miles, I am surprised it was not at the junkyard already."

"You think Robert Tyson Grant's billions are imposed on by you messing up some sheets and eating some of his squab? NFN, you make Dullsville more tolerable and are a fun guessing game."

"NFN?"

"Not for nothing. Morty, you have to give me a hint about your mission for the Church and why you were on that road."

"Can we not continue our conversation about murder? I wanted to add that while killing a despicable person may in the end make the killer the instrument of God's will, I am not sure the killer's soul would not have to pay penance in purgatory. The Church really should have rule books on such things, or perhaps a card for one's wallet with the highlights so one knows the exact cost of sin."

"Or a menu. Anyway, we agree that murder in certain contexts is not wrong." Purity held up a hand and ticked off her list on her fingers. "War is one."

"To include a government sniper killing a major terrorist, right?"

"Right."

"Number two: police shooting a dangerous criminal on the run."

"Three: capital punishment for mass murderers."

"Four: a doctor allowing the very old and/or terminally ill to perish and not prolong the life of those who are suffering."

"Five: Do you know Robert Tyson Grant?"

"I would not say I know him."

"You've *met* him, though, haven't you? Lying is a sin, Morty. Don't lie."

"Sex out of marriage and lying are not sins."

"Aren't those in the Ten Commandments?"

"I am happy to report that neither one is in the Ten Commandments. I committed all ten to memory when I was a child in parochial school. Bearing false witness is only a certain kind of lie, and adultery is only a certain kind of sex out of marriage. I can also tell you the Seven Wonders of the Ancient World."

"Awesome. So can you at least tell me whether you've met him or not?"

I sighed. "Yes, I met him once."

"Recently?"

"Recently."

"So were you on that road to see someone about my father or something? Were you trying to hit him up for charity for your parish?"

"Wine will not loosen my tongue, Purity."

"Hold it . . ." Purity sat forward. "Shit."

I, too, sat forward. "Is there an emergency?"

"Listen!"

Over the sound of the ocean there was a tapping noise echoing across the dunes and sea grass.

"Is that a motorcycle?"

Her eyes met mine. "FYI, that's a helicopter. A Bell 430 to be exact."

"How do you know this?"

"I'm kind of a helicopter freak. That's Robbie's chopper, headed this way. This is pretty late for them, but it's Robbie's copter."

I set my wine down. "Are you sure?"

She set her wine down. "Positive."

"You did not know he was coming?"

"The staff here is on orders not to tell me anything except whether my Vespa is gassed up when the car is wrecked like it is now."

"Well, is there anything we must do for his arrival?"

Purity leaped from her lounger. Cell phone to her ear, she reached under her robe and slid down her bikini bottom, which she kicked to one side as she dashed through the gauzy curtains and indoors.

"Downstairs in two minutes, Morty! Stat!"

THIRTY-FOUR

SO IT WAS THAT I went with Purity Grant in a car service to El Rolo and found myself at the door standing in front of Wilmer. He was in a light brown three-piece suit that must have taken three tailors and a squad of NASA engineers to construct. You could hear his muscles bunch as his giant head loomed down and planted a kiss atop Purity's blond head.

"Nice Pradas," the giant rumbled, but his shiny black eyes were on me. "Whosis?"

"Morty, this is Wilmer."

I smiled and put out my hand, but all Wilmer did was put out his palm, which was roughly the size of a serving platter. I at once realized that shaking this hand was impossible, like shaking the hand of a colossus, and a fist bump could have been fatal. I recognized the open palm gesture from East Brooklyn as a low five (as opposed to a high five) and reflexively swung my hand through the air, slapping Wilmer's palm loudly. Let's remember, I'd had a couple glasses of wine already. And I knew instinctively that there was less to fear from someone twice my size than from someone half my size. Wilmer had nothing to prove.

The colossus's eyes widened just enough that some of the white showed. "Where you from, Morty?"

"East 179th."

"East 163rd, myself. Where'd you go to school?"

"Holy Redeemer."

"I mean high school."

"East Brooklyn High."

"Me, too. Been back to the neighborhood recently?"

"Not for over a year."

"My ma still lives on the avenue, second story."

"I used to go to Oscar's on the boulevard."

"The feeler place?" Oscar's was a bar where house cleaners went. "You hear that Pete the Prick died?"

I had been at the house on Vanderhoosen Drive moments before Pete met his unfortunate end at the hands of Danny Kessel and an ice pick, but there was no sense telling Wilmer this and prolonging our entrance to El Rolo.

"That is a shame."

"Not really. He was a prick."

"I was merely being polite, because I of course hated Pete as much as anybody, and the Balkan Boys as well."

"They got a serious beating at a chica bar in Queens. Don't see them around anymore. Can't say I'm sorry about that, either."

"All good news for East Brooklyn."

Wilmer pivoted the door open with his heel. "Come on in, Morty. Glad to see Purity hanging with quality people."

"Nice suit." I gave him a thumbs-up as I passed into El Rolo behind Purity, who was eyeing me over her shoulder.

"You and Wilmer from the 'old neighborhood'? LMAO."

"Brooklyn is everywhere you look." I smiled. "*If* you look."

Of course, I was quite pleased with the scenery. El Rolo's interior was a dark sanctum furnished most notably with comely, expensive women. The brown lounges and tan sofas were an afterthought. In the corner was a curvy bar, behind which stood a petite Latino man in a tuxedo shirt and long sideburns. His eyes searched me carefully, and by the curl of his lip I did not guess that he liked what he saw. For purity, though, the corners of his mouth curled.

"The usual?"

"Thanks, Tito."

"And for the . . . gentleman?"

"I do not suppose you have cold duck?"

Tito's lip trembled. "*Très amusant.*"

"A glass of house red, then."

Purity curled her arm around mine. "So you want me to get you laid by a model, Morty?"

I laughed. "It is always best that these things happen of their own accord." Then I spotted a lovely brunette creature in the corner, and she was looking my way. A bored lout with a bottle of beer sat at her side.

"Shall we sit this way?" Purity had been heading one way, but I wheeled her in the direction of the brunette in the little black cocktail dress. As we approached she sat taller, her cleavage welcoming beacons in the gloom. The closer I got, the better I could see how magnificent a creature this was, perfectly formed, her lustrous hair cascading down her shoulders. The lout looked about ready to fall asleep, a Band-Aid across his cheek and a substantial unibrow across his forehead.

Cut away to this brunette whispering to the lout.

"Tony, that's definitely her."

"Who?"

"Purity Grant. Coming this way. Now remember what Helena told us?"

"I think so."

"Think so?"

"Gina, I was up all last night with the baby and then got chased . . . that's him."

"Who?"

"The Mexican, the guy who chased me. He's with her."

"Doesn't look too dangerous. Not with a gun, anyway."

I interrupted them, gesturing to the sofa adjoining theirs. "Forgive my intrusion. Would you and your husband mind if we sat here?"

The brunette put out her left hand, the one without a wedding ring. "I'm Gina, and this is my cousin Anthony."

I took her hand and pecked a courtly kiss to her knuckles. The scent of her hand was heavenly. Yes, you may think it is corny, but I have found a woman adores having her hand greeted with a kiss. I offered my hand to Anthony, and he tried to look awake.

"They call me Tony." He yawned and shook my hand.

"Your cousin Gina is quite ravishing, and as such I am sure you have been interrupted continually, so we will not disturb you any further."

Gina ignored my compliment and peered around me at Purity. "You're Purity Grant, am I right?"

I had tried to avoid introducing Purity, to spare her any unwanted attention.

Purity's focus had been across the room, no doubt where some of her acquaintances were gathered. She seemed to focus on Gina for the first time and grinned. "That's right."

"You're even prettier in person, I swear to God."

Tito arrived with a tray, and we took our drinks, Purity's in a martini glass.

"Not bad yourself. Morty? I have to go say hello to some friends." Purity made haste to the other side of the room.

"Until she returns, please, sit with us." Gina's hand waved at the adjoining sofa.

"Delighted, Gina." I sat. "So do you have a place here in East Hampton?"

"Just visiting. I actually thought I might run into Robert Tyson Grant, Purity's father. I drove for him today."

"Drove for him?"

"Yes, I'm a chauffeur, a limo driver."

"Your charm must delight your clients."

"Well, to tell you the truth, Morty, I think Mr. Grant was more delighted with my Shui Ping."

"Shui Ping?"

"A man in a white suit and stocking face mask attacked Mr. Grant, and I did my thing. Shui Ping is a martial art." Gina made short jabbing motions with her fists, and Tony winced.

"That is most unusual." I held my chin. "A man of that description attempted to assault Purity today, and I did my thing."

"Shui Ping?"

I shook my head. "I merely chased the coward off."

"Coward?" Tony leaned forward.

"Indeed. As soon as he saw me, he took off through the hedge like a rabbit."

"Is that so?" Tony was about to say something else, but Gina elbowed him and he sank back into the sofa, grumbling.

"This is amazing!" Gina chirped. "Where are you from, Morty? How do you know the Grants?"

"I am here on business, and to tell you the truth, I do not know the Grants well. I happened to be beside the road when Purity drove by and was attacked." I figured the short version was just easier. "My car is disabled, so in exchange for my valor Purity asked me to stay the night until I can make passage back to New York. It is really quite generous of her."

"You're not here on business with Mr. Grant?"

"I am here on behalf of my local parish in La Paz."

"Mexico?"

"You have heard of it?"

"Of course. Baja Sur, right?"

"That is a fascinating pendant." I leaned in close to inspect the cheap jewelry, and more. The smell of her hair was like a summer day. An intoxicating woman.

"It's onyx."

"It goes exquisitely with your hair."

"Maybe in this light. What does your parish have you doing in New York, Morty?"

"I am not at liberty to discuss church business, I apologize."

"So what do you do in La Paz?"

"I am gentry."

"Gentry?"

"I have made my fortune, so I no longer have a job. I help the church with sensitive matters such as the mission I am now engaged upon."

She batted her eyes, and my heart skipped a beat. "Sounds mysterious. Do tell?"

Were her idiot cousin not there I surely would have blurted out anything she wished to know, but even in the face of overwhelming pulchritude, I managed to cling to my last shred of decorum.

"I cannot tell you the circumstance at present, but would be delighted to do so at another time. You say you live in the city but are just visiting here?"

She put a hand on my knee and leaned her ear toward my lips. "Just whisper, I won't tell."

I have never been what you call a particular fan of the female ear one way or the other, but this one I could have spent all night caressing. Exquisite.

Her hand squeezed my knee, and I felt light-headed.

"I am here to recover a lost ring."

Her eyes met mine and blinked slowly, her tongue coursing her lips in anticipation of my continued betrayal.

"It went missing many years ago from a reliquary, where it reposed upon the finger of my ancestor the conquistador Hernando Martinez de Salvaterra. It is said the ring was fashioned from the golden Hapsburg medallion that encased a part of the true cross, and is embossed with the double cross of Caravaca."

Gina leaned in farther, that delectable tongue tracing the edge of those diaphanous lips, her eyes wide. "Is it Mr. Grant that has the ring?"

I finally blinked, and realized I needed to start breathing again to forestall unconsciousness. "How could you know this?"

"When I drove for him today, he was wearing a ring just like that! Do you think that the ring is cursed?"

"What makes you say this?"

"Mr. Grant was wearing a talisman around his neck, the kind to protect him from extreme danger. Something old like that ring, especially one having something to do with God . . . well, it could be cursed. He should give you back that ring."

"He has agreed to do this, only there has been a delay of some sort."

"Wait, though—when you have the ring, *you* will be cursed, won't you?"

"I have been deputized by the church for the recovery of the ring. I cannot be cursed when I am the instrument of God's will."

"Then I will get the ring from Mr. Grant and give it to you. He was in danger today, and from what you tell me, so was his daughter. We must end this."

"We?"

"Like you, I am already involved." She made the short Shui Ping jabs of her fists again.

I sipped my wine, trying to clear my head of Gina's hypnotic femininity. When faced with such a daunting beauty, I try to find some imperfection on which to focus, which helps me view her as human. One nostril seemed slightly larger than the other.

"Yes, but what I don't understand is, who is this masked man in the white suit attacking Purity and Robert Tyson Grant? What is his purpose?"

"It must be to obtain the ring, to keep you from your mission. This attacker must therefore be an agent of Satan."

"An agent of Satan?"

"Does that surprise you? Does it surprise you that you should be on a mission for the Holy See and that you might come up against Satan?"

Gina's ingenuity may seem surprising, but let's flash back quickly to her on a movie set. She stands script in hand with the crew, who are standing too close to her and leering. Gina is dressed in a safari outfit and staring straight ahead at the lead actress for whom she is the stunt double. This lead actress is in an identical safari outfit and seated at a desk in a set designed to look like a monastery library, gargantuan stage lights pouring fake sunlight through arched faux-stone windows in the background. The lead actor is in a white turtleneck and a shoulder holster, sitting on the chair next to hers. From under the table we can see he is sitting atop phone books so that he appears taller than the actress. The two of them are marveling at the text in a large dusty book splayed on the table in front of them. A hulking Panavision camera and its operator loom over the actors, closely flanked by the director and several technical people. One techie cantilevers a gourd-sized mic on a boom over the actors' heads; another techie steps forward with a black and white slate. On the slate in white chalk is written the title of the movie: KUNG FU TEMPLARS.

Techie: "Act Ten, Scene Four, Take Three."

Director: "Action."

Lead Actress, finger on the book: "So what this is telling us is . . ."

Lead Actor, one eyebrow raised: "Exactly. Satan himself!"

Director: "Cut. Good work, people."

Cut to a close-up of me, one eyebrow raised. "Satan himself!"

Close-up of Gina: "Mr. Grant is at the house tonight, isn't he? I drove him to the heliport myself earlier."

Close-up of me: "He was just arriving when I left."

Close-up of Gina: "Morty, I don't think we have any time to lose."

Close-up of me: "I suppose there isn't any time for another glass of wine."

Close-up of Gina: "Do you think Satan is taking time for another glass of wine when the ring is still vulnerable? We must get the ring and put it on the finger of the conquistador, whatsisname . . ."

Close-up of me: "Hernando Martinez de Salvaterra."

Close-up of Gina: "Yes, him."

Close-up of me: "The house is a half mile up on the right, with a lighthouse mailbox. I must remain with Purity and see her home."

Close-up of Gina: "Be careful. Come soon."

Close-up of me: "We must both look out for Satan, yes?"

Close-up of Gina: "Yes."

THIRTY-FIVE

PAN ACROSS THE FLUORESCENT CUBICLES in the *Daily Post* newsroom until we come to Skip's cubbyhole. He is leaning back in his chair, transfixed by his phone, a laptop at his elbow. An older man with bad acne scars, a mustache, and a PRESS windbreaker stops in the cubicle entry.

The man sneered. "The boss was right, you ain't busy."

"Hello, Bent." Skip glanced at the man.

"I sent you an e-mail."

"Mm hm."

"I got something for you to work on."

"I have Purity Grant to work on."

"Not breaking a sweat here, are yuh?"

"Bent, to the untrained eye of a crime reporter, what I'm doing may not look like work, but it is. Keeping track of Purity is a fulltime job."

"The boss doesn't think so. Work on what I sent you until something *real* happens with your girlfriend."

"Sorry, can't help you."

"Listen, punk, the boss says to give me a hand or he's holding back your expense vouchers."

"Eat me, Bent."

"Really? Tell the boss to fuck off if you want to, but I need a little help here, is that too much to ask?"

A wiry balding man in a sweater vest stepped next to Bent. "Skip? Something you want to tell me?"

Skip sat up. "No, boss, it's just that I'm busy with Purity and the Mexican guardian angel."

"What's up?"

"Well, she's out in the Hamptons with the Mexican."

"You send a photographer?"

"Yes, but there's not much to get, just a stretch of road."

"Then what are you doing?"

"Trying to locate someone who may have seen her. Waiting. But . . ."

"Help Bent until something happens."

"Yeah, but . . ."

The boss took a step into the cubicle and leaned down to within an inch of Skip's nose. "Didn't you hear me?"

"Yup, OK." Skip was trying not to cringe.

The boss retreated. Bent huffed and stalked off.

"Assholes," Skip hissed. He turned to his laptop, went to his e-mail, and clicked into the one from Bent. He then clicked a link. The small headline from the *Charlotte Sun* read: MEXICAN GANG BEHEADING NEAR CULPVILLE.

Skip's lips moved as he read down. The audience sees highlights of the story.

. . . South of the Border employees who were illegals . . . dormitory-style conditions and indentured to the victim . . . decapitated body found under a woodpile at the old Smith tobacco barns . . . head found in bus locker . . . three Mexican illegals who were witnesses apprehended . . . resembled cartel gangland beheadings . . . suspect has yellow eyes and carries a small hatchet . . .

Skip scrolled down to an artist rendering of Paco that was reasonably accurate, especially the eyes.

He clicked on the next link, and it was an article from the *Richmond Times,* and the small headline read: MOTOR LODGE OWNER ASSAULTED.

Skip scrolled down to another artist rendering, which was similar to the first.

The third link was a *Daily Post* police log entry for Manhattan: NEWSSTAND HATCHET ROBBER.

... *a newsstand outside Penn Station and described as a Hispanic male, 5'6" with hazel eyes* ...

A note from Bent at the bottom of the e-mail read: *Skip: Check this out. Same Mexican?*

THIRTY-SIX

CUT TO A WIDE ANGLE of the Grant mansion, limpid blue pool in the foreground. The silhouettes of Dixie followed by Paco pass in front of the pool, and as the camera pans right we see them walk quietly up to the guest cabana. The pool pump hums and waves crash on the beach off-camera.

Reverse angle: From inside the cabana, Dixie opens the door. She flicks on and then flicks off the interior light. She and Paco are in silhouette again in front of the pool, in the doorway.

"Stay in here until they get back, and keep the lights out," Dixie whispered. "You see that balcony up there?"

Paco nodded.

"The light will go on up there when she comes home. She'll be drunk. She always drinks a bottle of Perrier before bed, and we've laced it with sleeping pills. Wait five minutes until after the lights go out. Do you understand?"

Paco nodded again. "Light out. Five minute."

"Can you climb up the stonework to the balcony? Lord knows *she's* climbed up and down that stonework ever since she was a child."

"I do."

"The balcony door is unlocked. Climb up, pull her out of bed, drop her headfirst off the balcony onto the concrete."

Paco's silhouette made a stabbing gesture. "No knife?"

"*No!* It must look like an accident. She was drunk and took pills and fell off the balcony, that's what happens. Only *you* make it happen, understand?"

"I do."

"We've made sure the security cameras won't be pointing that way. The staff is all out for the night at a wedding. Nobody will be around to see anything. Next, you climb back down and come back in here and hide in the closet, understand? We'll get you some gardener's clothes and get you out of here in the morning, but stay in the closet, do you understand?"

"Closet. I stay."

"Good. Tomorrow afternoon, we'll be flying to Baja on our Gulfstream. We'll take you home."

"Good. My trip here not good. Question?"

"Yes?"

"I not cut her head?"

"*What?*"

Paco made a slicing gesture across his throat with his thumb.

"*No!* Just throw her off the balcony, headfirst, straight down into the patio. Do not cut her head off."

Paco's silhouette was bowed with disappointment.

"Paco? I want your promise you'll do exactly what we ask. Promise that you will not cut her, or cut her head off. Promise?" Dixie held up her hand as if swearing him in as a witness.

Paco sighed. "I promise."

From atop the mansion roof we see Paco and Dixie by the guest cabana off the pool. The camera pans over the ocean and dunes and down to the opposite side of the house and driveway. A limousine is pulling in.

Inside the limo, Gina turned away from the steering wheel and looked into the backseat, where Tony was asleep. She gave the mansion a calculating, squinty look before opening the driver's door and climbing out. She stepped up to the portico and rang the bell.

After a few beats, the window curtain parted.

Robert Tyson Grant's eye grew wide, and the door swung open. He was still in slacks, but his shirt was untucked and there were worn boat shoes on his feet.

"Gina!"

"There's no time. We must talk."

Grant shot a glance back into the house. It was the well-established glance all men have when worried that their girlfriend or wife will see them with another woman.

"Gina, how did you get here?"

"Not here, come." She jogged down the drive, her magnificent figure in the little black dress swaying. What man could possibly resist following this woman off into the dark? Well, there may be some. I am not one. Neither was Grant. He suppressed a smile and followed.

THIRTY-SEVEN

PURITY WAS AGAIN SITTING ON the beach nursing a bottle of rum. The light from the bar in the distance was splayed across the beach, and I followed it, shoes in hand, up to where Purity's hair glowed and fluttered in the breeze.

I dropped onto my knees in the sand next to her. "Something tells me you sit here often, yes?"

"Morty, why won't you fuck me?" Her eyes didn't leave the waves.

"We've been through that, darling. I am like a brother, nothing more."

"I could tell you liked that brunette."

"Yes, she is quite charming, I would bed her if I could, but that has nothing to do with you. No more than if you slept with someone else. Unless, of course, this person might harm you. We should go."

"Morty, would you do something for me?"

I shrugged. "That depends."

"Depends on what?"

"There are certain things I would do for you and others I would not."

"Would you break the Ten Commandments?"

I thought about that a moment. "I would not make a false idol, but I might use the Lord's name in vain if you insisted. I think God is made of tougher stuff and not that sensitive about such things."

"What about steal?"

"If your life depended on it, yes."

"Would you kill?"

"Same answer."

"Have you killed anybody before?"

I laughed. "If I had I would not tell you or anybody. I am not an idiot."

Her eyes met mine. "So you have?"

I smiled, shaking my head. "No, Purity."

"If Robert Tyson Grant tried to kill me, would you defend me?"

"Of course. If Robert tried to hurt you, I would not allow it. If you tried to kill him, I would try to prevent that as well. Killing is far too popular as it is."

Purity drained the rest of the rum from the bottle and threw it toward the ocean. "If you had to, would you kill Robert Tyson Grant to protect me?"

I stood with a groan. "Come, we should be going. Your father will be worried, and the Sixth Commandment says you shall not make your parents worry. Besides, I fear Satan is out tonight."

"I'll go if you answer."

"Fine, then my answer is yes."

"Yes what? Imagine now, you come in and Robbie is naked, on top of me, raping me, and has a gun to my head, and you have a gun. Would you shoot him?"

"I might, I really don't know, Purity. Come, let's go."

"Not until you answer. Would you kill Robert Tyson Grant to protect me?"

"Yes, I would kill Robert Tyson Grant to protect you. Come on, to your feet, young lady."

Purity uncrossed her legs and wobbled to her feet, sandals in hand.

"You think Satan is out tonight, do you, Morty?"

"Of course. I think it was one of his agents that attacked you this afternoon."

Purity took a halting step and wobbled again. "Carry me?"

I shrugged, lowered my shoulder into her crotch, locked my arms around her legs, and hefted Purity like a sack of expensive potatoes onto my shoulder.

She said, "Oof!"

Thus I trudged across the sand and black night toward the floodlights of El Rolo, the drunken heiress draped over my shoulder.

"Everything jake, Morty?" Wilmer's bulk was dominating the French back doors to the bar.

"Yes, it would seem so, I just need a car." I could feel Purity snoring on my shoulder blade.

"I usually carry her like this." Wilmer cradled his arms.

Behind my back, Purity was conscious enough to find an empty bottle of Visine in her cleavage and tuck it into my jacket pocket, all unseen.

"Hm, yes, well, I wish that I could, too. Is there a way around the side here so I don't have to go through the crowd?"

"I'll show you."

Wilmer thumped out of the floodlights into darkness, and I followed along a sandy path through scrub pine and grass that led to where the rides were out front.

Wilmer turned, bent, and put his arms out, and I jackknifed so that Purity rolled into his arms. He turned to one of the town cars where a kid had opened the back door. Resting Purity's shoulders on the leather backseat, he clamped her thighs in his hands and slid her like a casket into a hearse and shut the door.

"I'll be right back, I just have to pay the bill."

"No need, Morty, she has a running account, and we don't accept cash."

"Well, I am sure you do." I fished through my pocket for a twenty.
"You certainly seem to provide full service."

Wilmer held up a hand the size of a dinner plate. "I don't take
tips for doing my job. 'Sides, you're from the neighborhood. We
do solids."

I put the flat of my entire hand in the center of his palm. "Solid."

In East New York, it was understood that when you did someone a "solid" it was a favor that would be repaid, an open debt,
like when you got a buy-back from a bartender or a free coffee at
the deli. Solids were classic Brooklyn—people there were very
nice and helpful, but not at their own expense. You didn't get
something for nothing, and there was an underground economy
whose currency was favors and minor kickbacks at every level,
almost like bartering. You never knew if you would be paid back
for the favor, but there was a sense that it was good to have a lot
of unpaid favors out there, like uncashed checks or a 401(k) or
karma. There was a name for people who knew and honored this
system of checks and balances:

"You're a stand-up guy, Wilmer, thanks."

He just nodded his giant head and waved as he turned back to
El Rolo.

I found a term in this screenwriting book I'd never heard before,
something called a racing cutaway, where the screen is briefly
blurred by the camera turning quickly before it stops on a scene
somewhere else completely—let's try that here, because now we
have to get back to the mansion a half mile away. So the camera
pans quickly away from me, screen blurred, and when the camera

stops we see Tony in the back of the limo, peering over the seat
and whispering on his phone.

"She's going for the ring, that's what I'm saying. We saw Purity
at the bar just like Abbie said we would, but she was with the Mexican, the one who chased me off, and this Mexican told Gina that the
ring is magic, that it belonged to Jesus Christ, and he's a secret agent
from the pope or something trying to get it back from Grant. Hm?
I dunno. Anyway, she told him about when I attacked Grant in
Manhattan and stuff, and sold the Mexican on the curse idea, that
Satan is after the ring, she's here at Grant's mansion trying to get
the ring back and hand it over to Morty. Hm? Morty is the name of
the Mexican. I can't put her on the phone. I dunno where she is. I'm
in the limo. Hm? Well, I last saw her when she got out of the limo. I
was asleep, but I woke up. Hm? Well, she met Grant at the door, and
they run off down the road together. It's dark down there, I can't
see nobody. That's right, she said she'd get the ring from Grant and
hand it over to the Mexican to end the curse. Hm? Her dress doesn't
have no pockets, so I don't think she has the wax ring. Hm?" Tony's
eyes turned glassy. "Oh, she could put it there, huhn?"

Another racing cutaway, to a clearing in the scrub pines just off
the driveway. In a shaft of moonlight, Gina has Grant by the shirt
front, her large, dewy eyes looking up into his. Grant in turn is
holding her lightly by the shoulders, blinking rapidly, his lips churning alternately with resolve and longing.

Gina tears open his shirt and puts her hand on his chest.

"You have removed the amulet!"

"It itched," Grant mumbled.

"Robert, I had a vision, it all came to me, I know about the ring!
It is from the finger of the conquistador Hernando Martinez, and
fashioned from gold that once held the true cross! You must return

it! It is stolen, as if from Christ himself! How did you get it? Did *you* steal it?"

Grant winced, and was just about to kiss her when she pushed him away and cast her gaze on the ground.

"I see, you stole the ring."

Grant stepped forward, his breath coming faster. "I did not steal it. Someone else . . ."

"Then how did you come by it?"

"It was Pasqual, he stole the ring. We were boys at the La Paz orphanage, we didn't know any better. Pasqual, he had the ring, and when a home and family was found for him in Brooklyn, and he was to leave the orphanage, he gave it to me, so that I would find parents." His lie was seamless.

"And you did?"

"Yes."

"And you did not return the ring then?"

Grant sighed. "No, I didn't."

"Then you must return it now." Gina turned, her palm out flat between them in the moonlight. "I will give it to the Mexican, to Morty."

Through the trees behind them, the headlights of a car coming down the drive flash. The car was Purity and me returning to the mansion.

The gold ring of Caravaca glistened in the blue light as Grant held the one hand up and gripped the ring with the other. Then he paused.

"Did you have any visions about us? About you and me?"

Gina's hand gracefully held his face. She stood on tiptoe and kissed him passionately on the mouth, the two of them one silhouette.

When she pulled away, Grant's hand was still where it was but the ring was gone. His face was aglow with infatuation, not moonlight. She opened her palm, and in it shone the holy ring of my ancestors.

"Come," she whispered, closing the ring into her one hand while leading him back to the house with the other.

Another racing cutaway, to Dixie entering Purity's bedroom and flicking on the lights. I followed behind Dixie, with Purity over my shoulder. I bent and flopped Purity onto the bed with more force than I intended. Dixie lunged for the Perrier bottle that almost tipped off the bed table.

Purity moaned and rolled over.

I arched my back. "Carrying her is not as easy as it looks."

"Just what do you think you're doing, Morty?" Dixie shot me a suspicious glare. "What were you doing out with her, staying here?"

I laughed. "As I recall, Dixie, you sent me out here in that crappy green car. I would just as soon be in Manhattan. So if I can just have the ring, and a ride to the train station, I think we can wrap this up." My mind was on the plump little desk clerk back at the hotel. Perhaps she was working late.

"Let me find Robert." Dixie thrust the Perrier bottle into my hand. "Could you see that Purity drinks this? She'll feel better for it in the morning. Then turn off the lights."

Cut away briefly to Paco peering through the cracked door of the guest cabana, his yellow predator eyes fixed on the illuminated balcony doors.

I sat on the bed next to Purity. "Purity, you want to drink this?" I gave her a shake, but she just moaned. With a sigh I set the bottle back on the nightstand. "Well, it is here if you want it."

I draped the comforter over her and went to the French doors to the balcony. The curtains were blowing with the sea breeze, so I shut the doors, and latched them.

Cut away to Paco's yellow eyes going dark when I shut off the room light.

I came down the stairs, jacket over my shoulder, and found Dixie crossing the foyer from the living room.

"Robert? Robert??"

"Is he not here?" I stopped at the bottom of the stairs.

"We arrived together," she barked from the other room, reappearing in the foyer, her hips swaying with determination in the purple jungle print pants, those amazing implants bouncing ever so slightly under the lavender pleated bustier. What can I say? The notion that perhaps Grant had gone out for ice cream gave me ideas. After all, it was only the previous evening that Dixie and I were as one, so the images of passion were fresh in my mind. Let us remember that I had consumed my share of wine, and that the previous year in Mexico had not exactly been a bonanza of beauties.

Impulsively, I took her by the hand as she passed and twirled her toward me.

"*Querida,* I am sure he just stepped out to the Dairy Queen. Perhaps we should just relax with a glass of wine and wait for his return."

Cut to Purity in bed, moonlight through the window making crosses on the wall. She lifts her head and scans the room through the veil of her hair.

Rolling off the side of the bed, she popped deftly to her feet and tossed her hair back. On a side table she found an elastic next to the Perrier bottle and put her hair into a ponytail. Her eyes were bright and determined—it would seem she had not been drunk after all, yes? From the dresser she pulled out a pair of black sweatpants and pulled them on under her dress. Then she pulled the dress over her head, dropped it to the floor, and kicked it under the bed. She turned to the dresser so that our R-rated film audience is not cheated the sight of her lovely tanned breasts. I think we'd only seen these breasts when she was tanning in the first part of the movie. Or did we see them when she was in bed with Skip? The same cup size as Dixie's, they had a very pleasing and decidedly fruitlike, fresh, young shape, and did not stand rigidly at attention like the implants, if you know what I mean.

If you don't, well, more's the pity.

Cut away to Paco leaving the confines of the cabana and making a beeline for the rock wall next to the balcony.

Dixie yanked her hand away from mine. "*Please*, Morty."

She turned from me toward the front door.

"Dixie, really, it is a sin not to make the best of every predicament."

I stepped up behind her and cupped my hand on her bottom just as she opened the door.

She yelped, both from the surprise of my fingers caressing her fruit and from the sight of Robert on the stoop. His shirt was torn open, and he wore a giddy twist to his lips. Next to him stood the curvaceous and utterly stunning fortune-teller's niece, Gina.

To be honest, I am not sure how best to capture Dixie's emotions on film. I did not witness her expression. How could I have seen it from where I stood, her delightful rosy buttock in my grasp?

Ah, but I think we all know human nature well enough and women in particular to know that it must have been an exceptional moment. It did not matter to her that she had transgressed with me, or that I was fondling her pear. She was focused entirely on trying to calculate—in an instant—the tableau before her. I think, however, the equation "one plus one" was the obvious formula at hand, so Dixie was not puzzled for long.

I have flipped through the screenwriting manual, and nothing seems satisfactory to capture her surge of emotion. The book suggests the use of metaphor. So are we to insert the image of a snarling tigress? Would that overplay the moment for our audience? I fear so. The audience might imagine that somehow an actual tiger had arrived at the mansion to further confuse things, and was ready to devour the cast and end the story here. The manual also mentions the use of flash fantasies to translate the action Dixie would like to have taken were she at complete liberty to express herself in any manner whatsoever. So we see Robert suddenly standing in a desert munitions testing ground, Gina at his side. An approaching jet fighter lines up the crosshairs on his chest, Dixie in the pilot's seat with her thumb over the red button. Missiles burst from the jet and snake down to where the target vanishes in a boom and a mushroom cloud. Again, this may overplay our hand.

Perhaps our best option is to underplay the moment, because Dixie didn't burst into the flames of a jealous tirade or give her lover a knuckle sandwich. Yes, I believe what she did was smile brightly. This is what she had trained herself to do during all those years as a fund-raiser listening to boring old rich people and letting them fondle her as I was doing at that moment. This makes sense, too, because she put out her hand to Gina and cocked her head. Perhaps her smile was a little too strong, but other than that, I think she managed not to let laser beams shoot from her eyes.

"Hi, I'm Dixie. Have we met?"

Cut back to Purity's shadowy bedroom. I know there are a lot of cutaways, but there was much that was happening all at once. A split screen might work, but chapter 12 says cutaways build more suspense in a motion picture.

At this point, Purity was dressed in black sweatpants and matching hoodie, with tennis shoes on her feet. She was holding her phone and played back my voice, from when we spoke on the beach.

"Killing a despicable person may in the end make the killer the instrument of God's will . . . If Robert tried to hurt you, I would not allow it . . . I would kill Robert Tyson Grant to protect you."

With a sly smile, she put the phone back in her purse and turned toward the dark bathroom, where she found a fresh bottle of eyedrops that she stuffed into her hoodie pocket. She headed for the balcony doors, then unlatched them and opened them.

Paco was halfway up the rock wall, and his cat eyes went wide.

Cut back to the foyer, and Dixie.

"You'll have to excuse me if I've forgotten, I meet so many people. Bobbie, really, you should introduce your friend."

By this time my hands had retreated behind my back, and I did my best to look like my only thoughts were of kittens and buttercups.

"I'm Gina, and I know all about the ring. I saved Robert's life today, and we've made a connection."

"A connection?" Dixie sounded like she was seeing the same kittens and buttercups I was.

I doubt it.

Cut back to Purity, who pauses at the balcony railing and trots to the bed table, where she opens the green bottle of Perrier and starts to gulp.

About halfway through the bottle, she knit her brow and took the bottle from her grimacing lips.

"Blech!" She set the bottle back on the bed table and made for the balcony. Stepping out into the moonlight, she deftly threw a leg over the railing and swung herself around to the rock wall.

Cut to a close-up of Gina's face.

"A vision. I know about the ring, about the curse, all of it, and the ring must go back on the finger of Hernando Martinez immediately. Morty, do you have the finger?"

"My bags are still in the green car," I said, with my buttock-grabbing hand in the air where it could not possibly have had any chance of fondling Dixie's bottom. "You have the ring?"

She opened her hand and showed us all the ring.

"Excellent!" I moved past Dixie and the couple on the porch. "Let us get this done with and end this merry-go-round, yes?"

I marched over to the car, and Dixie looped her arm around Robert's, leading him in my wake. She gave him a searching look, and he nodded almost imperceptibly and winked. Gina trailed behind them.

Do we need to show Gina switching out the counterfeit ring that Robert gave her for the trick one from the magic shop? I will leave that to your creative people, but it would be a good chance to see her perhaps lift her dress to access a hiding place in her underwear, or perhaps reach deep into the velvet chasm of her bosom. Let us keep that R rating alive and well.

I opened the trunk and pulled the little humidor from my bag. It creaked when I opened it, and the finger made a slight crunch as I plucked it from its recess.

Gina came forward. Eyes were wide all around, so let's get that in extreme close-ups as I slowly extended the mummified finger toward Gina's cupped hands.

At that moment, Purity was descending the wall just as Paco was ascending the wall. What happened?

Purity jumped the last few feet down from the wall, checked the pool-lit surroundings, then slid around the side of the house to the sliding glass patio doors. She peeked into the living room, lit only by light coming from the adjoining foyer. With a shove, she silently slid the door open. In a camera shot from the bushes, we see her slink into the house.

The camera in the bushes pulls back until we find Paco, who was crouched behind and next to the pool pump enclosure. He turned his yellow eyes from where Purity had vanished back toward the balcony. Emerging from the bushes, he trotted toward the rock wall and the balcony.

Cut back to the action by the green car.

Eyes were wide all around, remember? I slowly extended the mummified finger toward Gina's cupped hands.

A foot from the finger, Gina slid one hand over the other, exposing a gold ring that dimly hummed in the fractured porch light.

Flame burst from Gina's hand. She yelped.

The ring fell to the macadam, sizzling and shooting sparks before it made a loud pop.

Only a scorch mark and a puff of smoke remained where the ring had been.

All four of us stared down at the ground, mouths agape, and perhaps the camera can capture this by looking up at us looking down.

Grant: "Holy . . ."

Dixie: "My stars!"

Grant: "What was that?"

Dixie: "It exploded!"

Me: "You do not see that every day. Wow."

"That smarts." Gina was waving her hand in the air—I don't think she expected the trick ring to get so hot.

Dixie looked at Grant in amazement. "The ring just exploded when she put it near the finger!"

Grant shrugged, a squint gripping his eyes.

I looked cautiously at the finger, a little uncertain as to whether it, too, might explode, and gently placed it back in the humidor, snapping the lid shut.

Gina was trying to ignore her burned hand.

"The curse is over. The ring is no more."

Of course the ring was in her underpants, next to where almost any man would forfeit his worldly possessions to be. Perhaps we can do an X-ray shot of the counterfeit ring in her undies?

Dixie's eyes stopped wobbling with wonder when she hit upon what this all meant. The fake ring had been destroyed, so Morty would stop asking for the real one. She glanced over to where we see another X-ray shot of the *real* ring in Grant's pocket. OK, I did not know where he had it at that moment, but he never liked to be separated from it, and it was not on his finger or on a chain around his neck. Next, she imagined an X-ray shot through the house, to where Purity lay dead in a crumpled heap on the patio, Paco sneaking back into the cabana.

Dixie smiled and extended her hands to either side, to Robert and myself.

"I think we should pray," she chirped.

Cut away to a close-up of the Visine bottle. It is upside down over an open decanter of amber Scotch, blue pool light playing on the wall in the background. Purity's fingers squeeze the entire contents into the Scotch, the surface of the Scotch foaming lightly. We hear Purity yawn in the background.

Cut to Tony peeking over the backseat of the limo, a phone to his ear.

"I think she did it. Yeah, the ring exploded and everything, they were all standing around watching. She must have the ring. Hm? Praying. That's what I said. Yeah, they're all standing around where the ring burned up holding hands in a circle, their heads down. I think they're praying."

Cut to Paco, his face sandwiched by clothing and dimly lit through slats in the closet door. In a POV or "point of view" shot, we see what he sees: Purity's bed and room.

Paco mumbled to himself in Spanish, so insert subtitles:

"Oh, Santa Muerte, I call upon you so that through your image, you may free me from failure in my mission. Do not abandon me from your protection, and I ask your blessing upon your devotee Paco, and that I am blessed with wealth for accomplishing what has been denied me. I go without fear, but if they direct that I should die and you do not protect me from failure, come and take me. So be it."

He lifted his Santa Muerte amulet to his lips and kissed it.

"Amen," Dixie said, raising her head.

Now that's a cutaway and a half, don't you think?

Dixie sidled up to Gina, turning her toward the limo. "You have been an absolute lifesaver, Gina, do you know that? You saved Bobbie's life and then you come all the way out here to act on your vision and end the curse. How can we repay you for all your troubles? Are you OK to drive all the way back to the city? Perhaps you can take Morty with you?"

"Nonsense." Robert stepped forward. "It's late, everybody should stay the night. If she drove back now they wouldn't be home until three in the morning. That's not safe. Please, Gina, Morty, stay the night, we have plenty of room. In fact, come on in and have a drink. I for one could go for a Scotch."

Remember those laser beams in Dixie's eyes? Now we see them, and they are boring right through Grant.

"*Sweetheart,* I'm sure these people have better things to do than—"

"Hey, I could go for a drink!" I smiled and turned to Gina. "Let us both stay and then drive together back to Manhattan in daylight. It has been far too long a day, yes? I am sure you would not refuse the hospitality of the man who is so indebted to you."

I could see Gina hesitate and avert her eyes. "You're very kind, but I have this aunt who needs me."

"Who is with her now?" I asked.

"Well, my other aunt, but . . ."

I persisted. "This other aunt—is she the kind to abandon the other aunt?"

What was I up to? Yes, I did not want to miss the opportunity—

however remote—for some sort of hanky-panky, preferably with
Gina, though Dixie remained a possibility. Still, my motive to stay
the night was more than that. I may be an idiot at times, like with
allowing myself to be taken for a ride by Purity, but I am from
East Brooklyn, after all. Street smarts count.

Gina still hesitated, but without much hope: "Well . . ."

"I insist!" Grant put his arm around Gina on one side and me
on the other, guiding us toward the house. "Dixie? Perhaps you
could go upstairs and check on Purity. I'm guessing she was probably pretty drunk, am I right?"

The look of dismay on Dixie's face melted to reveal a sly smile.

"Yes, *of course*, Bobbie, I'll go right up and make sure she's OK."

Cut to Paco's POV of Purity coming through the balcony doors,
hurriedly stripping off her clothes. She headed for the closet and the
deadly headhunter Paco.

Footsteps on the stair made Purity stop and pivot back toward
the bed, where she kicked her clothes under the bed and dashed
off-screen to the bathroom, closing the door behind her.

Paco sees the bedroom door open. Dixie cautiously put her
head around the corner and peered at the bed.

"Purity?" She stepped into the room, a smile spreading on her face
as she surveyed the bed, then locked eyes on the open balcony doors.

Slowly, almost reverently, Dixie stepped toward the balcony.
From outside and below the balcony, we see her approach, looking over the edge, expecting to see Purity's crumpled body on the
patio. Behind her, we see Paco. He said, "Psst!"

Dixie looked like she'd been electrocuted—but Paco slapped a
hand on her mouth before she could scream.

"Girl no sleep." Paco jerked his head in the direction of the
bathroom. "No drunk."

From the bathroom, there was the sound of the shower coming on.

In the living room, from behind the fancy polished bar, Grant had fixed Gina and me up with glasses of wine. And for himself?

He had just poured Dixie and himself a big fat Scotch from the poisoned decanter. Yes, eyedrops are a deadly poison. The prostitutes in Tijuana sometimes use it on their undesirable clients to avoid actually having to have sex with them.

It was at that juncture that I patted my jacket pocket and found an empty bottle of Visine. I thought this curious, but shrugged it off and tossed the small plastic bottle with my thumb and forefinger prints into a waste can next to the bar. Purity's trail of evidence pointing to me was impeccable, yes?

Grant raised his glass. "Well, here's to being rid of the curse. Hazzah!"

Dixie appeared in the doorway, trying not to look frazzled. "Thank goodness, darling."

"Dixie? Is, uh, is Purity sleeping?" Grant's glass hand went half mast.

"She's fine." Dixie patted her hair, her voice quavering ever so slightly. "She's in the shower, of all things, poor dear."

The glass slipped from Grant's hand, shattering both Dixie's drink and the decanter on the bar.

Cut to Purity, conked out in the corner of the white tile shower.

Cut to Paco, sacked out among sacks of grass seed in the murky gardener's shed.

Cut to Tony, laid out on the leather in the back of the limo.

THIRTY-EIGHT

ONCE THE BROKEN GLASSWARE WAS swept up and tossed, Grant and Dixie excused themselves to bed after an exhausting day. We were directed to the guest cabanas by the pool for our lodging.

Had they had that glass of Scotch, the entire story would have ended differently, and I would of course not be awaiting my execution. A long prison term in a New York State penitentiary, perhaps. The Visine bottle with my fingerprints on it in the wastebasket and the recording on Purity's phone may have done the trick.

Grant's cheating the Reaper had the advantage of leaving me alone with Gina. Unfortunately, she wasn't touching her wine. I will be brutally honest: Like most men, beyond the initial flirt to compel a woman to join me for a drink or dinner, I have almost no game unless a woman is half-snookered. It is a mystery to me how Mormons and the Amish seduce their women. One of those nature shows on public television should study this.

Yet as I suggested, this East Brooklyn kid knew there was more going on here than met the eye. This was my opportunity to explore exactly what this something was.

Gina was quick to set her untouched goblet of wine on the bar. "Well, I should turn in. Good night."

"I'll turn in, too." I poured her glass into mine.

"You don't have to."

"Do you like spiders?"

I would like to see the statistics on this, but I would bet you that only one in a hundred women do not find clumsy, nearsighted little spiders terrifying. These sad creatures are minding their own business when suddenly they are demolished into a paste by a shoe a thousand times their size. I think spiders would be flattered to know how much fear they instill in humans, who are perhaps a million times bigger than them, while at the same time more than a little mortified at how indifferent we are to destroying a fellow life form.

"*Spiders?*" Gina's pupils went wide.

"Pool cabanas are usually home to a few, especially in the bathroom." I took a gulp of my wine. "I will come and destroy however many there are if you would like."

Her eyes shot back toward the mansion's front door and the limo. It was obvious she was thinking of changing her mind about staying.

I guided her by the elbow to the sliding glass doors. "Besides, we need to talk about that ring."

"Not *big* spiders, right?"

"I would not expect any of the ten-pound variety like we have in La Paz, no." I flashed her a smile as I opened the door of the first cabana and flicked on the lights. It was like a quality motel room—just a bedroom, writing desk, and bathroom. "I would like to know why you have stolen the ring, Gina."

Lies are in the eyes, as they say. This is why men will not look a woman in the eyes when discussing serious relationship matters.

If you never look a woman in the eyes during one of these excru-
ciating interviews, it merely looks like a mannerism. Men know
that if you do actually look women in the eyes when they ask ridiculous questions like "How much do you love me?" or "How often
do you watch porno?" they will be able to tell from your eyes that
you are not telling the entire truth. Or worse still, they will in-
terpret apprehension as an indication of untruthfulness. I have
found women, on the other hand, convinced that the reverse tac-
tic is to their advantage. Specifically, I believe women think that if
they *always* look a man straight in the eye when lying or telling
the truth, we will not easily tell the difference. To their credit, this
is largely true because most men are not detail-oriented. Have you
ever seen a man try to fold a fitted sheet? I rest my case.

"The ring exploded, you saw it." Gina suppressed a blink, her
eyes locked on mine, arms folded across her chest. Alas, Gina was
not as good a liar as she was an actress.

I laughed softly and patted her warm brown shoulder. "I am
from East Brooklyn, Gina. As we say on the boulevard, five-pound
salami, four-pound bag."

I turned and entered the bathroom.

Sure enough, I found and vanquished a tiny helpless spider sleeping next to the bathroom sink. I came back into the main room
with the tissue in hand. "They do the exploding ring trick on the
boardwalk at Coney Island."

Gina was rigid in the doorway, arms crossed tightly, yet still
delectable. "I don't know what you're talking about."

It was not easy outing this devastatingly beautiful girl's
subterfuge—had she burst into tears, I probably would have re-
canted my accusations. I kept looking at that nostril of hers, the
one that looked slightly larger than the other.

"I think you do, and would bet you that the ring would magically reappear if you dropped your panties. I would imagine that perhaps you put it in your cleavage except that without a bra that would be a less secure place to have hidden the relic."

"I think you should leave." They say hell hath no fury like a woman scorned. They should also say heaven knows no disappointment like a woman caught in a lie.

"Very well, I will go wake the Grants and tell them of your deception. While I do so, you can go wake your cousin or whoever he really is, the one in the limo, and start your escape. However, if you ask me, this would be an unfortunate choice on your part. People like Grant can really get the police and district attorney motivated. You will not likely get as far as the expressway."

Her face was flushed red, which looked unusual on such a stunning woman, mostly because it made her look mortal.

She stepped farther into the room and gently kicked the door closed.

Her eyes were still on mine, cheeks flushed. With her thumbs she hiked her dress up and jerked her panties to her knees.

The ring bounced to the carpet.

She stood legs apart, panties down, head slightly cocked, her eyes twinkling lightly.

THE CAMERA PROVIDES US WITH an overhead shot of Grant and Dixie in a bed with far too many fancy pillows, the way rich people like them. He is in navy pajamas; she is in a pink nightgown. Both stare blankly at the ceiling, wide awake.

Dixie shakes her head slowly. "OK, I see why you asked them to stay, more witnesses of where we were when Purity fell off the balcony. I get that. What I don't get is that the ring exploded. Gracious, I mean, who is this girl? Why is she suddenly running off to the bushes with you?"

"I told you, nothing happened."

"Then why was your shirt torn open?"

"I told you, she wanted to see if I was wearing the whatchama-callit, the talisman."

"And you took it off? After what happened?"

"I told you, it itches. You try wearing it for a while."

"So now we have to cancel the Gulfstream jet to Baja and come up with another plan."

"At least the ring part of it is solved. I really don't care if the ring actually exploded or not so long as I have the original."

"We certainly can't take Paco and Purity on the jet down to Baja, can we?"

"I'm looking forward to putting the ring back on my finger. I feel naked."

"Although if we did take them both down to Baja, it might be easier to kill her there. The police investigations would certainly be a cinch, and there are snakes and things down there."

"Gee, Dix, then why not just invite Morty and Gina while you're at it?"

Dixie and Grant looked at each other.

"Bobbie, that's brilliant."

"It is?"

"We get Morty back to Mexico lickety-split, for one, and we should probably give him ten thousand or so for the parish, just to smooth things out."

"Or instead of making Purity's death look like an accident, make it look like Morty did it."

Dixie knit her brow and looked back to the camera in the ceiling. "I don't know about that."

"What, you like him?"

"No, of course not, he's nouveau riche. Just the same, I think that makes a frame-up complicated. Accidents happen all the time and are harder to disprove."

"You may have had a jealous moment about me this evening, but I have to admit I didn't like you meeting all the time with that greaser. I didn't like the way he was so close behind you when you opened the door this evening."

"You're sweet." Dixie kissed him on the cheek before resuming her study of the ceiling. "I definitely think we should deliver Morty back to Mexico, and Paco, too. If Paco is here in New York when he does the dirty deed, he has to get all the way back to Mexico to completely vanish back into the shark tank. I think we'd rather have him back there as soon as possible, and how much sooner could that be if he committed the crime in Baja?"

"We'd have to get him past customs in Mexico."

Dixie smirked. "Was there ever a Mexican customs agent that could not be persuaded to do a tycoon a favor? I don't see any problems."

"True."

Dixie clasped her hands, her excitement over this new plan growing. "I think drowning."

"Drowning?"

"Same plan pretty much as before. She gets drunk and does pills, the way everybody knows she does. Then she falls off the yacht, or takes the yacht out by herself, and Paco pushes her in. Shoot, I don't have it all worked out, but think of how easy and natural it is for drunk rock stars and celebrities like Purity to drown, happens every day. It doesn't leave a stain, either."

"No, we tried the accident, too uncertain. We use Morty as the fall guy. I don't like him. He's made a pest of himself." A crafty squint wrinkled his face—he despised me because he knew somewhere deep down that I had cuckolded him and was in the way of him bedding Gina. "The papers would love it. He goes from savior to sicko stalker."

"You're the boss." Dixie sighed, uncertainly. "I'll see what I can figure out."

CHAPTER

FORTY

THE CAMERA PROVIDES US WITH an overhead shot of
Gina and me mostly naked in the simple cabana bed. I am staring
blankly at the ceiling, wide awake. Gina is curled around me like
a question mark, looking sleepy.

"Morty, that was wonderful. It sounds like a line from a movie,
but I mean it, nobody's made love to me like that before."

Yes, she did actually say this, I am not puffing myself up.

"Ah, yes, well, you are an astounding lover, too."

In truth, making love to Gina was good, not astounding. In the
clinches, her best attribute was her remarkably alluring aroma,
that of summer and sunshine and that fresh-baked-bread-type
smell. Yet she had unfortunately given foundation to a theory of
mine. The prettier and the younger the woman, the less good she
is as a lover. How could this be? You would think that a stunning
creature such as this had been with a number of men and refined
her game, even at the tender age of the early thirties. Yes, but what
kind of men? These are men who have bedded her for her looks almost exclusively, for the sex, not for passion or genuine chemis-
try. So while I will not argue with Gina's assertion regarding my
skill, I wish to add that I don't think I was up against very stiff
competition, if you'll excuse the pun. Her past lovers clearly did

not train her well in the arts of give and take and the basic mechanics. Perhaps my expectations were unreasonably high, as well
they might be with a beauty such as hers. To be brutally honest, I
would wager the finger of my ancestor that the plump desk clerk
back at the hotel would have been a more compelling and frolicking
lover.

Never worship a woman, my friends, especially a stunner: She
will not respect you for it. Did you see? The moment I stopped letting her twist me around her finger—such as at El Rolo—but instead used the nostril and dominated her by confronting her with
the exploding ring gimmick, she found me immensely attractive.
She did not hop in the sack purely to get out of a jam about the
ring. It is like what I said earlier in the film about not letting a
woman know you care too much. Perhaps it is also true for the
women—never throw yourself at a man. You know, I think this is
probably true. It is better to play hard to get and not be gotten than
to play for keeps and only get kept.

Anyway, let's break the freeze frame of Gina and me and continue, but perhaps fast-forward a little through some of the more
explicit sex talk, to the point where we see me roll out of her arms
and return with the ring and the humidor, and the camera rolls
to one side as Gina gathers the sheets around herself and sits up,
her hair an unruly cascade.

I sat on the edge of the bed and put the humidor on the night
table. The finger in one hand, the ring in the other, I paused and
shot a look back at Gina.

"If the ring explodes this time, we can all just go home, how
does that sound?"

With a broad grin she bowed her head. "I guess I had that
coming."

I slid the ring on the finger.

It stopped at the first knuckle.

I pushed.

The finger creaked.

The ring would go no farther.

"This is most curious."

"Maybe Hernando's finger swelled from the ocean air?"

"The finger is in the ocean air in La Paz. Besides, it is kept in this smelly box. Yet the ring of my ancestor no longer fits on his finger, where it has been for five hundred years."

Gina sat forward. "Let me see."

I gave her the finger and the ring. She, too, found the ring no longer fit, and handed me back the finger. Scowling at the ring, she put it in her palm to gauge its weight.

"Morty, bring the bedside lamp."

Lifting the lamp off the table and jiggling the cord free, I held the lamp close to where she held the ring and switched it on. Gina turned the ring this way and that to the light.

She bit her lip. "Wouldn't they have used twenty-four-carat gold back in the conquistador age?"

"It would be pure gold, yes."

"Then why is this stamped fourteen carat on the inside?"

I cocked my head. "I am surprised they would have stamped rings at all back in those days."

"Oh, and it also says HAPPY GRADUATION, SON."

Gina and I locked suspicious eyes, the meaning of the inscription and what had happened taking a long moment to sink in.

Flashback: From behind the counter at a Forty-seventh Street jewelry factory, we see a plump Hassidic Jew waving good-bye to Robert Tyson Grant as he gets onto an elevator. The Hassid turns and pushes through a swinging door into a buzzing factory floor chockablock with jewelers hunched over their benches, some with unset diamonds and empty wedding rings spread out before them. The Hassid walks down a row to a metal shelf at the end, where he slides out a shoe box. He stirs his hand around in the box until he comes up with a large graduation ring with a chunky red stone in it. He eyes it and seems satisfied he has found what he wanted. Turning, he trudges down a row of jewelers until he stops at one of them.

"Jojo!"

A small dark man with thick magnifying goggles, a flexible shaft drill in his hand, looks up at the Hassid.

"Here!" The Hassid hands him the graduation ring and an eight-by-ten photo of the gold double-crossbarred crucifix ring of Hernando Martinez de Salvaterra.

"When?" Jojo's magnified eyes blinked.

"Chop chop. Now. Noon."

Jojo shrugged, and through his goggles the magnified inner band of the ring reads: HAPPY GRADUATION, SON.

Flash forward.

Gina and I are still staring at each other.

"The bastard gypped us," Gina spat.

I squinted, idly tossing the fake ring in my palm. "It is clear what we must do."

"Let's go wake the bastard." She started to get out of bed, but I put up a hand.

"Not so fast, my sweet." I cocked an eye at the gorgeous girl. "First of all, I need to know if you will help me, and not try to steal the ring again if we get it." She threw a hand in the air. "To be honest, I was only getting the ring for my aunt. For me it was more like an acting job."

"Your aunt?"

"She's a fortune-teller and had these two, Grant and the boobs, on the hook."

"You must be joking!"

With lips rolled, she nodded to indicate the affirmative.

"So your aunt—and I assume your cousin Tony got wrapped into this as well—was working a curse?"

Gina continued nodding.

"Let me guess. Tony was the masked man who you chased from Grant, and the same one I chased from Purity. Only he thought Grant was in the limo."

"It wasn't Satan, it was Tony."

"Where did he go last night?"

"I think he's still in the limo."

"These rich people think they are so smart. First they fall for the curse scam, then a jeweler passes them a fourteen-carat graduation ring for what is supposed to be a relic made from pure Hapsburg medallion gold." I held up the ring. "As Lincoln used to say, better to be a wise wretch than a rich fool."

"That sounds more like Benjamin Franklin."

"Maybe, but you see what I am trying to say, yes?"

"Do tell?"

"It sometimes astounds me that people who pay so little attention to detail and lack any street smarts do not have all their money taken from them overnight. So will you help me switch this ring for the other one?"

"Don't count on Tony, but I'm in." Gina smiled and bounced gently on the bed. "Sounds like fun. You're not mad at me?"

"We are all as God made us, and in a way, you may be part of His plan to pry the ring out of this deceitful tycoon and his wily paramour. You say you are an actress?" I put the finger back in its humidor and latched the lid shut.

"Yeah, but I'm not the right shape." She continued to bounce, and in a most delightful way. "Same reason I'm not a model. The clothes don't fit."

"That is, of course, quite insane." I cocked an eyebrow. "In Baja you *would* be the right shape, and they like it when the clothes on a woman are too small. I should help you to find work acting in movies there."

"Do they do martial arts movies? That's what I have on my résumé. I'm a yellow belt in Shui Ping."

"In Mexico they adore wrestling movies, which are almost the same thing. Very popular."

"I do speak some Spanish."

"Your exquisite shape is the only language you'll need in Mexican cinema."

She kept bouncing. I was still deep in thought, trying to figure out our next move, how to find out where Grant had the ring and how to swap it out with the graduation ring.

"Señor Morty?" *Bounce, bounce, bounce . . .*

"Yes, *querida*?"

"*Uno más, por favor?*"

FORTY-ONE

WE HAVEN'T HAD MANY SCENIC shots in this movie, except perhaps of Manhattan when we went zipping from one place to the next. I am running out of time with writing this story, my execution is next week, so I need to jump ahead to breakfast. Let us do as chapter 9 of *Screenwriting: Yes You Can!* suggests and insert a time lapse of the starry night over the ocean brightening until the horizon gives birth to an orange gooey sun. This will suggest the passage of time while setting the stage for the next scene, which was indeed quite a scene because all the major characters were finally assembled in one place: the poolside patio.

Beneath a sun umbrella, Grant sat at one end of an oblong glass-top patio table, Dixie at the other. He was in a white polo shirt and navy swim trunks; she was in a striped turquoise halter-top sun-dress. On one side was Purity in pigtails, large sunglasses, artfully torn black T-shirt, and matching pleather bikini bottom. She sat cross-legged in her chair and had not touched her scrambled eggs or the fruit or any of what had been plated for her.

Gina and I sat opposite Purity, she back in her black cocktail dress as she had no change of clothes, and I back in my tan suit.

Conversation had been sparse up to that point. Grant was expansive and hungry, but only when he was looking at Gina. Dixie was cautious and polite, the gears in her head clearly at work. Gina and I were sleepy but reviving from our escapades. She was much livelier *uno más* time around.

Purity was still trying to recover from the sleeping pills, a cigarette smoldering languidly between her lips. She cradled a large mug of coffee, texting on her phone and seeming to ignore the rest of us.

Topics of conversation had been limited to the kind of day that it was: classic summer beach weather, not too hot, breezy, sunny. All agreed that it was indeed a nice day.

I dabbed my lips with my napkin. "I must say that this has been a most unusual visit to the States, and the demise of the ring a most remarkable conclusion."

Grant gestured to Gina with a smile that made Dixie frown. "For me the ring hardly tops the way Gina saved my life."

"Yes, that is *remarkable*." Dixie beamed. "I mean, who was this mysterious attacker? Was he the same one that attacked Purity? What a coincidence."

"I am not so sure that it was coincidence." I held up a finger. "It is quite possible that this apparition was the agent of Satan himself, as Gina has suggested. After all, my mission to recover the ring was as an agent for the diocese, for Father Gomez of Nuestra Señora de Cortez, and thus by proxy for God Himself, yes? So who else would intercede against God other than Satan?"

Grant focused on me for the first time since I'd met him. "You are quite a religious man, aren't you, Mr. Martinez? You honestly believe in the devil?"

"How can I not when his work is all around us?"

"Let me ask you: If there is a God, why doesn't He do away with the devil? Why does He allow tragedy?" Grant's thumb worked the vacant spot on the finger where the ring used to be.

"It is not God who allows evil. Man allows it by inviting Satan and his works into his heart. If there were not God, only bad things would happen. There would be no good in men's hearts at all. As I believe Lincoln once said, men are men because they are free to do evil as well as good."

Purity mumbled, "John Burroughs, not Lincoln."

Grant pointed his fork at me. "This attacker could be almost anyone with a grudge against me, an insane person, a stalker. Isn't that easier to believe than he was Satan's manifestation?"

"I'm not sure I see the difference, actually, between the man you describe and Satan's agent. They could be one and the same." Grant's smug manner told me he had the ring on him and that he was talking about the ring being gone even while it was right here in the room with us, that he could feel the smooth gold relic against his skin. *Somewhere.*

"Yes, but why would this ring be so important to Satan?"

"An excellent question, Señor Grant. I would answer that question with another question: Why is the ring so important to *you*?"

"It was a gift, from a childhood friend who said it would bring me good fortune."

"Was it the ring or your business acumen that brought you the good fortune and the many riches you enjoy?"

"Like most people, I hedge my bets when it comes to luck. The success I made the old-fashioned way through hard work, determination, and timing. I'm sentimental about the ring. It reminds me of where I came from and how far I've come."

"Perhaps all the way from the orphanage in La Paz?"

"That's correct. One of the other orphans gave it to me. I had no idea of the ring's provenance, that it was a relic. I was hesitant to give it to you until we had verified your credentials with Father Gomez. You must understand that a lot of crackpots approach me with various ventures and start-ups, so I have to have everybody I meet vetted."

"But of course."

Dixie gasped. "Babykins, you never told me that story about the ring."

"Sorry, Dix, it's a very personal story, but what with all this fuss, and the ring being gone, well, I felt it was time to air it out, that's all. It is a shame the relic can't be restored, though it seems clear God wanted it this way. Perhaps that conquistador was never meant to have the ring in the first place." Somehow I think the conquistador he was talking about was me.

"Perhaps, though, its rightful place is with the church, guardian of all things sacred."

"Its rightful place *was* with the church until it burned up." To me it was as if he were saying, *I am way too clever for you. We both know I still have it, but there isn't a thing you can do about it. I am the rich and powerful tycoon, and you are but a lowly Mexican who has come scratching. You never even had a chance.* "In any case, I'm prepared to authorize a charitable donation from the Grant Foundation to your parish in the amount of ten thousand dollars. It is a gesture of regret that I was unable to return the ring and perhaps some compensation for the loss of such an important and rare relic." He was looking at Gina as he said this, trying to impress the girl with his largesse.

I sipped my coffee. "That is very generous, Señor Grant, and I'm sure Father Gomez will be able to put that money to good use, perhaps even toward the orphanage from which you originated." I was being outmaneuvered, and to be honest, had he turned me out then, I did not have a viable plan for discovering the ring's location and switching it with the graduation ring. "In fact, I am indebted myself to the Nuestra Señora de Cortez orphanage. You see, my father—"

"I know you made personal sacrifices to recover the ring for the church, and for that I'm sure Father Gomez is grateful. The least I can do, then, is to fly you back to Baja Sur this afternoon.

Dixie, Purity, and I are headed to Cabo San Lucas on my Gulf-stream this morning. Will you join us?"

"WTF?" Purity looked up from her phone, an inch-long ash from her cigarette dropping to her lap. "I'm going *where*? I was asked about this *when*?"

Dixie put a sympathetic hand on the table in Purity's direction. "Sweetheart, we know you were having trouble deciding on which rehab center to choose, so we picked one for you in Cabo."

"What's wrong with the one less than a mile from here?" Purity pointed a finger up the beach in dismay.

"The lawyers felt it would be better if you went out of the country this time. It is a little too easy for you to escape from the one here."

"Escape? What, am I a *prisoner*?"

Dixie smiled sweetly. "Either a prisoner in rehab or a prisoner in prison, take your choice."

"Hold the phone. *I asked to go to prison*."

"I think somehow a beach resort rehab will be a lot nicer than a state institution where you share a room with another woman whom you don't know. Sooner you go, the sooner you'll be out."

Grant raised his chin at me. "So can we give you a lift, Martinez?"

"Can I come?" Gina blurted, smiling at Grant. "Morty said he wanted to introduce me to some people in the film industry down there."

A brilliant tactical move by Gina, yes? She put Grant in direct competition with me, and he would not casually lose the prospect of Gina. Not to someone like me. Also, of course, if she came along she could help me recover the ring while in the evenings we *uno más*.

Dixie blinked rapidly. "Surely you don't have your passport with you, Gina?"

"Actually, I do, it's in my purse. I got back from some stunt work in Toronto yesterday, and it's still in my bag."

"Robert, is your Gulfstream large enough for all of us?" Dixie thought she was giving him an out, or possibly a mild put-down—but she was making it more difficult because she was making him admit that his jet wasn't big enough. Men inherently despise admitting anything belonging to them is not big enough, and if you need to know why that is so or need it explained, then you really should be watching SpongeBob instead of this movie.

Grant steeled himself. "The airport here can't accommodate *my airliner,* but the Gulfstream seats six."

Purity stubbed out her cigarette on the side of her chair. "BTW, if you need extra room, peeps, I volunteer to take one for the team and stay behind." Her comment was ignored.

"Gina, you haven't any luggage. What will you wear?"

"Who needs to wear much at the beach?" Gina threw up her hands. "Sometimes I like to just wear nothing at all. It's very liberating."

"I'll drink to that." Purity toasted the air with her coffee. "FYI, your limo disappeared overnight. What's up with that, Gina?"

"My cousin Tony slept in it because he had to drive home to his wife last night. They have a baby girl that keeps them up all night. He's a limo driver, too. We switch off." Gina turned and put a hand on Grant's forearm. "So, Robbie, is your jet big enough? Can we fly to Cabo with you?"

Grant patted her hand and flashed his toothy white smile. "Absolutely positively."

"This is most generous of you, Señor Grant." I dropped my napkin on my plate and stood. "After all Gina has been through on your behalf, your help in furthering her acting career is most appropriate, and I am sure she will be most grateful. I will gather my things."

"How about a swim?" Gina beamed at Grant but tugged my pant leg under the table, signaling me. About her swim? Ah! Grant would have to take his shirt and shoes off. I would then be able to search them, and we would be able to see if he was wearing the ring, or if he was reluctant to take his shirt off.

Dixie looked at her watch. "Honeybun, it's getting late, and the plane is waiting."

"My plane, my pilot, my crew." Grant slid his chair back. "There are suits in the cabana, Gina. Should be one your size, or close to it."

Gina giggled strategically and sashayed off to the cabana.

"I'm liking this girl more and more." Purity snickered under her breath, while continuing to peck away at her phone with her thumbs.

Just who was Purity texting? What was she discussing? Perhaps during the previous scene we can scroll Purity's conversation with Skip down one side of the screen while the rest of the scene plays out in live action. I could not find this technique in the screenplay book, so do not know if it is an innovation, but how else are we to capture on film what she was texting?

Skip: Working hatchet murder story. Wassup?

Purity: @ El Rollo w Morty last nite

Skip: U hook up?

Purity: LMAO vry fny

Skip: Out L8?

Purity: Not 2—Bobbie here w Dixweed whn we got home, Morty w a brunette

Skip: Get out WTF?

Purity: I was saved by Morty, grl saved Bobbie, same attacker

Skip: U dint rel8 this last nite!

Purity: I dint meet this grl til L8R

Skip: So this grl came home w Morty n hooked up?

Purity: YGAGA m9—Morty came 4 a ring from Bobbie, grl involved

Skip: ??? ring

Purity: spooky old relic magic ring w a curse

Purity: If u can bleeve it, Bobbie and Morty r now discussing God vs Devil over bfast

Skip: Put conv on the phone so I can hear

Purity: no time—ring went bang smhow

Skip: I cant follow this—whut?

Purity: Bobbie had sacred ring, relic, belonged to church in la paz, Morty sent here to get it

Purity: B gave ring to M but it blew up

Purity: Hly sht! Taking me to mex rehab! NFW!!!

Skip: When?

Skip: Hello?

Purity: fck—going to Cabo like NOW, Morty 2

Skip: U, Bob, Dix, Morty?

Purity: LMAO. Grl coming too, Dix iz pissed!

Purity: ROTFLMAO grl sez dznt need clothes, Bobbie in heat

Skip: when do u leave??? I will come down

Purity: come! Mi8 b big story, catch Bobbie fckg grl Dix freaks

Purity: Morty joker in deck, and I have a plan

Skip: grl name?

Purity: gina, limo driver, actress

Skip: last name?

Purity: dunno CUL8R n cabo

We see Purity's screen as she exits her messaging center and logs on to her Web browser. In the Google search box she types: INBOARD BOAT ACCIDENTS EXPLOSIONS.

CHAPTER

FORTY-TWO

SKIP'S BOSS AT THE *DAILY Post*—the wiry balding man in a sweater vest—was perched at his computer in a small, immaculate office with a narrow window view of another office building. He was typing extremely fast, studying the screen intently.

"Boss?" Skip knocked on the door frame as he stepped into it. "I worked that Mexican story for Bent pretty good, but—"

The boss kept typing. "Pretty *well*."

"—something has come up with Purity, something big. I need to get to Cabo San Lucas ASAP."

"Shut the door, have a seat."

When both were accomplished, the boss swiveled mechanically away from his computer and eyed Skip cautiously. "You've done well with the Purity story, but circulation thinks the story is wearing thin. Some in the industry are joking that we're in bed with Purity. Are you?"

"What? No!"

"Word around here is that you're actually sleeping with her." The boss held up a hand. "Not that there's *necessarily* anything wrong with that. That's a terrific way to stay on top of that story, if you'll excuse the pun. What's wrong is that it is beginning to show. Her antics are overexposed. We're taking a break from bedding with

Purity to find something for the readers to panic about. You'll work the Mexican story, see if we can find us a serial killer. If not, take assignments from Bent until you do find a serial killer that the readers can worry about. Readers don't worry about Purity."

"Work for Bent?"

"Until you find a story you can sink your teeth into."

"Boss, I'm telling you, something big is coming off in Cabo. Grant is there with Purity, and it looks like Papa Bear has found himself some sort of beach bunny. Meanwhile, there's some sort of business with Grant and a magic ring that's a holy relic that the church is trying to get back. Anyway, Purity is bound to pull a really big stunt. I just gotta get down there."

"Did you hear anything I said, Skip?"

"Well . . ."

"Did you?"

"I did, yes, but . . ."

"Beach bunnies? Magic rings? Purity crashes a Porsche into the Cabo San Lucas marina? That's TN2.com celebrity gossip. *Daily Post* is slap and tickle, Skip. We tickled them with Purity for a while, now it's time to slap them with a hatchet-wielding Mexican immigrant psycho killer. Purity might manage to kill herself somehow a couple months from now. We'll get back on her then. Get out of my office."

Like a machine, the boss swiveled back to his computer and began clacking away.

Out in the hall, the camera follows Skip as he walks slowly back to his cubicle and slumps down into his chair.

He wiggled his mouse. The computer screen came back on with one of the police sketches of Paco. Skip stared at the picture a moment, then lurched forward, moved his mouse around, and clicked his way to a Web site called Last Minute Travel.

FORTY-THREE

PAN ACROSS THE SUNNY EAST Hampton airport run-
ways and a small propeller plane taking off. Keep turning the camera until you come to Gina and me behind a fence at the airport's
drop-off, the limo fifty feet behind us. You can see Gina is now
wearing a colorful bikini top under her little black dress, and her
hair is up and obviously post swim.

"I checked, the ring was not in his shoes or his shirt," I whispered.

"He's got it on him," she hissed.

"On him? He was only wearing swim trunks."

"On him." Gina pointed down at her own lovely groin.

"There?"

"He's got it tucked under his nut sack."

Behind us, the limo trunk opens, and we see Grant and Dixie
help Paco out of the trunk. El Cabezador was now in black pants,
white shirt, and red vest. They stealthily huddle Paco off-screen.

"Impossible! How do you know this?"

"How do you think?"

"You . . ."

"I goosed him. Don't look at me like that! How else were we to
make sure he didn't have it on him?"

"So it is tied with string, or what?"

"I didn't exactly give him a Brazilian, Morty, I'm not sure how it's held there. String?"

I laughed. "Gina, I think I love you. That is amazing. You know, you really are fantastically deceptive—and you sure as hell have him on the hook!"

"I'm deceptive when I need to be." Gina dropped her sunglasses and favored me with her sapphire eyes, the kind that make men buy diamonds. "How about you?"

"I think you know me a little bit by now, yes? I am probably one of the more brutally honest people you will ever meet, especially with women. Honesty and trust is what makes me a good lover."

She raised her sunglasses, a devilish smile rippling across her most succulent lips. "An *awesome* lover."

Purity appeared next to us in shorts, low moccasins, shirt, and bikini top, her braids jutting out to either side of a Panama hat. Aviator sunglasses and cigarette completed her ensemble. Following her into frame is a nervous young paralegal in suit and tie.

"Morty! Turn around!" Purity held up a document and a pen. I turned.

She slapped the Ultravibe Media contract up against my back and began furiously signing page after page. "The paparazzi aren't here yet, but it's only AMOT. Let's roll."

FORTY-FOUR

I THINK THE BEST WAY to capture the flight to Cabo
would be as a vignette. *Screenwriting: Yes You Can!* mentions this
as a way to accelerate the storytelling without skipping over certain details that may be important or amusing. It is done without dialogue, usually to the accompaniment of music, which we
haven't discussed yet at all for this movie. There is much for me
to relate in this story, and little time, so I have not been able to fully
embellish my tale, though I am sure that the choice of music depends on whether you wish to have somebody like John Williams
or Lalo Schiffrin write an original musical score or you intend to
use Top Forty hits off the shelf. I perhaps am not entirely quali-
fied to choose music, as I am not what you would call a music buff.
I do not even own an MP3 player and those little white earplugs.
However, when I think about traveling to Mexico, how could I not
think of the instrumental music of Herb Alpert and the Tijuana
Brass? This is merely a suggestion, but I would think "Tijuana
Taxi" or "Spanish Flea" would be ideal for this vignette. If you do
not know these songs, they are catchy, and include horns like one
would find in a mariachi band. So cue the Herb Alpert.

The Gulfstream jet ripped down the runway and sliced into
the Hamptons summer sky. The jet's interior was spacious and

like a living room that happened to have luxurious swiveling leather seats bolted to the floor. Gina sat at the window on the right side, me next to her, Dixie across the aisle from me, and Grant next to the window on the left. Purity was in the seat behind me, sleeping with her sunglasses on, curled in a fully reclined seat.

Meanwhile, Paco, in his red vest, braced himself in the jet's galley. His yellow eyes studied the liquor bottles, the Perrier, the glassware, the wine cabinet and chilling champagne.

In the passenger cabin, we all unbuckled our seat belts. Dixie got up and went to the galley. She gave Paco instructions, pointing to the same features of the galley that he had been studying. The task of waiter did not seem to faze him, but he lifted his Santa Muerte amulet from his shirt and said a quick prayer that he perform the task of making cocktails adequately.

Dixie returned to her seat, making pleasantries across the aisle to me while Grant flipped pages in the *Wall Street Journal*. Gina studied the terrain below the jet with interest.

Paco strode purposefully down the aisle and bowed to Dixie. He listened to her order, Grant's, mine, and then Gina's. Purity declined any beverage and rolled over and went back to sleep.

In the galley, Paco found the ice, but the cubes were frozen into a mass. Out came his blood-rusted beheading hatchet, and ice chunks flew about the galley as he hacked away to free the cubes.

In the main cabin, I was politely listening to Dixie, but looked down when an ice cube came bouncing up the aisle.

In the galley, the cocktail steward hacked limes to pieces, cramming the wedges and ice into three large water glasses. Then he picked a bottle at random and sloshed a cup of dark liquor into each glass.

I continued to listen politely to Dixie when a champagne cork zipped up the aisle, bounced off the fuselage, and landed in my lap. Nobody saw this but me.

Paco appeared with a rolling drink cart, the champagne bottle overflowing. He handed Grant, me, and Gina the gargantuan cocktails, which he'd chosen to garnish with a tree-sized stalk of celery. Wiping out the champagne glass with the corner of his vest, he poured Dixie a glass of bubbly before retreating to the galley.

Dixie smiled apologetically and explained that Paco was new.

We all tasted our drinks with interest.

There seemed to be some unique flavor that we could not identify.

FORTY-FIVE

OUR CAMERA PROVIDES US WITH a wide shot out over a sea of tourists. They are standing in a serpentine line for Mexican customs at the cavernous Cabo San Lucas International Airport.

Zoom in on our troop: Grant and Dixie, me and Gina, Purity last and by herself. We are flanked by luggage.

Medium close-up of Grant and Dixie—she whispers to him, "I've got it, sugar."

"Hm?" Grant's mind is elsewhere, probably on Gina and how she cupped his balls in the pool.

"We send Morty a note from Purity asking him to meet her at the Ramparts, at night. We send her a note from Morty asking *her* to meet *him* at the Ramparts, same time. This puts them together. We just have to adjust the timing so that Paco arrives first, Morty second, and Purity third. When Morty arrives, I'll be dressed as Purity and lure him into the shadows, where Paco will be waiting to club Morty, knock him out, and plant evidence on him once Purity comes. I will hide up on the path to the villa and wait for Purity to pass me, to make sure she's headed to the Ramparts. Once she passes me, I'll come meet you on the yacht, while Paco does the dirty deed, makes it look like Morty did it, and joins us on the yacht, where we'll set sail, pay Paco, and drop him off somewhere else. Morty will awake and go back to the villa and report the murder but try to claim he didn't do it, yet all the evidence will implicate him. Case closed!"

"I like it!" Grant particularly liked it for his own reasons. "The timing is crucial, though. We'd better say we're going on an after-dinner boat ride in the speedboat, and that's how I'll transport you to the beach at the Ramparts. That way I'll be able to get back to the yacht quickly and get her ready to go."

Grant quickly imagines a scene in the yacht bedroom, Gina naked and straddling him. The door opens, and Dixie rages into the room with a gun. Cut to a newspaper spinning out toward our audience, and when it stops the *Daily Post* headline reads: GRANT MURDERED IN BOATY LOVE MEX-NEST. *Skip Baker, reporting from Mexico.* There is a picture of Dixie on the cover being led away in handcuffs by Mexican Federal Police.

"How long do you think all this will take?" Grant asked.

"I think from the time you drop me off maybe an hour? Purity is often late, as we know."

"An hour should do it."

"Do what?"

"Hm? Oh, should do it to warm up the yacht's diesel engine. You know how it stalls."

"Brilliant, sugar pie!"

Track the camera back in the customs line to a medium close-up of Gina and me. Men in the background crane their necks to sneak a look at Gina.

"I've got it, Morty."

"Hm? What is it you have?"

"Shrinkage."

"Shrinkage?"

"A man's package. In cold water, it shrinks."

I knit my brow. Penis abuse in any form is an instant affront to all men. "What exactly are you suggesting?"

"Well, if I were to lure Grant into some cold water, his package would shrink. The Li'l Guy goes *schwermp*." Gina illustrated with her fingers. "Don't the testicles also run for the hills, bunch back up into the body?"

I shifted uncomfortably. *"Schwermp?"*

"Exactly! Then the ring will fall off. I scoop it up and drop the fake in its place. That way I don't have to get close to his Li'l Guy. I mean, let's face it, if he thinks he's going to actually screw me he's got another thing coming, and there's a line I won't cross to get that thing out from under his nut sack."

"I am glad to hear you say that, *querida,* because I would not ask you to do such a thing and would think less of you if you would."

"Well, if the roles were reversed, and the ring were up inside Dixie's kitten, would you do whatever was necessary to get it?"

Women's capacity to ask men questions they must lie to answer never ceases to astound me.

"If you are clever and play upon someone's appetite and charm them, it is usually sufficient to gain whatever advantage you seek."

"So you think if you were going to boink her she'd pull it out in advance."

"Precisely so. Which is why you must arrange for this shrinkage to be a surprise, so that he does not have time to remove the ring."

"You don't think he'd be tempted to mambo with the ring tied around his nut sack?"

I shifted uncomfortably again. "Having not tried a stunt such as that, I can only speculate that it would indeed be possible to achieve. However, constricting the package at the place where it attaches like that might have unintended consequences."

Gina raised an eyebrow. "Do tell?"

"As I said, I have not attempted this stunt, so I do not know. Restricting blood flow in that region at critical junctures could prolong, delay, or even defer the culmination."

"Really?"

I eyed her suspiciously and directed the conversation elsewhere. "In any case, yes, I like your plan. Surely he is so smitten with you that you could lure him into a vat of molten lava, much less arctic waters."

"And you?"

"Me?"

"Yeah." Gina shifted her weight to one marvelously curved hip and squirmed seductively. A man behind her lost his balance and fell down.

I returned her gesture with smoldering eyes and a jaunty jut of my jaw. "I would add Tabasco to the lava, and icebergs to the icy water."

"See, this is why I like you so much." She smiled. "Unlike any man I have ever met, you're *not* smitten. You're just unbelievably charming, and unlike most men, you lie and flatter like you really mean it. Women really like that in a man. And you're from *Brooklyn*?"

"*East* Brooklyn."

Track the camera back in the customs line to a medium close-up of Purity, who glances in the direction of Gina and me and mumbles, "Get a room."

Her attention returns to her phone, where her thumbs peck away like angry chickens.

I guess we must write the text of what she is texting and scroll it down the screen. Can you imagine if you made a movie entirely about the youth of today? The entire dialogue of the movie would have to be scrolled down the screen, because I honestly do not think they speak directly with one another at all anymore, except for the intermittent "awesome" or "dude."

Skip: arrive 2nite

Purity: 2day!

Skip: no r-lier flts

Purity: time?

Skip: 6

Purity: Better hurry or u miss the show

Skip: show?

Purity: FYSBIGTBABN

Better put the translation on the screen, because even the most ardent and jaded texters may not know that one: *Fasten your seat belts it's going to be a bumpy night.*

FORTY-SIX

CABO SAN LUCAS IS MANHATTAN to La Paz's Brooklyn. Both are worthy seaside towns, yet people mostly visit one rather than the other. True, the terrains are similar: dry coastal town on a gentle slope leading to a wide bay, mountains in the background. Yet unlike La Paz, Cabo's downtown marina and the ocean beaches are mostly glitzy hotels and resorts. At the southern end of the town is a thin peninsula called Land's End that angles into the Pacific Ocean from the southern tip of Baja Sur. One finds various small beaches on this peninsula with a natural rock arch near the very end. People whale watch, Jet Ski, parasail, shop, eat, drink, and basically vacation in Cabo. So maybe we should do a montage like on the opening credits of the hit TV show *Hawaii Five-0* or possibly *Baywatch*. We show all the local attractions quickly so we can turn the camera across the bay to Grant's Italian villa on a cliff east of town.

Man, this place had it all. Three pools were built into the cliff in front and to one side, each cascading into the next with waterfalls. Stairs cut into the side of the cliff spiraled down to a protected cove and a private marina just big enough for Grant's vintage motor yacht and a slick red speedboat. There was a sauna, steam bath, and gym; the whole place was wired for surround sound.

Why anybody would want to work there I have no idea, but it had a business center conference room. Servants' quarters and a four-car garage were landside. As if that were not enough, it was of course, an Italian villa with five bedrooms, all of which had balconies with awesome views of the Pacific and Cabo itself. The sun set beyond Land's End. The living room had a huge teak bar that opened up to a large veranda with a fire pit and a Jacuzzi next to the pool and a trap range for shooting clay pigeons out over the ocean. Believe me, this place kicked butt, and would be the kind of spread anybody with Grant's money would be crazy *not* to own. All it needed was an airport, though I suppose the private helipad and sleek helicopter across the street sufficed.

He had named this place Villa del Destino Ganado, and these words were carved into the bleached stone arch of the villa's entryway. I stood looking up at the arch as the Mexican caretaker carted our luggage into the villa.

"That is most interesting." I pointed at the words. Gina stepped up next to me with a shopping bag. She'd shopped in the airport for clothes. Most women take a day to buy a simple blouse that makes them look fat. In ten minutes Gina threw together a wardrobe of tourist beach crap that on her looked like a million bucks.

"OK, so why is that interesting, Morty?"

"*Destino Ganado* is written in my family's crest. It is carved into the fountain that is in my villa in La Paz. It means—"

"Earn Destiny."

"I must ask Grant about that."

"Where did he go?"

"He and Dixie said they had some errands in town and that they would see us back here for dinner. I suppose that gives us time to freshen up. Those lines at customs are brutal."

"Think they put us in rooms near each other?" Gina grinned and began to walk backward into the villa.

I grinned back at her. "Could it be far enough?"

"Far enough?"

"To keep me from coming by to check for spiders?"

"Uno más?"

The camera looks down from a balcony and captures me pursuing Gina into the villa. The shot widens to capture Purity on the villa balcony, spying on us. Gina and I had our mischief, Purity had hers.

"That takes care of them for a while," she whispered and pivoted back into the villa.

Let us do a traveling shot and follow Purity as she jogs her way through the villa. The screenwriting manual says this can be done with a Steadicam, which allows the cameraman to jog directly behind her and follow her wherever she goes without making the audience feel like there is an earthquake. The use of a Steadicam will allow us a delightful view of Purity jogging from behind, those pigtails bouncing and her compact shape swaying splendidly. It might also be an excellent way to relate all the information above on the opulence of the villa without a *Hawaii Five-0* montage.

Purity jogged down the upstairs hall, through a beaded curtain, and down the steep and narrow back stairs, into a pantry. She opened the refrigerator and removed a large fish from a platter. Purity turned through a side door and went around a garden path and past a bespectacled gardener, down some rock stairs next to a waterfall, and around the base of one swimming pool. The blue Pacific was spread out to the right, rays of late-day sun streaming in behind her. On the left, she passed the entrance to the sauna and steam bath, both built in under the upper pool. Beyond was an intersection with a stairway going down and a promontory containing the trap range hut and shooting stations. Down the stair she went, steeply, the frothy ocean crashing on the rocks below and to her right.

Curving left around the cliff face, she came to a rock landing, the protected cove, and the top of a long aluminum staircase down to the private marina. Below, the vintage motor yacht and slick red speedboat bobbed gently at the dock. Purity stopped and looked up to the left, as does the camera. Mounted on a bracket bolted to the cliff face was a security camera pointed down at the boats below.

Purity took the large fish and speared it onto the bracket under the camera, but without letting the camera see her.

A flock of terns mobbed the fish, and their feasting obscured the camera's lens.

Purity jogged down the stairs, sunlight dappling the far wall of the cove.

Jumping down the last few steps onto the dock, she stopped to look behind her, sweat staining her shirt, her breath coming fast as much from the jog as from excitement. Satisfied the birds were still blocking the camera and that nobody had followed her, she turned and hopped aboard the wooden motor yacht.

Purity ducked into a passageway and then immediately went down some steep stairs into the bowels of the yacht. She hit a light switch and followed a series of caged bulbs that illuminated a low paneled passage. Past a stainless steel galley and vented teak doors, and at the end of the passage, was a door bearing the brass plaque ENGINE ROOM.

Opening the engine room door, she flicked the light on. The room gently gurgled to the sound of the bilge pump. Dimly glimmering in the center of the narrow room was an engine the size of a coffin. Various pipes and conduits ascended from the coffin to the ceiling on a column.

Let's go to a series of close-ups.

Her hand coursed the length of a small aluminum pipe as it twisted along the ceiling and down the column until it turned away from the column and came to a gap in the pipe bridged by a black rubber hose. Purity twisted the hose until one end slid off its aluminum counterpart. Gasoline spurted from the detached hose but trickled to a stop.

Next: Purity's hand plucked an ignition wire from the top of a spark plug and tucked it next to the engine block.

Next: Purity's hands held a gasoline can and poured gallons of fuel onto the floor around the engine and where the ignition wire was tucked next to the engine block.

Next: Her finger shut off the switch on the wall labeled BILGE PUMP. The gurgling stopped.

Next: Her fingers shoved rags into the door vent.

Next: Purity's hand on the brass knob gently closed the door to the engine room.

Cut to Purity on deck, where she entered the bridge and removed her dangling diamond earrings. A St. Christopher's medal hung from an electronic compass next to the ship's wheel, and she hooked her earrings onto the chain.

Jumping down from the boat onto the dock, she jogged to the stairs but stopped to look back. Flash fantasy time, a quickie.

We see Grant in full yachting togs and white captain's hat at the helm of the boat, Dixie by his side, lovebirds cooing at each other. Grant's hand turns the boat's ignition switch.

Cut to the engine room half filled with water, a gasoline slick on the surface, and then a close-up of the ignition wire tucked next to the engine block. A bright blue spark fires from the spark plug to the engine block.

Cut to a shot of the yacht from above as it erupts in flame, splinters of wood, and the white captain's hat cast high into the air as the boat is destroyed by the fireball.

Back to Purity's wild, excited eyes as she imagines this great moment. She turned and charged back up the stairs to the villa, the birds still flocking around the camera.

FORTY-SEVEN

IN TIME LAPSE, WE SEE the sun sink low over Land's End from the veranda at Villa del Destino Ganado. Cabo San Lucas is in purple shadow, the festive lights of the resorts beginning to twinkle.

We must end the time lapse at sunset for some important action.

Gina and I stepped out onto the veranda, goblets of wine in hand. She was in a simple white cotton peasant dress that on her could just as soon have been something from a Paris runway. I was in a black collared shirt and my white suit pants.

"Beautiful!" Gina smiled at the sunset, the orange light dazzling in her blue eyes.

"Yes, very beautiful." I said this looking at her.

"Now don't go getting all smitten on me, Morty."

"Do I look smitten? Nonetheless, I think you should know I appreciate your beauty *almost* as much as your cunning."

She looked at me suspiciously, but laughed. "That's really nice. Thank you."

"No, thank *you*. A most passionate afternoon." If I do say so, she was coming along nicely.

"Back at you."

We clinked glasses.

My mood shifted as I looked back in the direction of the living room, and then led Gina to the veranda railing. "I have to show you something. It was in my room when I returned to change for dinner."

I handed her a folded note, which she unfolded and read in a whisper.

"*Meet me on the west end of the Ramparts at 9:00 P.M. I have something important for you, Purity.* What's this about?"

I shrugged. "I cannot imagine."

"But you just left a note for Dixie to meet you at the helipad to lure her away so I could get at Grant."

"Yes, now there are three notes."

"Purity is trying to cozy up to my guy? And my guy is trying to cozy up to Dixie. And Grant is trying to cozy up to me."

I began to say one thing, cocked an eyebrow at her, and said something else. "Three notes?"

"I got a note of my own, shoved under the door when I took a shower. Here."

I unfolded a very similar piece of paper and whispered aloud. "*I have not forgotten our kiss or swim, and wish to continue. Meet me on the yacht at 9:00 P.M. RTG.*"

We shared a mutual moment of perplexity, holding each other's notes and squinting. Or is it perplexion?

The camera is on Dixie as she enters the living room and sidles up to where Grant is pouring himself a Scotch. The audience can see Gina and me on the veranda in the background.

Dixie had a wary eye on us. "Cuddlekins, take a look at this." She handed Grant a folded piece of paper.

Grant knitted his brow and whispered the note. "*Querida, we must meet, the helipad at 9:00. 9:30, I have some important information about Grant you should know. Regards—Sr. MM.* Information about me? Like what?" He probably suspected I was going to spill the beans about Gina's stolen moonlight kiss.

Dixie looked vexed. "Robbie, Morty is merely saying that to get me to meet him. We're in the home stretch here, so try to stay sharp."

"Why would he want to meet you?"

"Why do you think?" Dixie wiggled her hips. "When you came in the other night, with Gina, I have to tell you, Morty was making advances."

Grant scowled, his face red, his eyes turning to me on the veranda.

She patted his arm. "Now, now, sugar, nothing happened, and I'm only meeting him down at the Ramparts briefly to lure him."

"He did *something*! What?"

"He felt my bottom."

Once again, Dixie thought she was pulling Grant one way, keeping him focused and determined in the stretch. Yet at the same time she was pushing him toward Gina. Grant not only wanted me convicted of murdering Purity, but he also wanted to make sure I didn't get Gina. His spite meter was in the red zone.

I know it may seem a little odd that he was angry at me for trying to *cheat with* Dixie when he in fact was intending to *cheat on* Dixie. Alas, this is the way men's minds work sometimes.

Cut back to Gina's and my thoughtful pause on the veranda.

Gina spoke first. "Imagine if I gave Grant a note—then there would be four notes and probably four meetings at nine o'clock."

"I changed my appointment with Dixie to nine thirty. That should still keep her out of your hair so you can meet Grant at nine."

"So you're going to meet both Purity and Dixie?"

"I think I must. For all I know, Purity has something genuinely

important to tell me. She is troubled, and I admit to feeling somewhat protective of her since I have saved her life twice."

"Mm hm. Just keep it zipped, bubby. I know how charming
you like to be."

"*Querida,* you have my word. Three notes. Coincidences like
this are like a tarantula in the bathtub. Obvious but unwelcome.
You kissed Grant?"

"It was the only way to get him to cough up the ring."

"The *fake* ring."

"Are you saying I'm cheap?"

"I'm saying that you are cunning and yet beautiful."

"You two arguing?" Purity limped out onto the veranda with
a green margarita glass. She was in a blue patterned bikini and
matching shawl skirt. "Morty, could you do me a favor?"

"Of course."

"I have some earrings, and I think they're down at the yacht,
down that path. I twisted my ankle. Could you go down and get
them? I remember hooking them onto a chain hanging from the
compass in the bridge."

"At your service." I smiled, set my wineglass on a table, and
went off to retrieve the earrings.

Purity and Gina were alone.

"So did you and Morty fuck really hard this afternoon?" Purity said this as casually as if she'd remarked upon the weather.
She sipped her drink.

"Hm." Gina could give as good as she got. "On the hard-fuckness
meter, I'd say it was about an eight. Night's early, though. What do
you have planned?"

"Vivisection, the usual." Purity's phone chimed, and she peeled
away from Gina just as Grant and Dixie emerged from the bar
area. Grant looked like he was ready to play tennis, with a sweater
tied around his shoulders and a Scotch in his hand. Dixie was in

a snazzy orange jumpsuit with a halter top and a glass of white wine.

We see her texts witten on the screen.

Skip: M here—hotel mar del cruz—CU n town?

Purity: yoyo [you're on your own]

"Looks like we just made it in time for sunset over Land's End!" Dixie tilted her head at Grant and then blinked at Gina. "We're so glad you could join us here at Villa Destino."

"I certainly appreciate you having me. This is quite a treat."

Skip: ??? wrud [what are you doing]

Purity: OMW out

"Where's our Mr. Martinez?" Grant asked, hoping that I had gone back to La Paz.

"Went to fetch something. He should be right back."

Dixie adjusted her halter top. "He's missing a nice sunset. Life's too short to miss nice sunsets. We're going on a romantic boat ride later to see the lights of the town. We'd invite you along but it's just the two of us."

Skip: with Morty?

Purity: he left me a note, wants me 2 meet him @ 9 @ ramparts

Purity was in the background and looked up from where she was texting on her phone. "You should take the yacht and do a hot tub."

Grant shifted uncomfortably. "Not a bad idea."

"A sailing yacht?" Gina sipped.

"She's called *Premiere*." Grant puffed with pride. "A motor yacht, a classic from the fifties, she was built by a shipbuilding magnate who had it custom built. Later it was owned by a Hollywood producer. He entertained many famous movie stars and personalities of that era on *Premiere*, in fact some even motored with him to Cannes."

Gina acted impressed. "She sounds like a one of a kind."

"She is." Dixie grinned, and turned. "Purity, what are your plans this evening? You're not planning on taking that scooter out on the local roads, I hope."

Skip: Ramparts a bar?

Purity: CD9 [parents in room] VCDA [vaya con Dios, amigo]

"My plans are to chill."

I may have been missing the sunset, but I was becoming more familiar with the geography. On my way back from retrieving Purity's earrings, I became lost, which with all the paths around the grounds of Villa del Destino Ganado was not hard to do. When I came up the stairs, I zigged instead of zagged, and found myself at the edge of the garden and property where the land abruptly returned from the lush plantings to an arid scrubland. I found a signpost there with an arrow marked THE RAMPARTS. It pointed along a path that wound down the cliff face to a small beach in the distance. Looming over this beach were towering pointy rocks that isolated the little beach from all but Grant's villa.

I squinted, wondering about that note. Did Purity want me to service her on that little beach? Would I once again have to explain to her that I was not attracted to her sexually? If she wanted me alone, and it was not about sex, why would she want me to come all the way down that path at that little beach? I also had to think about Dixie. When I met her at the heliport, how was I to delay her there without attempting to make love to her? *If so, should I?* To be brutally honest, even though you may not believe it based on my roving eye, I have never been one to double up on my women. I simply do not enjoy charming two women back and forth. No matter which one I am with, I imagine I am with the other. I end up only half as passionate with both, which serves nobody's purposes. Besides, what kind of idiot would I be to jeopardize what I had going with Gina, one of the world's great beauties, for an overly mannered southern belle slipping past her prime? Yes, even considering her notable bedroom skills and that whole thing she did with the silk scarf. Besides, I was genuinely coming to feel Gina and I were on the same page, that after a couple weeks our relationship would not become a protracted shopping spree punctuated by afterthought sex, and that she would not attempt to lower my cholesterol or enroll me in a tantric yoga course. To many women, every man is a fixer-upper, and when they have him fixer-upped, they have no further use for him other than as the bearer of their shopping bags.

Gina was disadvantaged by being overly attractive. She did not trust men because few to none of them had been able to get beyond her utterly devastating outward appearance in order to actually listen to any of the words that came out of her mouth. She did not trust women because few of them had ever been able to forgive her for her utterly devastating outward appearance. This disability had ruined her chances for both love and a career.

I am perfectly suited for this type of woman, and I will tell you why. From this film treatment you have seen that I genuinely love all types of women, and I get a great deal of satisfaction charming them and making them feel special, whether it is the plump one from the hotel desk, Dixie with the implants, or Gina, the very picture of female perfection. I greatly appreciate Gina's body, don't get me wrong. She is one of the few women I've ever encountered who was more spectacular naked than partially clothed, and that says a lot, but looks and sex appeal are not an end-all for me. Crazy, I know. I can be with Gina and not be smitten, which is the only kind of man she can trust.

Anyway, time is short. I had better get off my soap container and relate my wanderings through that garden, along the winding path, past the gardener's shed not far from the trail to the Ramparts.

I heard a low and serious voice from within the shed, speaking in Spanish, almost like a chant. Curious, I put an eye to the partially open door.

Shadows of rakes and pitchforks and scythes danced on the walls by the light of a candle. Kneeling before the candle on a packing crate was the clumsy airline steward. In front of the candle on the crate was a crude hatchet. I recognized it as the type Mexican field hands use to harvest pineapples. Held reverently in his hands was the amulet, and even from where I stood I recognized it as the image of Santa Muerte.

I stepped back from the door and continued on my way. Hey, whatever floats your boat, right? Live and let live. Or whatever.

FORTY-EIGHT

LET US FAST-FORWARD THROUGH DINNER at the oversized Moorish dinner table because it was a formality. Everybody's mind was elsewhere, yet conversation was necessary. Of course, Dixie did most of the heavy lifting in that department, complete with mild put-downs to Gina and regular boasts about the ardor she and Grant shared for each other.

Purity texted through most of the meal and said nothing and was pretty much ignored as she had been on the flight. Grant and she never even looked at each other. Not then, not ever that I saw.

So we zip through the meal, candles burning down, the wine bottles being depleted in direct proportion to the growing tension and anticipation over the evening to come. I would venture that if there were any lapses in judgment that fateful evening, ones that seem curious in hindsight, you might ascribe some of that to the wine. Everybody was half in the bag when we scuttled away from the table.

I think we can see the initial deployment of various schemes best using a crane shot at the back of the villa. Panning slowly right to left. Grant and Dixie—carrying a small duffel bag—trot down the path toward the marina.

As we pan farther left, Gina, seen through her balcony in her bedroom, is holding the fake ring and tucks it into her most delectable bikini top, adjusting it so it doesn't show in the mirror. The mere thought of her doing so gives me a manly shudder. The ring secure, she picks a tropical shawl off the bed and wraps it over her shoulders for warmth.

The camera comes to my room, and me seen from my veranda. I am brushing my teeth and checking the whiteness of my smile in the mirror, adjusting my testicles. Yes, ladies, they need adjusting, it isn't something we do for fun.

Then the camera comes to Purity's room, where we see her slip into a flashy short dress, her hair carefully messed and moussed for a night out on the town. A clever girl, spirited, and I admit that I still like her spunk even if she did make the effort to frame me, the man who more or less saved her life twice.

As we pan farther left, we leave the house behind and see the gardens. We zoom into the gardens, until we see the candlelight flickering in the gardener's shed, Paco muttering his prayers in Spanish. Cue subtitles:

"I go without fear, but if they direct that I should die and you do not protect me from failure, come and take me. So be it."

We hear the candle blown out and the screen goes dark.

FORTY-NINE

WAVES GUSH ONTO THE SHORES of Rampart Beach by starlight. Grant's motorboat emerges from the darkness, the engine shutting down as it slides with a sizzle onto the beach. The towering spires of rock look over the silhouette of Grant and someone in pigtails. Purity? No: She speaks and it is Dixie, and we see her adjust her wig as she whispers to Grant.

"So do we have it straight, smoochie? With the ether from *la farmacia,* Paco and I will subdue Morty. Then I go down the path and hide and make sure Purity comes down the path before heading back to meet you at the yacht. Paco will do what he does, leave the weapon with Morty, and follow me to the yacht to be paid. We motor him up the coast to San José San Cabo, send him on his way, make sure we are seen at the marina for the alibi."

"So what time do you think you'll be back?"

"Ten-ish. Purity is not exactly punctual."

"Got it. Good luck—and be careful!"

Dixie patted him on the check. "I *am* a force to be reckoned with, or hadn't you noticed?"

Grant gave her a quick kiss, and in silhouette we can see by her hesitance that she expected a longer embrace. She clambered over the front of the boat and into the waves, giving the boat a shove back out into the ocean. Grant started the motor, waved, and sped away. Dixie stood on the beach, small duffel over her shoulder, wearing a blond pigtail wig and Purity's wardrobe.

"Señorita?"

Dixie shrieked, startled:

Paco was standing behind her. He was dressed in dark coveralls, perfect camouflage for the shadows of the rocks. In one hand he held his curved pineapple hatchet. In the other, a gardener's sickle.

Even as I began my hike down to the Ramparts, Gina started down the steps to the yacht, and Purity wheeled a Vespa out of the garage.

BY TEN O'CLOCK, THE CLOAKED specter of fate had
begun his dastardly plan for us all.

I arrived at the beach a little after nine, and by starlight alone
saw who I thought was Purity in the shadows. I went in that direction, and that is the last thing I remember. I am not sure how
I was subdued other than by the ether, as my only injury was four
scratches across my chest. They were meant to look like those
suffered by a rapist being clawed by his victim.

By ten I lay on the sand in a dark, hidden crevice of the rocks.
Paco squatted next to me. In one hand he held the sickle, and in
the other the ether, ready to make sure I did not awake until Purity
was dead next to me. He was waiting to make his kill.

Dixie was halfway along the path to the villa, up a ledge, checking her watch. Her impatience got the better of her. She clambered
down and began hiking back to the villa.

Cut away to the yacht, where Grant had Gina cornered on a sofa,
his arm around her where he could keep an eye on his watch and
the time. Glasses of champagne were in their hands.

"Robert, you know I like you, but I can't have a relationship with you. It can only be for sex, you know that?"

"That's a good place to start." He giggled and moved in for a kiss. She turned her neck to him and he began slobbering on it. Well, perhaps I should say he was kissing her neck, but I don't like imagining this.

"You have to know something, Robert. I like sex in the water."

That bastard giggled again from the confines of her nape. "Great, the Jacuzzi is all warmed up."

"Oh. I was going to say I don't mind cold water." Gina winced, her eye searching her surroundings for some recourse other than having to let him grope her in the hot tub.

He stood, pulling Gina to her feet with one hand and wrapping his other arm around the champagne bucket. "Let's go!"

Dixie stood in the garage staring at where the Vespa had been. She bent down and picked up Purity's phone, which was on the ground, obviously dropped by accident.

Dixie hissed, "That *bitch!*"

We see Dixie heading back down the path to the Ramparts, cursing under her breath, cell phone in her hand.

Grant led Gina out to the aft deck and flipped a switch. The Jacuzzi glowed green, plumes of bubbles erupting from the depths. With a beguiling smile, Gina dropped her skirt. In only a bikini, she placed her lovely behind on the edge of the tub and rotated her legs into the water.

"Coming?"

Still holding the champagne bucket, Grant was momentarily

hypnotized by Gina's otherworldly pulchritude, second only to Aphrodite on a good day.

"Here." Gina reached out her hands. "Give me the champagne so you can undress."

He did so hurriedly, and Gina plunked the bucket on the edge of the tub.

Before he could step back she let the bucket tip forward, then pretended to try to catch the bucket from falling.

Instead she sloshed the icy water on the front of his pants.

Grant's whoop of penile surprise echoed through the cove.

Paco peeked around the corner of his cubbyhole and did a double take.

He saw the approach of a woman in blond pigtails and jumped to his feet. His back flat against the rock wall, Paco brandished both the sickle and the hatchet, me sprawled at his feet.

Paco whispered in Spanish, "Santa Muerte, do not abandon me from your protection, and I ask your blessing upon your devotee, Paco, and that I am blessed with wealth for accomplishing what has been denied me."

"I am so sorry, Robert!" Gina splashed out of the tub and to where Grant stood hissing and waving his hands at his sides. "You want me to rub it?"

Like any man who has had a penile surprise, Grant was in too much shock to hear what she was saying or to do anything but hope the moment would pass quickly. He had hunched over and was making woofing sounds, one eye closed.

"Let's get you into the warm tub just the way you are!" Gina guided Grant in shuffling steps back to the edge of the tub. "One leg, then the other, that's the boy."

She heard a plunk and looked back.

The gold Caravaca ring of Hernando Martinez de Salvaterra was in a puddle on the deck behind her.

As Grant lowered himself into the Jacuzzi, he shuttered violently.

"Oops! My suppository fell out!" Gina crouched out of view for perhaps five seconds.

When she reappeared, Grant had recovered enough from his penile surprise to ask, "Suppository?"

Gina had battled men's advances her entire adult life, and unfortunately some of her childhood as well. With women of lesser beauty, feigning a menstrual cycle would be an adequate defense against the onslaught. Gina had learned that for her there was really only one thing that would absolutely, positively make men not want to slip her the wood.

Gina lifted one leg and then the other into the glowing green Jacuzzi. "Oh, it's nothing, you'll hardly feel it." She handed Grant his champagne glass and settled in next to him.

"Hardly feel what, where?"

"It's just medicine. Now where were we?"

"Medicine?" Grant's brow was a tower of furrows. "Medicine for what?"

"I mean, once you've got it, it really isn't that bad. People make such a big deal."

"They do?"

Gina had wrapped herself around Grant, which under any sort of ordinary circumstances should have put him instantly back into an amorous mood. However, even as he may have recovered from one variety of penile peril, he was now experiencing another.

"Make a big deal about what?" he asked.

"The *sores,* silly, and the occasional discharge. It's nothing. You'll see."

Head hung low, Paco knelt at the starry water's edge. Waves crashed before him, ocean foam surging forward and swirling around his legs. He was shirtless, an elaborate tattoo of Santa Muerte's grim scythe-bearing visage on his chest. In his hands was the pineapple hatchet. The jagged, fanglike rocks of the Ramparts rose ominously behind him.

In subtitles:

"Oh, Santa Muerte, I have called upon you for guidance but have accepted your will. You have helped me travel far, been my guiding light on my mission, and brought me full circle to this place in my homeland so that I might honorably complete my mission and return to my people with pride. It is not for me to question how or why you have done this only to abandon me from your protection at the most critical moment. No, I, Hermes Pacifico Diego Ramirez, El Cabezador, accept the meager destiny that you have bestowed, and I ask your blessing in returning me safely to my people, and hopefully with some small recompense for accomplishing the journey, despite the outcome, so that I might claim some small measure of success. I go without fear, but if you direct that I should die and you do not protect me from failure, come and take me. My soul is as ever always yours, Santa Muerte. So be it."

Paco unfolded himself and stood bare-chested in the starlight. He tucked the hatchet behind him in his waistband, the blade between his shoulder blades. With grim resolve, he turned and strode up the beach toward the path back to the villa.

As the camera pans with him, we see in the distance that he picks up something the size of a soccer ball wrapped in his shirt.

He tucks it under his arm and marches toward the lights of the villa.

Gina was on the dock, shawl around her shoulders, and back in her skirt.

Robert was on the yacht, at the railing. "I'm sorry, Gina, I hadn't realized it was so late. I'm expecting Dixie. If you see her on the path just tell her you came down for a look at the Hollywood yacht, OK?"

Gina nodded and blew him a kiss.

Her beautiful legs made quick work of the stairs, and as soon as she turned the corner out of sight of the yacht she pulled the Caravaca ring from her bikini top. It dangled from a loop of string, and she favored the trinket with a radiant smile. "Gotcha!"

Footsteps approached, and her eyebrows shot up in alarm.

Gina crouched, making herself small in a crevice in the rock and hiding her face.

Paco tromped past on his way to the yacht, his shirt-wrapped package tucked securely under his arm.

Goggle-eyed from his close encounter with sores and discharges, Grant stepped up to the yacht's bar and sloshed Scotch into a glass from a decanter.

He took a sip, closed his eyes, and shuddered.

His eyes popped open, and he put a hand on his pants front.

Grant shoved his hand down his pants, feeling for the ring under his nut sack. His eyes darted this way and that as he retraced what had happened that evening. He hurried out to the Jacuzzi and turned it off. His face glowed green as he searched the depths of the tub for his ring. Turning, he began looking on the floor.

"Ouch!"

He stepped on something hard, wheeled, and stooped down out of frame.

He came back up into frame, fake ring in his hands, a smile of relief on his face.

"Gotcha!"

A close-up of the ring dissolves into a quick flashback, of young Robert being led by a young Father Gomez through the courtyard of the orphanage. Ahead stood a man and a woman, smiling, clearly the couple that had adopted him. The gold ring was clutched tight in Robert's hand, his eyes darting to the empty windows of the orphanage on either side. Yet one of the windows ahead was not empty. In the window was Pasqual, his eyes hooded, a scowl upon his lips.

Silently, Pasqual's lips mouthed the words *Destino Ganado*.

The yacht rocked, and Grant snapped out of his reverie.

Feet tromped up the gangplank.

"Dixie? How'd it go?"

From the darkness, Paco stepped on deck, the reaper tattoo on his chest.

The shirt-wrapped package was in one hand, the pineapple hatchet in the other.

In a rented Ford compact, Skip Baker arrived at the gates to Villa del Destino Ganado. He leaned out and pushed the intercom button.

After a long pause, the box crackled with the voice of the caretaker.

"*Qué?*"

"I'm here to see Purity. My name is Skip Baker."

The box buzzed. "*No está en casa.*"

BRIAN M. WIPRUD

Through the gate, Skip spotted Gina in the distance trotting up the path from the yacht.

"Excuse me! Hello?" Skip got out of the car, waving.

Gina stopped and peered toward Skip. She hesitated.

"I'm here to see Purity. Can you tell me where she went? I'm here from New York."

Yellow flashed the night sky.

From the marina's cove an orange tongue of fire licked the sky, vanishing back into the cliff's maw in a swirl of sparks. The ground jolted.

Mini cutaway: We see the calludaroo on Grant's dresser jump from the explosion's thump.

Both Skip and Gina were dumbstruck by the pillar of fire boiling into the sky.

"Oh my God!" Gina muttered.

She turned and ran back toward the marina.

Skip leaped onto the hood of his car and rolled over the top of the gate, charging across the lawn after her.

The camera tracks behind Gina as she dashes down the path and curves around the cliff face. Ahead, the path pulses with firelight, and as she turns the corner we see the yacht below, a cauldron of flame in a hull and nothing else. The entire inside of the vintage boat had been blown out, and anybody on board obliterated. Fragments of falling wood and metal chunked and clanked against the cliff walls, all eventually splashing into the fiery waters below.

On the column of smoke, smoldering twenty-dollar bills flickered and danced through the air.

Gina had a hand to her mouth, sinking to her knees.

Skip skidded to a stop next to her.

He pointed. "What happened?"

"*Premiere*. It's gone."

"A boat exploded, is that it? Was anybody on it?"

With downcast eyes, she said, "Robert Tyson Grant."

"Holy shit!" Skip pulled a point-and-shoot from his jacket and began taking pictures furiously. "Anybody else with him?"

"Dixie."

"Where's Purity?"

"She was meeting Morty. At the beach."

"At the beach? What about the Ramparts? She said she was going to meet him at the Ramparts."

"That is the beach."

The Mexican caretaker appeared next to them in just shorts and a T-shirt.

"*Mi Dios!*" He started down the stairs.

"Come on." Skip reached a hand out to Gina. "We need to call the Federales, and to make sure Purity and Morty are OK."

Gina cast a tearful eye back at the flaming yacht and followed Skip up the dark path.

At the villa's shadowy veranda, the camera zooms in on Skip and Gina coming from the path to the yacht.

The camera slowly zooms out to include a silhouette of me on the end of a lounge chair, crooked like a question mark, panting. Skip and Gina jogged up onto the veranda, headed for the living room—but Gina stopped short. She leaned in my direction.

"Morty?"

Switch to their perspective as they draw near.

They see me as I turn toward them, half cast in shadow.

Eyes: bloodshot from the ether but also with tears.

Hair: matted with blood and sand.

Shirt: torn open to reveal four crimson scratches across my chest.

Pants: splattered with blood like a butcher's apron.

"She's dead," I gurgle.

Cut to my blurred wobbly perspective.

Gina shrieks, "Morty!"

She rushes toward me, and the camera fades to black.

I pass out.

FIFTY-ONE

I ADMIT THAT AS MUCH as I would like to think of myself as an accomplished screenwriter, I am at a loss when it comes to describing the macabre. To be brutally honest, I don't remember much of anything of how I got back to the villa, or what I saw at the beach. The prison psychiatrists tell me that I have repressed memories, but I will not allow them to hypnotize me. I know whatever images I have of the headless body of Dixie on that beach are not ones I want to take with me for the rest of my short life and to the grave. There is a reason the memory is repressed. So be it.

The audience is wondering what exactly happened on that yacht.

Again, I could guess, but I am not sure I want that image with me, either. I am not capable of writing that gruesome scene. The thought that Paco may have displayed for Grant the head of his lover Dixie is far too chilling for me to contemplate. Grant was kind of a dick, true, but such grisly episodes should only plague our most ruthless killers and remorseless financial speculators.

My fate is pretty clear given where I am composing this cheery tale. Everybody's little scheme backfired on them and onto me.

The body at the beach was identified as Purity's—the manner of dress, her body type, the phone, and the fact that Purity was missing were sufficient for the Mexican navy.

Yes, the Mexican navy. I will return to that matter in a moment.

Dixie had set me up nicely by putting long fingernail scratches on my chest, which she did to make it look like Purity had struggled when I tried to kill her. What Dixie did in the process was to plant damning evidence under her own fingernails—which is where the forensics people found my flesh. Paco put my prints on the sickle and covered me in the victim's blood. Purity was kind enough to record me on her phone saying I would kill her father for her and to make sure I was on the security camera going down to the boat alone to sabotage it. She also left on her bed the note supposedly from me asking her to come to the Ramparts.

Making matters worse was that Gina did not see Paco go down to the yacht. Her face tucked into the rock crevice, Gina only heard the footsteps go past in the dark and assumed that it was Dixie. She also knew I was going to meet Purity down at the beach. So did Skip.

Yes, Skip came out of this in great shape. He was back on top at the paper, scooping every other tabloid on the triple murder of Robert Tyson Grant, beauty queen Dixie, and Purity Grant.

This was big, big news in the States, as everybody knows, and which is why you are interested in making this into a movie.

The news was even bigger in Mexico. As anybody knows, the *federales* are practically in the midst of a civil war with the drug cartels, and the violence and rash of senseless beheadings were creating a hue and cry in the congress to bring back the death penalty—which they had only abolished several years before.

The sensational nature of the Grant murder case caused a populist push by the politicians in the Mexican Congress to bring back the death penalty for those found guilty of beheadings.

See if you can guess who is the first to die under this new law.

Anyway, because the murders took place within tidal areas, the Mexican navy had jurisdiction, and my lawyers used this to get me out from under the civil death penalty and court system. I was to be tried by a tribunal. This created another giant controversy, and under political pressure the navy convened a commission that recommended they adopt civil statutes covering beheadings. Guess what? They did, and the tribunal found me guilty in a single day. In a country known for its sluggishness, they have handled my case with uncommon swiftness. So I guess I should feel special.

To be brutally honest, I am grateful the navy was swift, and I am grateful they will execute me by firing squad tomorrow instead of dangling me from a noose. I am spared the hopelessness of a lengthy trial I cannot win and the indignity of the gallows. There is something noble about a firing squad, even if I am a convicted murderer. I didn't want my last conscious memory to be pooping my pants.

Is there any bright side to this tale? Has God seen fit to trim with silver the dark and foreboding thunderheads that have gathered around the ill fate of Morty Martinez?

Gina, a girl who barely knew me three days before all this happened, has been fantastic and visits me all the time. Her beauty foils any attempt by the prison to forbid me contraband, like the occasional bottle of wine or Gruyère cheese. I would be an idiot if I did not admit that she and I have grown very close and that were there not an appointment to riddle my body with bullets I would ask her hand in marriage. I believe she would have said yes. What perfect irony that I should find the love of my life while on death row, yes? Tomorrow she will be set free to love another.

Oh, yes, I almost forgot. What of the gold Caravaca ring of Hernando Martinez de Salvaterra? Thanks to Gina, the ring was of course recovered and the relic returned to Father Gomez. He came to visit me, too, although reluctantly. I think he thinks I'm guilty, too, but mumbled something about saying a prayer for me. Gina said she was going to ask Father Gomez if she could wear the ring

for execution day in hopes God would somehow save me. I suppose it is worth a try.

You must be saying, "Morty, hold the phone! If Purity is still
missing, how do you know the body on the beach was Dixie's?
How—in fact—do you know all this about this soulless killer Paco?
Are you guilty and just making up all this shit or what?"

Until recently, I have been in the dark as much as everybody
else. Well, except about the palmist part; Gina filled me in on that.
In my defense, I've been guessing that the murder was committed by the cocktail steward I saw in the gardener's shed worshipping death. Of course, it was not for me to find out who did these
crimes, just to prove I did not do them. Yet it was hard for my defense attorneys, much less the prosecutors or the tribunal, to see
how anybody else *could* have done these heinous murders. My
premise about the clumsy devil-worshipping cocktail steward
sounded idiotic, and the crumpled Waffle House place mat they
found in the gardener's shed did little to substantiate my theory.

Skip Baker has been following this case closely, and I give him
the exclusive from my side of things. I figure, why not, he's a nice
enough guy; helping his career with my plight is just another
way to put a positive spin on all this.

Two weeks ago he came to me in an agitated state. I met with
him in my death row cell, a small ray of sunlight beaming through
the bars of my window. I was dressed as I have been for months, in
my dark gray prison jumpsuit with the stripe down the side. I lay
on my bunk, hands behind my head. Skip was in a windbreaker,
a tropical shirt, and chinos, documents in his hand. He waited for
the guard to leave earshot before sitting at my little writing desk
where I have been churning out this story. He leaned in, elbows
on knees.

"Huge news, dude. You didn't kill Purity Grant."

My smile was a weary, lopsided one. "Really?"

"I think you killed Dixie."

"Really?"

"Look at this." He pointed to the coroner's report in his hand. *"Implants.* I can't believe I missed this. It was on the back side of the report, and before I only had one side."

"And?"

"Purity Grant did not *have* implants."

"How do you know this?"

"Morty, I told you she and I hooked up. I know implants and these were not implants and I have it from her physician in New York that she in fact did not have implants! I've alerted the authorities, and they are exhuming the body to get the numbers off those implants."

"There are numbers on implants? I never noticed any."

"Inside the tit, on the silicone implant itself."

I furrowed my brow. "Then what was Dixie doing dressed as Purity down at the beach, with her phone?"

Skip slapped his knee and pointed a finger at me. *"That's what I'd like to know."* He jumped to his feet and began pacing, talking more to himself than me. "So I'm cleaning out some files from my laptop the other day, archiving them, when I came upon a little story I was working on just before we all ran off to Cabo. A little story about this guy."

He showed me sketches of Paco from the Memphis and Richmond police departments, and they looked quite similar.

"That's the clumsy cocktail steward!" I sat up. "The one worshipping death in the gardener's shed. Ask Gina, she'll tell you, this is the man who was on the plane."

"He left a trail of murders and robberies across the South—that's where these pictures came from. Now get this. You remember you said you first met Grant at the Red Flame Diner off of Sixth? We had a heeler follow up on that, as we do on a lot of small details.

Turns out Grant went there every day for lunch for weeks and had a table reserved. Then they mentioned the last time they saw him. They said he and Dixie were yelling at a busboy, only it wasn't a busboy, and that they left with him. It seemed odd that they would yell at a stranger and then leave with him, so we recovered their security camera images." He handed me a grainy photograph.

I looked from the photo to Skip. "They met this Satan worshipper at the diner. I don't understand."

"A prostitute named Firecracker spent the night with this guy in Richmond and told the cops he's Guatemalan, named Paco, works for the Juárez cartels, and was on his way to New York for a job." Skip put his hands on my shoulders. "I think Grant and Dixie hired this Mexican hit man to kill Purity. When you happened to show up before this dude, they thought—"

"That I was the hit man!" Now I was standing, too. "This all makes sense now, why they acted so strangely."

"Then when the real hit man did show up, they decided to take him and you along to Mexico to frame you for Purity's murder."

"My brain is exploding, Skip." I gripped my hair in astonishment.

"Don't you see? Purity also set you up for killing Grant! Dixie and Grant sent a note from you to Purity and from Purity to you, and used Dixie to lure you into the shadows, where they put you out and waited for Purity to show up. When she did show up, Paco would kill her and make it look like you did it. Only Purity didn't show up. Dixie probably went up to the house, found Purity's Vespa missing, and found where she'd dropped her phone. I think some of those reports that sighted Purity at a disco that night were actually true. Dixie picked up the phone and headed back to the beach to tell Paco Purity wasn't coming. Paco mistook Dixie—who was still disguised as Purity—for his victim. Realizing his mistake, he chopped off her head and went to a rendezvous at the yacht to get the money. Grant was on the yacht, and who knows what happened, except one of them turned the key and set off the diesel explosion in the aft of the ship. Both were obliterated with nary a trace."

"But, Skip, where is Purity? Are you saying that the woman I have been accused of beheading may still be alive? If so, I am free to leave, yes?"

"Where is Purity? That's the ten-million-dollar question. Get this: Right before she left New York, she signed a media deal, selling her image for things like jeans and perfume—fashion stuff. These companies have been making a ton of money off her while the murder investigation has gone on. So I got to wondering—where is all this money going now that she's dead?"

"Yes, where?"

"We contacted her lawyers about this, and our guys are in court now trying to force them to tell us. We think it is to an offshore account. If we can track any withdrawals, we'll know where she is."

I embraced Skip. "You have saved my life! Skip, how can I repay you?"

"Um, yeah, well, there's just one problem."

I held him at arm's length, a misspent tear rolling down my cheek. "Problem?"

"The Mexican authorities were quick to get you in front of a firing squad. That doesn't mean they're going to be quick to make themselves look incompetent."

"I . . . I don't understand."

"We've got the U.S. ambassador involved, and apparently the State Department is in discussions, but . . ."

"But what? I didn't kill who they say I killed."

"From their perspective, you at least may have killed Grant."

"But the video of me going to the boat showed I was there only a few moments, and the gardener saw Purity run past him with a fish in her hands headed for the yacht earlier that evening. That would account for the gulls flocking around the camera at that time. And remember Purity's phone? She had done a Web search about boat explosions."

"That's all a possibility, and circumstantial—it doesn't translate to fact. If Purity is found alive it will go a long way to diverting blame from you to her. Putting Grant's murder aside, the navy's position is that even if you didn't kill Purity, you killed Dixie thinking it was Purity."

"But the Mexican hit man—what of him?"

"It would be one thing if we knew something more about him, or at least had a body, but he and Grant were obliterated in that explosion. There's no actual evidence that Paco was here other than your eyewitness of him in the gardener's shed."

I groaned. "What about the Waffle House place mat in the gardener's shed?"

"That's probably your only hope. We're having less-than-perfect prints from that matched with those in the Richmond motel room and Grant's Gulfstream. It'll take time, and it's dicey."

"Still, there is a lot of doubt here. They cannot shoot bullets into me now can they?"

"Morty, the *Daily Post* is doing everything it can to save you. You have made so much money for the paper these last months, the editors don't want this story to die if it can be avoided."

"I see." I sank onto the edge of the cot and heaved a heavy sigh. "So I am to be executed after all, yes?"

"We're doing everything we can, Morty, but I'll give it to you straight: I think the Mexicans won't listen, and we don't have enough time—much less Purity Grant—to make them listen."

We shared a long pause.

"Well, Skip, I can only hope I am exonerated after my bullet-ridden corpse is buried. I want you and the *Daily Post* to know how much I appreciate that, and the efforts to free me."

"Um, could you write something up like that for us, Morty? You know, a farewell note, an exclusive that we could print? Once you are exonerated it will sell a ton more papers if you profess your innocence to the end and credit our paper with being the noble guardian of justice."

I nodded. "Of course."

A guard appeared at the bars to my cell.

"Looks like I have to go, Morty. Chin up, OK? If all else fails, when they say 'fire' . . . duck." He winked and smiled.

I returned his joke with a firm handshake and a wry grin.

Skip's footsteps faded down the long prison hallway, and so did my hopes.

Since that fateful day I have been working both day and night to revise this film treatment to reflect the truth of what happened, to fill in all the unknowns, to fit all the crazy pieces of this jigsaw into a hideous landscape that features an innocent man standing bravely before a firing squad.

FINAL CHAPTER

I THINK IT WAS LINCOLN who once said of an unfortunate predicament that he was too old to cry yet too sad to laugh.

It is now three in the morning, the day of my execution. I have had my last meal: a grilled cheese, of course, and it wasn't very good because Mexicans can only make quesadillas. They were nice enough to provide me with some tequila. In the USA they don't let condemned men drink, which if you ask me is perfectly insane. If ever there was any poor slob who really needed a drink it is a condemned man, wouldn't you say? Write your congressmen.

Gina came today, after Skip. I refused to see her; the prospect of witnessing her tears was too painful. Instead I have left her a note:

Dear Gina: I have left you my villa in La Paz, sell it, do whatever. My destiny is no longer in La Paz, but with God, who will hopefully look favorably upon His poor servant, the one who restored the relic of Hernando Martinez de Salvaterra at the expense of his life. My gratitude to you, dear Gina, for staying in Mexico and comforting me, is boundless. I have but one regret in my life, and that regret is that I cannot spend eternity cherishing my sweet Gina. Perhaps I will see you on the other side, but do not pine. Find a man as good as me if you can, but do not settle, and avoid men with elaborate facial hair. Just trust me on this one. Love always and forever—Morty.

As you might imagine, a condemned man cannot sleep at a time like this, and I have been quite busy trying to finish this film treatment. Soon, I will be sleeping for all time, with any luck in a bed with squishy pillows at God's feet.

To be brutally honest, I feel I have failed in my attempt to package this incident as a good screenplay because according to *Screenwriting: Yes You Can!* my story lacks catharsis. What have I, Morty Martinez, learned? How have these incidents altered my worldview and my soul? I keep going back to the words in my family crest, the ones on the fountain in the courtyard at my La Paz villa and oddly also above the entrance to Grant's much nicer Cabo San Lucas villa. *Destino Ganado.* Earn Destiny. I earned a firing squad for having restored a holy relic? Has He given me Gina—arguably one of history's greatest beauties with one slightly imperfect nostril—only to cruelly take her away? Is there some lesson in this ironic punishment? In my dark hour, I await some word from God, some sign, some piece of the puzzle that puts it all together so I see His grand design. Yet like a child who stays up late on Christmas Eve, my blank stare into the cold fireplace begins to make me feel foolish.

I'm going to end this film treatment now and contemplate what lies ahead, not behind. Even if I am not a very good screenwriter after all, I hope that what I have written here compels you to tell my story, and that it can inspire others who have been framed by two insane rich people who were hell-bent to kill each other.

Go with God, amigos.

STILL JUST 50¢!

THE DAILY POST

PAGE 6
SUBWAY GIRLS
IRT vs BMT

Monday June 20, 2011

IS THIS THE **REAL** CABO KILLER?
PAGE 8

FROM INSIDE THE WALLS- MORTY'S FAREWELL TO DAILY POST READERS
PAGE 4

POST EXCLUSIVE

NINE LIVES

Heiress Purr-rity Grant Alive

Innocent Man Faces Execution for her Murder

CABO SAN LUCAS, June 19
Skip Baker, Reporting

Creating an uproar in the already tumultuous Cabo Murder Mystery, The Daily Post has discovered one of the star victims, bratty heiress Purity Grant, alive and living anonymously in an isolated beach cabana near the seaside Mexican town of Posada del Calamar. When confronted by this Daily Post reporter and asked why she has not come forward during the last few months to intervene on behalf of her convicted murderer, Morty Martinez, she replied with four-letter words, and requested we speak with her legal counsel. The discovery of the Catty Heiress unharmed comes on the eve of her murderer's execution by firing squad at the hands of the Mexican navy. Amid a growing file of contradictory evidence, Daily Post lawyers have heroically pursued every legal avenue to delay Mr. Martinez's execution until his case can be reviewed. U.S. Embassy officials in Mexico City have been alerted to these latest developments by the Daily Post and are making a last-ditch appeal with Mexican authorities and admiralty.

FULL COVERAGE: PAGE 2

CITY COUNCILMAN IN LOVE NEST SCANDAL

PAGE 3

CHEWING GUM BOMBER RATS OUT AL-QAIDA

STAY 4 CABO SLAYER — MARTINEZ DODGES BULLET!

EXCLUSIVE

Posted June 20th 2011 12:41PM by TN2 Reporters

United States Embassy officials in Mexico City rushed today to stay the execution of Morty Martinez, accused murderer of heiress Purity Grant and her father Robert Tyson Grant, founder of the Grab-A-Lot discount stores. Mr. Martinez was to be executed at noon, yet the stay of execution was delivered to the Naval Detention Center in La Paz fifteen minutes after the scheduled execution. Mexican officials stated that a "technical complication" delayed the scheduled time of execution. Captain Roberto Blanco, a spokesman for the Mexican Navy, claimed the nature of the technical complication was that the condemned "eluded" the fusillade of bullets by "ducking." The stay of execution arrived at the prison as the soldiers were reloading. Mr. Martinez and his lawyers could not yet be reached for comment.

INFORMA.NET

• ver edición impresa
• SUSCRIBETE AHORA
• servicios del suscriptor

PROSECUTORS STRIKE DEAL WITH GRANT

Mexico City, June 29, 2012 ~ Lengthy negotiations between prosecutors, lawyers, and
Ultravibe Media consultants have spared the Mexican people from footing the bill for a
sensational murder case against Purity Grant. It was widely believed the prosecution had
little chance of success and relied exclusively on circumstantial evidence. The yacht
explosion that killed her stepfather effectively demolished all evidence at the crime scene,
and Señorita Grant has explained her disappearance after the event and murder of Dixie
Faltreau the same evening. She claims that when she heard that night that she'd been
murdered, she feared for her life should she come out of hiding. The prosecution has
contended that the murders that evening were orchestrated by Señorita Grant. The
defendant has claimed that the murders were a plot against her by her father and mistress
that went awry. Today's deal included a lifetime ban on Señorita Grant's travel to Mexico
and a forfeiture of all Mexican holdings, to include the Grant Cabo San Lucas villa
Destino Ganada. Señorita Grant recently became a majority shareholder and CEO of
Ultravibe Media, which elected to established a foundation in memory of her stepfather.
The R.T. Grant Foundation will fund a home for Mexican orphans at *Destino Ganada*
where girls will learn the trade of helicopter mechanics.

CLICK FOR FULL ARTICLE

The Times

Gina Stelianodaciselli, Mortimer Martinez

Published: July 29, 2012

Mortimer Martinez and Gina Stelianodaciselli were married Saturday at the Nuestra Señora de Cortez, Baja Sur, Mexico. Father Gomez Entropica officiated.

The bride, 32, is an actress with Telemundo Television for their hit drama "Cabo." She is a native New Yorker and former martial arts stunt double.

She is a daughter of Gerta and Stavros Stelianodaciselli of Brooklyn, New York. Her father is retired custodian for the New York City Public Schools. Her mother is a homemaker.

The bridegroom, 45, is a French cheese importer and philanthropic consultant to his local diocese in La Paz, Baja Sur, Mexico. He graduated from East Brooklyn High School in Brooklyn, New York.

He is the son of Ethel and Pasqual Martinez of East Brooklyn. Both are deceased. His father was a mechanic at Canarsie Car and Truck.

The groom attained considerable notoriety in the recent Grant murder trial in Mexico, and has since been vindicated.